Weavers of the
Land

Weavers of the Land

Judy McCall Chester

Library of Congress Control Number: 2017909990
ISBN: Hardcover   978-1-5434-3278-7
               Softcover   978-1-5434-3277-0
               eBook   978-1-5434-3276-3

Print information available on the last page.

Rev. date: 06/22/2017

To order additional copies of this book, contact:
Xlibris
1-888-795-4274
www.Xlibris.com
Orders@Xlibris.com
762878

Chapter 1

THE LOW-HANGING CLOUDS TRAVELING INWARD from the southwest of the Atlantic Ocean brought with them a fine rain, contributing to a misty, cold spring morning in Northern Ireland. The glistening green grasses beneath the fast-moving clouds transformed the valleys into an emerald backdrop. On top of rounded rolling hills, surrounded by a looming mote, was one of the many majestic castles in the British Empire of King George III. The castle walls and floors were constructed of gray granite hewn from the jagged mountains. Of all the castles in the empire, this was the favorite of the Princess Mary Katherine.

Mary Katherine, the only child of King George III and next in line to the throne, came bounding from her room in a half-run, half-walk down the long chilly, gloomy corridor. It was past dawn, and the heavy morning fog had not yet lifted. Her every exhale could be seen in the early light. Mary Katherine could not understand why anyone would begin the day so early. But King George had summoned a fabric weaver by the name of Robert McCall to the throne room. The king's wish was to commission the weaving of a fine royal tablecloth. The young princess found a great interest in all new visitors to the castle. She made her way to the high arch adjoining the stately throne room as she had done on so many prior occasions. Hanging from the twenty-foot arch were royal-blue drapes which the curious princess wrapped around herself to escape the chill of the morning. She was unaware that the toes of her slippers were always exposed beneath the drapes, thus alerting the king of her presence. He allowed her to play this little game because he desired that she learn governing skills, which would be of great benefit to her as the future queen. She thought of her approaching eighteenth birthday and realized that this was somewhat of a childish game, one she would soon give up.

Peering from behind her secure place, she could see the back of this Robert McCall. To her surprise, he was not as old as she had imagined a weaver to be. He had a commandingly strong but polite voice. He was tall in stature but lean. His hair was blond, wavy, and long to his broad shoulders.

Yes, he is most interesting, she thought. *I wonder about his eyes. Eyes tell you a lot about a person.* Whatever the color might be, she would love to know.

Suddenly, at her most befuddled moment, there was a loud crash. The drapes had collapsed, and the ever-so-charming princess found herself facedown on the stone floor. She could hear roaring thunderous laughter from her father. Somehow, he had known this day would come.

Robert McCall quickly bowed to the king and went to the aid of whomever it was that had put themselves in such a precarious position. Lifting the person from an enormous amount of heavy fabric was difficult.

"Oh, Your Grace." He quickly but politely bowed. "Art thou?"

Before he could express his concern, the princess, still somewhat tangled in the yards of fabric, fell unexpectedly into his arms. At that moment, their eyes met. It wasn't as she had imagined it might be to be in the arms of someone so handsome. In fact, it was quite the opposite, however; she found it to be most humiliating. Yes, there they were looking at her, blue eyes as blue as the royal drapes she so clumsily had fallen into.

Her first thought was to escape. What must he think of her? Abruptly, she acknowledged the king. Off she ran back to her chambers where she always found those who were waiting to be at her beck and call. Breathing deeply, she stepped into a nearby alcove to gain her composure. It seemed word had reached her ladies-in-waiting before she arrived. Her hair was a jumble, and the shortness of her breath revealed how mortified she was by the whole ordeal. Breathing deeply, she calmly took to her needlework, hoping the entire incident would not be the talk of the day. For some reason at this moment, the palace did not seem as cold as before.

The king decided to commission Robert McCall the task of designing the royal tablecloth. This could be of enormous value to Robert's reputation. Robert returned to his studio to commence the work on perhaps the most important fabric he would ever design, but he could not dismiss the beauty and fairness of the young princess. She was as fair and delicate as the roses he so often wove into his tapestries. He found himself fascinated by her curiosity. He discovered himself thinking of her throughout the course of his day's work. Would he ever have the occasion to be in her company again? Should he allow himself to think of her? He was positive he was some years her senior and notwithstanding the fact that she was of royal birth.

The princess, after being so shamelessly embarrassed by her own curiosity and clumsiness, remained in her chambers the entirety of the next day, allowing her feelings to adjust to her own self-induced humiliation. What else could she do? Try as hard as she might, she could not erase the weaver, Robert McCall, from her mind, nor could she forget the strength and depth of his deep-blue eyes.

Mary Katherine continued to do what all the ladies of nobility did. She studied astrology, the laws of the land, math, and the fine arts. Playing the harpsichord was one of her favorite pastimes. She especially enjoyed doing fine handiwork, such as lace making, tatting, and very fine needlework. While working on a very ornate needlepoint, she wondered if Robert McCall enjoyed the same satisfaction as herself in seeing the blending of colors and threads taking place as they evolved into a panorama of amazing beauty. Such work lent itself to a lot of contemplation.

The weeks passed into late spring. Enough of the royal cloth had been woven to allow Robert to request an audience with His Majesty that he might judge the quality of the work.

The days were no longer cold, so Mary Katherine found herself more and more out of the palace and in the front gardens. The warmth of the spring sunshine was greatly welcomed and appreciated as opposed to the coldness of the castle rooms. She knew that being in the front gardens would keep her informed of all the comings and goings of those who visited the palace. One day, her wishes were realized when a rider approached the great front doors of the castle at a slow gallop. Could it be? Was it who she had so long hoped might visit with the king? Positioning herself in the right place at the right time had certainly paid off. It was Robert McCall. He did not realize that she was in the garden, for he could not see her. She was well hidden by all the foliage. She wondered if he would even take notice that someone was in the garden. Watching him very intently gave her reason to recall his strikingly handsome features. She watched closely as he dismounted his horse and gave the reins to the attending doorman. He then brushed and tidied himself to enter the castle. Mary Katherine knew she must find a way to present herself in a more dignified and fitting way, one that is becoming of her position.

After all, I am a princess, she thought. Her thoughts were how she might arrange being in his company without being so obvious. This would require some planning. If only she could speak with her mother about such a thing. But the queen was out of the country, so she had to rely on her own intuition, whatever that might be.

Think, think, I must think, I must be quick, she thought in a panicked breath. *The king does not hold an audience for long periods. Should I fall again or have the vapors? No, that would be a much too common thing to do. Time is fleeting, think, think again, surely you have some thoughts. I know! I will just stand outside the throne room door. He must acknowledge my presence. Who would not recognize the princess?*

Untying her bonnet and pushing the hair from her face, she then pinched her cheeks to give herself a more radiant glow. She pretended to be coming from the garden just as Robert bid the king a formal good-bye.

"I can hear him approaching. His boots have a loud clatter on the stone floors. Don't allow your feeling to be so revealing, stand erect, be regal," she told herself.

"Robert McCall," she called as she handed her bonnet to one of her ladies. She approached Robert while taking in his penetrating eyes and noticed that he was taller than she had even remembered, perhaps he was more than a head taller than herself. Searching for words, she then again addressed him, "Robert McCall, I trust your audience with the king went well?"

Bowing and being somewhat caught off guard by the presence of the princess, with a thickness in his throat, he replied, "Your Grace. Quite well, thank you. The audience with the king was of great benefit."

"I trust the king liked the design of the tablecloth," uttered the princess as she again admired the blueness of his eyes.

"The king does like the sample of my work and is anxious to have the cloth completed." Robert remembered the best of protocol when in the presence of royalty and asked, "I trust my lady is doing well?"

"Quite well, thank you," she answered, knowing they were engaging in small talk. She thought, *I wonder if he recalls that most dreadful day when we first met. To my chagrin, it was not the most flattering day of my life.* The images of that day raced through her mind. *Oh well, we are in conversation, and he makes no mention of it. I know he has not forgotten, but what gentlemen would make mention of such things? Somehow, I must make it possible for us to meet. I know.* She became excited with her thoughts. *I shall invite him to tea, yes, that is a grand idea. It must be after the queen returns from her journey. Now, I must gather the nerve to extend the invitation. He must suspect I have an interest in him.*

"Robert McCall, Her Majesty, the queen, is expected to arrive any day from her journey to London. We would be most pleasured if you would join us for tea one afternoon."

"It would be my honor to grace the queen and the princess on such an occasion."

"Well done. We will make the arrangements soon." Mary Katherine straightened the ruffles on her dress. It was obviously a nervous gesture.

Bowing to make his exit, he said, "I bid my lady a pleasant afternoon."

The princess extended her hand and allowed Robert to kiss it tenderly.

"Good day, Robert."

She turned, leaving his presence with a most satisfied smile on her face.

Mary Katherine found it difficult to await the return of her mother so that she might share with her the acquaintance of this new friend. Her biggest fear was how her mother would react to the fact that she had taken upon herself the liberty of extending an invitation without the approval of the queen. Such matters were usually considered with great care.

Chapter 2

E VERYONE IN THE PALACE WAS busy making ready for the queen's arrival. The cooks and bakers had been working all day in preparation of a family banquet. Fresh flowers were in abundance; they adorned the bedrooms, sitting parlors, and the very large foyers. Crisp new linens and bath essentials were placed in the bedchambers. All windows were opened to air the rooms from a long damp winter, adding a freshness of fragrant sweet lilacs only spring can bring.

The marriage of the king and queen was an arranged one that never lent itself to a true romantic relationship. Their marriage did reveal one of common and mutual respect. Very little time was spent in the company of each other, so this made it easy for the princess to visit with her mother.

She found herself becoming very excited as she waited for their quiet private time. They had so long been apart, and she wished the horse and carriage would hurry along. "How surprised Mother will be to know that I have met an interesting young man."

The following day, the queen visited Mary Katherine in her chambers to catch up on many things that had transpired during the queen's absence.

Mary Katherine told her mother how she had met Robert, the weaver, revealing the fiasco in the throne room, the fall and entanglement in the draperies, which brought about the accompanying humiliation. She described how she had tried her best to make it as graceful as possible. They laughed at how ridiculous this had been. Mary Katherine was not feeling so forlorn and had become much more at ease with their reunion.

This is a good time, she thought to inform her mother of her interest in Robert. *I feel faint when I think how this might evolve. I know Robert is not of high nobility, but surely, Mother will allow me to extend the invitation,* realizing that it has all but been confirmed.

"Mother, during your absence . . ." She stumbled as she chose her words most carefully. "I took it upon myself to extend an invitation to tea, inviting Robert McCall."

This was not easy for the young princess. Her hands were cold and sweating as they so often felt when she had an intense question for her parents. Mary Katherine was waiting with great anticipation for a reaction from her mother. The queen could be quite firm as well as rigid on occasion.

"A mere commoner . . . to have such an audience with the queen is not highly probable. I am not sure how the king will view the proposal for such a sitting. In due time, I will take this matter up with His Majesty" was the Queen's unpromising reply.

Mary Katherine changed the subject as she knew the impatience of her mother when pressed too hard and long on any issue. "Mother, I have been quite busy with my needlework." She motioned for her work to be handed to her. "Would you care to see what has been accomplished thus far?"

The queen was quite pleased with the fine quality of her daughter's work.

Mary Katherine found herself with high anxiety as she awaited the reply of her parents. *I do pray they will not make it too long before they render their decision,* she thought.

Several rainy days passed. Mary Katherine, due to the weather, was captive in her chambers. She kept herself busy with her studies, trying hard not to think of the tumultuous decision to be made.

There was a knock on her door.

"Enter."

It was the queen's chambermaid. She was bearing a message from the queen. "Your Highness, the queen wishes that you should come to the queen's chambers."

Was this the answer Mary Katherine was anxiously waiting for? She hurried to the queen's chambers, stopping at the door to straighten her clothes and smoothen her hair. The queen was very particular about personal appearances. The princess knew this was not the time to annoy her mother with trivial things. Bowing most gracefully, as she had been taught in royal protocol, she addressed the queen.

"Your Majesty, you summoned me?"

"Yes, my dear. The king and I have made our decision regarding your interest in this Robert Mc Call."

Detecting a firm tone in her mother's voice, she surmised the worst.

Her mother continued, "The king informs me Robert McCall seems to be a very nice gentleman and presents himself very well before the court. However, he is not of high nobility. Your position as future queen is of great concern. Such a relationship is not advisable. Therefore, we do not encourage your interest to continue toward Robert McCall."

Mary Katherine let out a deep sigh, preparing herself for an overwhelming letdown. To her delight, her mother continued, "However, we will honor your request for afternoon tea to save you from further embarrassment."

Mary Katherine was elated with the news. Realizing it might not be wise to allow her feelings for Robert to be manifested, she kissed her mother on the cheek, thanked her most graciously, curtsied, then left the room. Filled with excitement over such good news, she bounced and twirled once or twice back to her chambers. She busied herself with just the right invitation to be sent. Just as quickly, she thought, *What would they serve?* She decided that mint tea would be most refreshing with the weather turning warmer. Afternoon tea must be accompanied with sweet tea biscuits. Watercress sandwiches with cheese would go well since watercress is in great abundance in the spring. She found the hours passing. The evening was beautiful. The vaulted sky was bright and clear with illuminating stars as the clouds melted away after the heavy rains. As she leaned from her window, she breathed the fresh air that only spring rains can deliver. The cool evening breeze blew the sheer curtains in and onto her face. Pulling the curtains back, she located familiar constellations. Mary Katherine found it very difficult to go to sleep. She tossed and turned until early morning.

The invitation, which was sent by a palace footman, read as follows:

Her Majesty Queen Mary Margaret
and
Her Royal Highness Princess Mary Katherine
Request the honor of your presence
To join them for tea.
2:00 p.m.
May Twentieth
The year of our Lord 1775
RSVP

Robert accepted and returned the invitation by the palace footman.

The tea table was placed on the grassy west lawn of the palace grounds, allowing the guest to enjoy the warmth of the afternoon sun. The palace was surrounded by beautiful flower gardens with immaculately trimmed hedge mazes, which added to the ambiance. Gracing the tea table was an elegant Irish linen table covering with rolled tea towels. A centerpiece of yellow and pink roses accented with sprigs of baby's breath. Great care had been given to the polishing of the finest silver, which reflected a lustrous shine in the sun.

The two o'clock hour was quickly approaching. Mary Katherine, with the help of her ladies-in-waiting, chose a pale yellow cotton day dress with lace adorning a low-cut neck and long sleeves. Her red hair was in a loose upsweep, the twist and plates were intertwined with yellow ribbon and sprigs of the same tiny flower that added to the rose centerpieces.

Robert arrived by carriage and was escorted to the west garden by the queen's footman. His hair was pulled back and tied with a black satin bow. He was wearing a very ruffled white shirt and a gray wool coat. He did not sit, for he knew the queen would arrive shortly. Among other things, the queen was most punctual.

The queen entered the garden where she greeted Robert. She extended her right hand, carrying a silk fan in the left. Robert bowed with one arm behind his back; he leaned forward, then took the queen's right hand and politely brought it to his lips. "Your Majesty."

"Robert McCall, we are most delighted you are here this afternoon."

At that moment, the princess made her entrance. "Good afternoon, Robert McCall, we are pleased you accepted our invitation to tea this day."

All greetings and formalities were extended.

Holding her hand was most pleasing to Robert. His feelings for the princess were beginning to emerge. The feeling he was experiencing frightened him, knowing that he was but a commoner and any further feelings toward the princess could, no doubt, prove to be a problem.

"Your Grace is most lovely this afternoon." He could not help but to once again admire her beauty.

They continued with tea and talked of the weather, enjoying the balmy warmth of spring as blossoms from the apple trees fell like snow on the green lawns. The queen asked of the tablecloth and its progress while fanning ever so gently.

Mary Katherine could not allow the time to pass without being with Robert alone. She asked if they might be excused to view the gardens. Excusing themselves, they began their walk. Mary Katherine knew many eyes would be upon them, watching their every move, but they could talk in private.

Robert admiringly could not but take in the graciousness of Mary Katherine. She was small and petite with velvet-like skin. He especially liked the way the sunlight made her red hair look like shining copper. He thought, *Yes, she is most lovely. Dare I allow myself to be so smitten by her loveliness?*

They walked the gardens, talking, remembering not to hold hands. Mary Katherine asked Robert, "Do you like horses?"

Robert, enjoying the walk and especially the company of the beautiful princess, replied with a soft voice, "Yes, I do. Why do you ask?"

"I have a favorite friend I would like you to meet."

They made their way to the back gardens and then on to the stables. Mary Katherine had planned this, knowing it would give a bit more time for their visit.

"I love to ride to feel the wind on my face, to feel the freedom it brings."

Coming to the stable door, Mary Katherine bid the stableman to open the door. Stepping in, she caught the horse by his bridle, then rubbed under his jaw while continuing the conversation, "This is Diamond, my personal horse, given to me on my twelfth birthday. I named him Diamond because of the white marking on his chest."

Mary Katherine, still in conversation, petted the horse on his front shoulder, then gave him a handful of grain from the feed bucket. Diamond responded with his familiar neigh.

Robert rubbed Diamond affectionately on the nose and told Mary Katherine, "He is a fine animal."

Mary Katherine went nose to nose with her horse, telling Robert, "I have a forthcoming eighteenth birthday. I expect my parents will hold a very elaborate celebration inviting many foreign nobles. It is rumored that they are in search of a suitable suitor for me." Looking up into Robert's face with a soft but confirming voice, she continued, "I will make sure you are among the invited."

"I would be most honored to be among your guests," answered Robert as he closed the stable door after the princess.

The afternoon was coming to a close. Each hoped that this would not be their last encounter, as they bid each other a cordial good-bye.

Chapter 3

THE KING AND QUEEN DID indeed intend to use Mary Katherine's birthday as an opportunity to pursue a suitor for the princess. They were fearful of her interest in Robert.

Elaborate plans were being made for the princess's birthday celebration. She was in committee meetings almost every day with her mother, planning a lavish gala. The castle needed to be cleaned top to bottom. Much food preparation had begun. A royal plea for local musicians was sent out among the kingdom, along with the need of a very carefully arranged selection of music.

Many foreign noblemen would spend a week after making such a long journey. Entertainment would be a big requirement: lawn games, fencing, archery, and fox hunting. Included would be the biggest of events, horse racing. Long evenings featuring dancing and political commentary would also be expected by their guests.

Rice paper was chosen for individual invitations; they were designed, handwritten, and bore the king's seal.

Mary Katherine had a challenging assignment to choose fine fabrics for a formal gown. Many clothes were to be considered for all the entertainment and activities that would take place.

Weeks passed, and the castle bustled with final preparations and arrangements as they came together for the biggest event of the year.

The guest list had been finalized. Invitations were in the process of being delivered. Mary Katherine was most excited that Robert would be among the guests. It would be very rude to exclude him because he had so recently been entertained by the queen.

The princess and Robert had not been in the company of each other since the tea.

The weather could not have been more fitting for the forthcoming festivities. Various nobilities were beginning to arrive. The earliest guests received the best rooms.

Mary Katherine was required to entertain any number of possible suitors. She found them all to be self-centered, spoiled, and quite boring. She could only think of Robert and wondered if he was thinking of her as well. The only thing interesting to her about the entire affair was seeing Robert again.

She had the last fitting of her formal gown. It was as beautiful as she could have possibly hoped for. Time was drawing closer.

The baking and roasting aromas were beginning to escape the great kitchen. The smell of cinnamon and rosemary permeated the air.

Mary Katherine took one last ride on Diamond to escape and to clear her head of all that was taking place. *Much ado about nothing. Everyone turns eighteen if they live long enough. It is getting late. The ladies-in-waiting will be very nervous if I do not return soon,* she thought.

Arriving back at her chambers, she found her bathwater drawn and prepared with soothing salts and peppermint oil. Slipping into the warm water was most needed and relaxing. The evening was too quickly upon her. Everyone around her was in a tither; they were busy preparing her clothes, styling her hair, and dressing her. She held on to the ceiling-high bedpost while her bone-staved corset was being drawn, making her waist all twenty-two inches. It was customary for a woman's waist to be small enough for a man's hands to wrap around. The queen entered to check that all was in unison with the schedule. Everyone stopped what they were doing and turned to formality. That was, all except Mary Katherine; she was still clutching the bedpost. She did manage to squeeze out a very high-pitched "Hello, Mother."

"Hello, dear. I have brought the royal jewels for you. You have several choices."

All the ladies-in-waiting were stunned by their beauty.

"Thank you, Mother. Would you please be so kind as to help me make a decision?"

Released from her holding position, the princess, with the help of three servants, stepped into her many petticoats. The gown was the most tedious with small ivory bone buttons down the back and sleeves. Each had to be pulled with a button hook. The princess turned and took one final approval check. In the oval mirror, she adjusted her comfort in the tight corset. The ladies-in-waiting gasped at her stunning beauty and fell back with exhaustion. Their murmurs were ebbed with their curtsies as Mary Katherine left her chambers. It was now time for the beautiful princess to make her grand entrance.

The banquet tables were covered with the finest of Irish linen and lace cloths. Tall vases filled with bouquets of flowers, along with large silver candelabras and goblets, added the finishing touches to the table settings.

Massive selections of breads, cakes, cheeses, roasted lamb, pig, fowl, figs, apples, and nuts, along with kegs of wine and ale, were for the taking.

The trumpets sounded.

"Make way for the king!" announced the palace crier.

The music stopped. Everyone quickly took a position of bowing as His Majesty entered through the great, heavy, double-wide doors. His left arm extended forward, supporting the right hand of the princess. Everyone was in awe at Mary Katherine's youthful but stunning beauty. The queen followed behind with an escort, giving this time to her daughter. This was Mary Katherine's shining moment. The king and queen proudly presented their lovely daughter to the court.

The marble floors were so polished they reflected the emerald-green taffeta gown worn by the princess. The gown was very full with yards and yards of ruffles that lay over large hoop petticoats. The off-shoulder neckline was adorned with an emerald and diamond necklace with matching earrings. The dress featured puffed-to-the-elbow, long, slimming, over-the-hand buttoned sleeves. The princess wore her hair in a fashionable upsweep with a neatly tucked diamond tiara. She chose the shimmering emerald-green fabric to reflect the love she had for the lush emerald-green vegetation that surrounded Ireland, her most favorite of places in the British Empire. Her red hair and the green of the dress was a beauty all its own. As she made her grand entrance, her eyes were ever searching for Robert, though knowing he would not be in the front line as it was for the nobility. He would be in the back, perhaps closer to a wall.

The king opened the great ball by dancing with his daughter. He then presented her to his chosen suitor. Mary Katherine danced with one suitor after another. While dancing with the Prince of Spain, or that's who she thought him to be, she could not help but notice that his height matched hers exactly. He had a very ruddy completion, thinning hair, with a squeaky voice that was as annoying as his stumbling feet.

My father cannot be serious about this prince, she thought as she struggled through the dance. *I could never in a lifetime be interested in this person for he certainly is not to be compared to Robert.*

Looking over the shoulder of her dance partner, she caught sight of Robert. He was the most handsome.

Robert was in a hypnotic trance, his eyes fixed on the princess. The music stopped, forcing him back to reality. He thought for the moment and decided it was his opportunity to approach Mary Katherine. Moving through the festivities of people eating and laughing along with the circus of jesters, Robert made his way to Mary Katherine.

"Your Grace, may I have the honor of this dance?"

"Thank you, Robert. With great pleasure. I would love to dance." Her hand was shaking as she extended it while they moved to the dance floor.

"Your Grace is most lovely this evening," Robert quietly whispered.

"Thank you. It pleases me you think so."

She placed her hand on his shoulder, and they gently glided across the floor in a waltz. Mary Katherine was once again thinking all the while of his handsomeness, but she dared not tell him so. During dancing a waltz and two reels, at every opportunity, they allowed their eyes to meet, searching for the deepest inner thoughts of each other.

The king and queen watched their daughter intently.

"Our daughter is most lovely this evening. I am sure we will be successful in our search for the proper suitor for the princess."

Delighted, the king leaned toward the queen, holding his handkerchief close to his mouth as he spoke in private to her.

"Yes, I do agree she is most lovely tonight" was the Queen's dutiful reply while fanning, smiling, nodding, and greeting their guests.

"It is quite warm in here," Mary Katherine commented, hoping Robert would pick up on her thoughts.

"Would my lady care to step into the gardens for some fresh air?"

"That would be most refreshing," replied Mary Katherine. She was relieved that he could be so sensitive to her thoughts.

They walked and talked quietly about the festivities, stopping at the water fountain.

"The evening is quite beautiful, actually quite perfect." Letting Robert know it was just as she hoped it to be, to have time alone with him.

Robert knew that the time for Mary Katherine's parents to find a suitor for her was approaching. He felt compelled to let her know of his affections. He realized his opportunity would soon pass. Robert reached for her hand, kissing it. Unable to resist the temptation, he drew her closer to him. Mary Katherine had never been so close to a man other than her father. She felt a warmness she had never before experienced. *What is happening? Is he going to kiss me? Should I allow it?* With these questions reeling in her head, she found herself hopelessly giving in to her feelings.

Robert took her face tenderly into his hands. She could feel their strength. He then kissed her, embracing her. He told her, "You are so lovely. You are especially beautiful this night."

His hands brushed over her tightly braided hair. To him, it felt like strands of woven silk.

Mary Katherine had never been kissed before; she stood quite rigid and in shock at what had just taken place. Things were moving too quickly for the both of them.

"I am sorry, Your Grace, would you forgive me, but a lowly commoner?" Robert waited for her reaction.

"Whatever for? What is there to forgive, Robert?"

Robert continued, "The king has sent for many suitors for your hand. Does my lady find them to be interesting?"

"I find them to be hopelessly boring and prudish. I cannot find myself forever living in a loveless marriage." She was reflecting on the marriage of her own parents.

"I cannot bear to think of you having to finish the evening with those prudes as you so call them." He held her hand.

"We must return before we are missed."

Mary Katherine leaned into Robert for a good-bye kiss.

Robert was most encouraged by her action; he asked, "When might we meet again?"

"I will send you a message very soon." And she hurried away.

Gathering her composure and leaving the garden before Robert, the princess returned to her proper place alongside her parents for the finalities of the evening, which ended with an enormous fireworks display.

The king again leaned into the ear of the queen, bringing to her attention. "Our daughter seems to be a bit flushed, don't you think?"

"Yes, my lord, I do believe you to be correct in this matter. I shall converse with her concerning her absence these last few minutes."

The queen once again called for the princess to come to her chambers. "My dear, your father and I could not help but notice you spent a great deal of time with Robert McCall the evening of the great ball. I must again remind you, pursuing this relationship would not be to your advantage or that of the monarchy."

Mary Katherine took to heart the words of her mother; she knew her feelings for Robert were deep, and this made her heart ache.

The palace was now vacant of its guests, leaving the princess with a feeling of sadness and loneliness. She would always remember the evening of the great ball. She could not erase the enchantment she was left with after the most magical night of her life. She kept thinking about how to arrange a meeting with Robert. It was up to her to decide when and where.

Chapter 4

SINCE HER BIRTH, THE PRINCESS has had a nanny named Elizabeth. Mary Katherine shortened her name to Liz. Liz was tall, very slim, with dark hair, and flushed cheeks, giving her a natural warm glow. A confidante to Mary Katherine, she knew everything about the princess. Liz had long known the day would come that the princess would turn her attention and interest toward a young man. She felt her intuition to be correct about Robert and sensed trouble soon to come.

Sitting at her desk for most of the morning, Mary Katherine, with pen in hand, tried to compose a note to Robert, asking him to join her for an afternoon of horseback riding. She stood and began nervously pacing back and forth, writing and then tearing the note into pieces. Finally, after a struggle, she arrived at just the right composition.

"Liz, I have a note for Robert McCall, would you please deliver it for me?

Liz was very reluctant. "Your Grace, are you sure this is a wise choice?"

"Liz, you can leave the castle quite easily without question."

"I ask my lady to reconsider," begged Liz. "The king and queen are most concerned about your affections for this weaver."

"Be gone with you, Liz, do as I have asked," ordered Mary Katherine as she relaxed from the morning of composing the note.

Liz knew that if they were caught, the king and queen would be most displeased with all concerned.

However, after much persuasion, the note was delivered to Robert.

The day came for the rendezvous; Mary Katherine went to the stables to have Diamond saddled for the afternoon. She had planned to meet Robert by the river. Somehow, she convinced her attendants that she did not need an escort, which proved to be an exhausting task in itself.

Mary Katherine arrived before Robert and sat on a rock, her mind reeling as she tossed small pebbles into the shallow clear water watching them settle to the bottom.

"Will he come?" she kept asking herself over and over. Sitting alone, she could hear the light gallop of a horse as it rounded the bend. Her heart took a leap as though it skipped a beat in the hopes that it was not someone else. On impulse, she almost bounced to her feet, but then with great restraint, she held back, not wanting to reveal her eagerness for his arrival.

Robert jumped from his horse and dropped the reins close to Diamond. The two horses acknowledged each other with a neigh and a light one-foot action in the soft grass as though they themselves were embarking on the beginning of a romance.

Mary Katherine rose to her feet. Robert removed his hat as he approached her. Mary Katherine extended her hand, not in the fashion for a formal royal kiss, but as a tender gesture of hand holding.

Robert realized the gesture was not a formal one and reached for Mary Katherine's hand, then pulling her close to him before embracing her. This time, Robert kissed her longer and with more passion. They rode their horses, jumping boulders, laughing, and racing in the green meadows. Robert helped Mary Katherine down from Diamond to water and rest the animals. He was unable to resist the temptation to kiss her. Walking and leading the horses, they talked.

"Mary Katherine, are you feeling the same as I?"

"Yes, I think so, Robert. I know I find myself thinking of you. I wonder what you might be doing. I find myself wondering if I will be able to see you again. Robert, are these the things you think of?"

Robert felt an inward sigh of relief, for he did not want this to be awkward for Mary Katherine.

Holding her hand, he gently and softly began, "Mary Katherine, I know this is fast, but I do believe this is called love. I love you, Kate."

"And I love you, Robert."

Before she could think, should she or should she not hold back her feelings, Robert kissed Kate with a desire to assure her of his love and affection.

"Robert, no one has ever called me Kate. I like it. Say it again, please."

"Kate," he whispered it slowly and sensuously. He then kissed her on the forehead.

"This is the most beautiful afternoon. It is good to know that we think alike about our relationship," confided Kate. With a bit of reluctance in her voice, Kate continued, "You know, Robert, this is going to be very difficult for us. As next in line to the throne, I am expected to marry nobility."

Catching herself, she realized she was perhaps putting words in Robert's mind by mentioning marriage; after all, their relationship is such a new one. She wanted him to understand what could possibly lie ahead for them.

"I am sure the king will do all he can to discourage our love."

"Kate, my love, we will not allow anything to destroy the love we have found."

Kate leaned into Robert for a reassuring caress. "I am sure Liz will help us stay in touch."

The afternoon passed with the two continuing their talk of their newfound love and the complications that it was sure to create.

"It is getting late. I must return Diamond to the stables."

They embraced with a lingering kiss. Robert tenderly brushed her red hair back from her eyes as she tied her bonnet.

"I will have Liz continue delivering our notes. She is very fearful for us."

Robert helped her mount Diamond. Their parting seemed to be harder each time.

The princess knew she had to have the help of Liz to carry on any secret rendezvous between her and Robert. Her fear was how long Liz would be willing to keep up the charade.

Liz was anxiously awaiting Mary Katherine's return. Liz, who was now involved in the secret relationship, asked the princess, "Your Highness, how deep are your affections for Robert McCall?"

"Liz, I do so love him. Oh, Liz, we do enjoy each other's company. He is most certainly a gentleman. We have declared our affections for each other. It is so good to tell someone of our love."

The princess crossed the very large bedroom chamber, answering Liz as she went.

Liz followed the princess. "Your Grace, all these years I have raised you as if you were my child. Your happiness is of great concern to me. I am sure you will agree, His Majesty will be most displeased that you have chosen Robert McCall as a suitor."

"I know, Liz, that there are dangers in this relationship as far as the king is concerned, but I do love Robert so and he loves me."

"Your Grace, please be careful. You are leading with your heart and not your mind. Much is required of you as the future ruler of this empire," Liz tried to give some parenting advice.

"It is most apparent my parents led with their minds and not their hearts." Mary Katherine quickly turned in a high-nosed fashion, throwing her bonnet on the bed.

The long days of summer lent many opportunities for Mary Katherine and Robert to meet. They found with each new encounter that their lives were being filled with a deepening romance. Liz, with great unease, assisted in making many of these meetings available for the two of them.

One particular summer day, Liz had the kitchen pack a picnic of cheeses, breads, sausages, wine, and cool watermelon. This day, Kate met Robert.

"Robert, it is so good to be with you again. I do so enjoy your company."

"Kate, I miss not being able to caress you and tell you of my love every day." His kiss was tender and inviting.

Upon finishing their picnic lunch, Robert asked, "Kate, what should we do for the afternoon?"

Kate paused with a gleam in her eyes. "Robert, I have all my life been behind the castle walls. I have never been down in the village alone to walk the streets, see and mingle with the people of my kingdom. Liz has always been with me in the royal carriage. I would love to go to the village and to the shipping docks. I won't be recognized because I have on a most simple dress. It will not draw attention."

"If that is what my lady wants, then that is what my lady shall have," answered Robert, very pleased.

They walked the market streets, enjoying the camaraderie among the villagers. The princess loved the jesters with their alluring talents and the merchants selling their fresh summer vegetables and exploiting their bartering skills. Mary Katherine was thrilled with the exuberant life the people on the streets exhibited. The children were running, playing ball and stick games. She thought how much she had missed always being shielded by the castle walls, having spent many days alone without the pleasure of a playmate.

Robert took her hand as they walked through the crowded street, pulling her close, protecting her from being shoved about. Stopping by a flower vendor, he reached for a nosegay and paid the merchant. He handed the flowers to Kate and whispered in her ear so no one else could hear, "Flowers for a most beautiful princess."

Kate once again melted into him. They then walked down the hill to the coast where they saw the merchant ships docked. Among the exports were barrels and barrels of Irish potatoes. The fishing ships were in for the evening with their sea catch. Excited, Mary Katherine had an interest in the village and its people. She had never before seen the citizens hard at work. The stirring air had the blended smell of sea salt and fresh fish. Laid along the docks in meticulous rows were the fishing nets and buoys in need of repair.

The day was drawing to a close. Robert and Kate lingered as long as they dared. Liz cautioned them that dark would soon be upon them. The setting sun cast shadows on the jagged rock hills and on the sandy gray coastline.

Kate was reminded of the royal tablecloth and asked Robert of its progress. Robert told her, "It is finished. I need to present it to the king."

Kate excitedly replied, "Very good, then I shall be able to see you soon."

Their embraces and kisses were longer and revealed their pain in parting.

Chapter 5

I T WAS AN EARLY MORNING in late summer, and the air was moist and warm as Robert rode across the drawbridge over the mote surrounding the castle. Over his shoulders, bundled in a canvas string sack, was the finished royal tablecloth made of the finest Irish linen. The cloth featured the rich design of the American eagle with its wings spread wide. Robert was feeling a great deal of anxiety. He deeply felt this to be his greatest weaving accomplishment and hoped it would be received well by the king. He drew a deep breath as he approached the doorman for permission to enter through the great castle doors, all the while hoping he might catch sight of Kate. He walked down a long corridor, passing a number of doors, each with a guardsman, before coming to the throne room door. Pausing, he pulled in a second deep breath, completely filling his diaphragm, while drawing his hands over his hair. He was dressed in his finest attire. He was hoping his nervousness would not be evident to His Majesty.

The doorman announced, "Your Majesty, Robert McCall."

Robert approached the throne. He bowed and addressed the king, "Your Majesty. I have finished the royal tablecloth. I trust it will be to His Majesty's liking." Taking the sack from around his shoulder, he untied the drawstring, and removing the cloth, he asked the king, "Your Grace, if someone could help unroll the cloth?"

The king motioned a guardsman to assist Robert. King George stepped down the three stone steps from the throne to further inspect the tablecloth. Admiring the fine linen and the quality of the weave, his eyes fixed upon the eagle. His face turned a flushed red, his eyes bulged, and his jaw tightened. He then exploded into a furious rage.

"Arrest this man! Off with his head! The charge is treason."

King George III was highly insulted that Robert McCall would design a tablecloth using an American eagle. The relationship between the British Empire and the Americas was strained at best. The American Revolution was unfolding. The palace guards grabbed Robert by the arms and dragged him from the presence of the king.

Robert declared, "Your Majesty, I meant no harm to Your Lordship or to the Mighty British Empire."

Robert found himself in the darkest of dark places. Not used to such dismal surroundings, he concluded that this had to be the most bewildering moment in his lifetime. The guards threw him into the dark damp room, forcing him to his hands and knees. As he crouched in one corner of the room, he felt straw on the floor as an animal would in a stall. The loud, screeching, deafening sound of strong metal-to-metal doors closed behind him and left him with a desperate sick feeling. He knew he was in the castle dungeon. It was not at all comfortable; there was not even a bed.

"How had it come to this?" he asked himself.

He could not help but wonder if he would ever see Kate again. Was this the king's way to end his relationship with Kate? The day grew long, and he saw no one. He had no one with whom to defend himself. He was uncertain if he would ever see the light of day.

The noise of a pounding hammer against wood awakened him from a semiconscious sleep. He could hear voices, but they were not clear enough to distinguish the words. In his wildest fears, he could only imagine it to be the building of scaffolding to support the spectators for his own beheading. So soon, he thought, and without even a constable to plead his case. Unable to see light, he had lost his connection to the time of day. Crawling about on his hands and knees, he was able to find a water bucket. Lifting it to his face, he made sure it was clean water and not waste. The thought sickened him, and he was only able to quench the dryness of his mouth.

Meanwhile, Mary Katherine was in her chambers. The news of Robert's fate had reached her by way of the servants. The princess overheard the chambermaids talking about the handsome fabric weaver held in the dungeon, awaiting the beheading orders from the king. She was in disbelief of all that had manifested itself this day, and she was uncontrollable with anguish and fear for Robert.

Liz tried desperately to console her, knowing the time was short for Robert.

Mary Katherine wept, declaring to Liz between outcries, "This cannot happen. I shall not live without Robert. I will die, should my father carry through with his declaration of death by beheading Robert."

Liz was fearful for the princess; she knew of her deep and abiding love for Robert. She knew Mary Katherine would will her own demise through grief.

Liz tried to comfort the princess. "Your Grace, your sorrow and grief saddens me. We must talk quickly where we cannot be heard."

Liz gently guided the weeping princess into a small linen closet.

"I have a plan. It can be very dangerous for all of us." The princess, still in a state of shock and crying uncontrollably, was taken by the shoulders of her lifelong servant and shaken. "Mary Katherine, you must stop crying so you can listen and help me if we are to free Robert. It requires you to make a lifetime of sacrifices. My question to you is this: Is your love strong enough to withstand a lifetime of sacrifices?"

Mary Katherine lifted her skirts to dry the tears from her face. "Oh yes, yes, I do so love him. I will do whatever it takes to free him."

"Listen to me, Your Grace, you will have to abdicate. You will no longer be a royal heir to the throne." With great urgency and concern, Liz asked again, "Mary Katherine, do you understand me? Do you truly understand what this action means?"

"Yes, Liz, I do realize the meaning of abdication." The princess listened more attentively to her confidante.

Together, they devised a plan, one that, if they were caught, would be fatal to all three. It would require that they wait until early morning before it could be implemented.

Chapter 6

I T WAS A VERY FOGGY early morning. The carriage Liz had ordered the evening before was waiting for her at the castle door nearest the dungeon. Since Liz was a direct servant to the princess, she had access to most of the castle. She went to the great kitchen and prepared a food tray for Robert, which she covered with a towel. Passing a wall rack holding kitchen aprons, she grabbed one, tying it on and covering her head with a scarf. Liz knew the guard would be heavily armed with a metal helmet, thus making it impossible to render him unconscious. Sadly, she concluded there was only one way. Meanwhile, Kate packed some traveling essentials in two valises. She put on her heavy cape and then, in a rush, gathered one for Liz as well for the morning was cool and misty. At this point, she did not know where they would go, but knowing they would need something of value to sustain them, she went down to the magnificent dining hall to the china closet and packed as much of the palace silver as she alone could carry. Then struggling, making her way in and out of recessed halls and doorways, she was careful not to be seen. She quietly found her way to the waiting carriage. There she waited for Liz and Robert. She was not sure how Liz was going to free Robert; time had not allowed them to discuss Liz's role in the escape. Liz, still being the protector of the princess and with added caution, was very careful not to tell her of all the impending details.

Liz slipped her way out of the kitchen down the dark stairs to the dungeon, carrying the covered tray of food. Robert was the only prisoner, which made it easy to locate his door. Smiling at the sentry, she said, "Good sir, I have food for the prisoner and some bread and cheese for you, sir."

He turned his back on Liz and put the cast-iron key in the lock. Liz was positioned directly behind the guard. She drew a large kitchen knife from under the cloth and dragged the knife under his chin across his throat. Being taller than the guard gave Liz an advantage, but performing this gruesome act was something from which Liz would never recover. Dropping the knife quickly, she finished turning the lock, and not looking down for she dare not look at the bleeding guard, she hastily called to Robert, "It's Liz, quick, be quick."

Robert recognized her voice and followed her lead. Very carefully, they eased their way around the guards as they retraced the passageways. Upon reaching the door, Robert saw the awaiting carriage. Knowing he was a better horseman than Liz, he quickly took over the reins. Getting into the carriage, he was surprised when he saw Kate. There was no time for formalities, not even a kiss for Kate.

It would soon be daybreak. There was no turning back. Life now and forevermore would be changed for the three of them. Liz informed them of the rest of her plan. "We will go to the shipping dock where we can board a ship for America. We know we can never remain anywhere in the kingdom. We must do this thing as hard as it might be."

Leaving the country was the only way they could have escaped sure death, even that of the princess.

Liz was still quite shaken from the violence she had inflicted on the guard. She could not allow herself to think of it as murder. She rationalized her thinking as a choice between the imminent death of Robert, Mary Katherine's true love, or that of the guardsman. The princess was all she had as family, and she had spent her entire adult life caring for Mary Katherine. Now she must leave Ireland forever for a new and strange land. Having been a servant to the royal family had afforded her a lifestyle better than most people of the village. For the moment, she put these thoughts behind her for time was short. Soon, they would be missed at the castle, and an intense search would ensue.

Liz, knowing the danger, advised, "We must leave the carriage and book passage quickly before we are found. This I will do for fear of you being recognized, Your Highness." Looking directly into Mary Katherine's eyes and with a firm voice, she reiterated, "From this day forward, Mary Katherine, you will no longer be addressed as royalty. Do you understand what this means?"

Mary Katherine, with a trembling voice, replied, "For Robert, my love, I will give up all nobility."

Robert, unable to resist, gave Kate a tender kiss. "Kate, no man can be as fortunate as I to have the love of one as pure and giving." Robert reached to pull Kate's cape and hood secure around her face. "This so you stand a less chance of being recognized."

Liz, still being the caregiver to the princess, cautioned, "You stay very close to Robert while I secure our passage."

Robert, taking Kate by her hand and leading her, whispered, "Let's walk over and around the cargo as if we are looking for goods until Liz returns."

"Robert, I am dreadfully fearful for all of us."

"Kate, if we can board the ship soon, I feel we will be quite safe." He hoped this would ease Kate's fears while giving her hand a gentle squeeze.

"Good morning, good sir." Liz approached the ship's purser.

"And a fine morning it is, madam."

"I have very fine silver. How many passengers to board your ship will this purchase?"

Liz took from the valise all the silver, except for three goblet pieces, which she tucked under their garments.

With a facetious look, the purser studied the goods. "Fine silver it is, madam. You don't think this will be missed by the king, do you?" He recognized the king's emblem. "I will give you passage for two."

Liz was afraid to barter for three, realizing passage for two would perhaps be wiser. The king's guardsmen would be in search of and asking for three people.

"Very well, two it is," answered Liz.

Leaving the purser, she searched for Kate and Robert. Her head was still in a fog about all that had taken place these last few hours; she wished things could have been different. "How will I ever recover? Kate must never know the extremes this day has brought forth." Her head was reeling almost as if she was near fainting. "Robert saw the guard, the blood and the knife. Surely, he knows what I had to do." Looking about, Liz saw the pair at the end of the dock. She made her way to them, weaving in and out of the potato barrels which were waiting to be loaded. With an intense look on her face, she said, "We only had enough silver for the purchase of two boardings."

Kate once again became a little distraught. "Whatever shall we do?"

Robert looked about for those who might be in search of them, saying, "The two of you board the ship as quickly as you can. Find a good place to be out of the way that you might not be recognized."

Both Kate and Liz in unison spoke out, "What will you do, Robert?"

Kate choked up and, almost in tears, stammered, "I will not leave without you, Robert."

Seeing Kate's distress, Robert took her by the shoulders and looked her straight in the eyes. He calmly assured her, "See those potato barrels?"

"Whatever for?" whimpered Kate.

Liz got excited and immediately understood what Robert was thinking. "Yes, Robert, that will work! A stowaway."

Hugging Liz and giving Kate a very passionate kiss and hug, Robert bid them good-bye, telling them, "I will see you in a few days. That will give us time to be well out at sea. Liz, please take care of Kate and yourself."

"Do be very careful, Robert. I do love you, Robert."

"I love you, Kate. See you soon, my love." He broke their hand hold.

Kate, blinded by tears, left Robert. Liz was holding her hand and leading her as they made their way through the passengers. Robert watched from a distance, hoping they would not be recognized as the two pushed their way through those boarding and up to the gangplank. When he was sure they were aboard the ship, he went in search of an almost empty potato barrel.

Robert found a barrel with few potatoes. Climbing in, he covered himself by pulling the wooden lid back in place. He knew he was faced with another very uncomfortable day and night and that his biggest risk for discovery would be during the loading. Stowaways were not dealt with very kindly. His lot would be as dreadful as that which the king declared.

"Kate, keep your cloak around your face, and do not look anyone in the eye until we are safe," advised Liz.

She guided the young princess to a safe place aboard the ship, staying in front of her and shielding her, all the while leading her by the hand and not allowing anyone to look directly into Kate's face.

The ship carried sixty-six passengers, fourteen crewmen, and one stowaway. The ship's purser was a dirty, sweaty, little man with few teeth and a gruff deep voice that did not coincide with the mousey little man giving the departing orders. "The voyage will take about fifty-three days to cross the Atlantic, depending on head winds. We should dock in the Chesapeake Bay in late October. Storms can be mighty and demand more than a body can sometimes give. Everyone has to do their share of needed work to stay alive during the storms. They can come from hell and be guided by the devil himself. If you don't do your part, we will heave your body over the side to the sharks."

Reality quickly hit both women. This would be a very difficult voyage for both Mary Katherine and Liz for they were accustomed to the finer things. The two women had come aboard with very few provisions. Robert had nothing except the clothes on his back.

To the west, the sun was setting as the anchor was hoisted. The ship began to leave the harbor. It was very slow-moving as the vessel made its way out to sea and allowed the wind to fill its large ballooning sails.

Liz called Mary Katherine Kate more and more often. This was a hard thing for Liz to do after so many years of servitude, but she knew it was necessary for Kate to get used to a new life. And she needed to protect her identity.

Going below the main deck after several hours of slow sailing, Kate and Liz found their crude accommodations. They were not at all what they were accustomed to. Their sleeping quarters were bunk beds and hammocks and were shared with fifteen or more women along with crying children. The cabin was very small and cramped with an odor that could not be described by either woman.

Liz murmured to Kate, "I don't think we will be down here anymore than needful."

This was the first time sailing for most of the passengers. People were getting sick with the tossing movement of the ship. Small children and babies were crying, thus expelling all they had eaten that day.

Kate and Liz were reeling with exhaustion and hunger, for it had been all most two days since they had had rest or food.

They were trying to stay topside as long as possible before retiring. They leaned over the railing and watched the green mountains of Ireland slowly disappear and then rise again behind the rolling sea. Slowly, they sailed out into the deep waters ahead of them, leaving them with the sad realization that they would never return to their beloved Ireland.

The cook from the galley in the hold offered those who could eat warm mutton stew with potatoes, along with straight flour-and-water fried bread.

Kate was feeling very queasy and wasn't able to eat even with Liz's gentle persuasion. "Kate, we must eat to keep up our strength. I know it is not what we are accustomed to, but it is nourishment. It is what the people of the village eat."

"Perhaps tomorrow, Liz."

Kate then closed her eyes and pulled her cape tighter around herself. She kept shifting until she found a comfortable resting position leaning against the forecastle of the ship.

Liz accepted a bowl of stew and a piece of bread. She felt for Robert because she knew nothing would be offered to him and how hungry he must be by this time.

Robert tried to make his quarters in the very back of the potatoes, hoping those needed would be taken from the front. He once again found himself in a darker than dark place in the bowels of the ship. His body ached with paralyzing pain after being in a bent position, knees to nose. Without lifting the wooden lid to the potato barrel, he could smell an indescribable stench. It was coming from some rotten potatoes and was almost more then he could bear. Feeling very hungry, he finally began to eat the raw potatoes to quiet the growl of his stomach. He found the potatoes gave a fair amount of liquid which he desperately needed. He knew right away sleeping was going to be a difficult thing because of the rodents crawling over the potatoes. The ship did have cats aboard for this very reason, which was evident from the cat and mouse games going on. He himself, unlike his furry roommates, was quite exhausted. His thoughts were of Kate and how he wished that things could have been different for them. Her sacrifices had been enormous, her spirit strong, would she regret it? He wondered if he would ever find himself truly worthy of her affections. His thoughts were of Liz and the daring things she had done. How could he ever repay her? With these thoughts, he drifted into a much deserved sleep. He was awakened the next morning by the cook clamoring for supplies for the day's meals.

The ship was now out to sea, and the rough mountain peaks had fallen behind in exchange for the rolling white caps of the deep blue waters that left no visible land in sight. Nearly everyone was recovering from motion sickness and trying to gain their sea legs.

Kate and Liz left their quarters for the main deck. It was good to breath in the fresh salty sea air. The midday sun was now directly above them as they sailed due west. The two talked concerning Robert very softly and most privately for fear of being overheard. Liz spoke in a subdued tone to Kate. "I feel sure Robert can join us in a few days. It should be safe for him to mingle among the men for short periods. Most of the men slept on the main deck last night. Perhaps they will continue to do this on good sailing nights. It is hopeful Robert might be able to do this without being discovered."

The vessel had a minimal crew, and every man had to do his work plus that of another. This would be to Robert's advantage, hoping no one would take notice of him. Kate finally took a bowl of mutton and potato stew along with the flat bread.

"Is this leftover from the evening before?" She didn't realize that this would be the mainstay of nourishment for the entire trip. After a bite of the stew, she said, "It's not so bad." She sopped the flat bread in the stew, soaking up the hot broth.

From out of nowhere, she heard the shrill cry of a woman. Looking up, she saw a mother in a frantic struggle trying to reach to a small child who had found his way to the poop deck, the highest deck on the ship. The deck had very little railing around it, which made it most unsafe for little ones. With the quick thinking of a sailor on the deck, the child was rescued and handed over to the mother. Little did Kate know, this was but a small bit of the excitement that would follow in the remaining days at sea.

The day was drawing to a close, and they had been at sea for two beautiful golden Western sunsets. The waters were still, and the ship, with its sails full of the sea air, seemed to be in a gentle glide across the surface. The yellow, gold, and red rays from the setting sun shone over the looming deep, giving it the appearance of fine silk. Kate took in its amazing beauty and, for the first time, realized the enormity of the earth and all its varying compositions. She could feel the strength she was gaining from eating. She no longer felt dizzy and weak. She thought of Robert, knowing he had little or nothing to eat in that dark hole. Perhaps tomorrow, he could come from the bowels of the ship and they could talk. There was so much to talk about.

She was grateful the king's henchman had not discovered them during their sudden departure. She wondered of her parents. Had they realized all that had happened concerned the three of them? Were they connecting the pieces? She felt sure they knew she and Liz had escaped with Robert. She wondered if it had yet been discovered that the palace silver was missing. It was her hope that no one else would be blamed for its disappearance. This would be a very serious matter with dreadful repercussions. Kate was still unaware of all the details of their escape. She didn't know that if they were caught, their punishment would be much worse than for that of stolen silver.

Kate's thoughts were quickly changed when the winds began to pick up and the sky suddenly became very dark. The sea turned from blue-green waters to a deep mysterious gray. The sails filled with wind, becoming tight as they pushed the vessel faster. All the women gathered the children and headed below deck. The crew came from the forecastle to take their positions as they tethered the ropes.

"This is good, not a devastating storm, but one strong enough to move the vessel through the waters at a worthy speed!" yelled Captain Wallace at the helm. The captain was a rough weathered man with wrinkles sculptured by years at sea.

Kate and Liz went below with the other women. It was dark, forcing their eyes to adjust to a single candle in the room. The air was stale. The children were crying and fearful of the approaching storm. It was a restless night for all in the cramped quarters. Kate found herself in a dream. She was riding Diamond through the meadows of the royal estate. She could again feel the fresh air as it blew through her hair. She woke up in a sweat, her clothes damp. The room was hot from all the body heat generated by sleeping women and children. If only a good breeze could come from the one small window hatch. It must have been just after midnight, and the storm surely had passed because she could see stars, the night sky was clear. Finding it difficult to sleep, she turned over, trying to make herself more comfortable. The straw tick mattress made crunching sounds as she turned. Her bedding was very rough and lacked the freshness of a good laundry.

For two days and nights, Robert rolled and tossed with the potatoes. He was becoming sicker with the motion of the sea. His own vomit could not be detected because of the foul odors that overwhelmed him. The darkness, along with the never-ending motion of the rocking ship, gave him vertigo, disallowing him to stand on his feet. Would he ever be free of this misery and able go topside?

The third morning, Kate was hopeful Robert would feel safe to come from the depths of the ship.

Robert managed to pull himself up to the upper deck. He couldn't stand his own filthiness as he edged his way to the wake to allow the salty sea spray to wash away his disgust.

Everyone gathered around the ship's cook who had pots of mush with a little salt meat for breakfast. Standing in line with an empty bowl, Kate suddenly realized that never before had she ever waited for any of her wants. She caught a glimpse of Robert, and she knew how famished he must be. Receiving his mush, he moved alongside the bulkhead, and leaning into it, he began to eat. Kate, after receiving her mush, looked across the bow of the ship. As her eyes caught a glimpse of Robert, her heart leaped. He had survived his self-imprisonment. She moved over to Robert, recognizing his weakness due to his lack of food and water. She was so relieved to see him that she gave to him her bowl, still filled with the unappetizing mush. Robert took it without reservation. She gave him time to eat before they spoke. Robert was very careful not to draw attention to himself. Being discovered would certainly mean he would be thrown across the ship's waist and into the sea. His need for water was much greater than his need for food. Regaining strength, he wiped his face on his sleeve and looked at Kate.

"Kate, how are you doing? This must be so hard for you, leaving your home, your wealth, and your parents." He noticed tiredness in her that he had never before seen. "You look so tired. How are your quarters?"

"Robert, I will be much better now that I have seen you and know that you are all right. It is worth the sacrifice to know that you are alive and we have escaped the wrath of my father."

"Kate, I am so blessed to have a love such as yours. How will I ever be able to repay you and Liz?" He lifted her chin and gave her a very gentle kiss.

"Oh, Robert, I have so needed your affection. We have been through so much these last few days."

"Kate, it isn't as I had planned it to be." Robert took her hands in his. "I have nothing to offer you but my everlasting love. What kind of life lies ahead of us, I do not know or if you will have me. Will you do me the honor of becoming my wife?"

"Oh yes, Robert, I will be your wife." Kate smiled at Robert, once again looking into the depth of his gentle eyes.

Robert again kissed her tenderly. Kate returned the kiss with adoration.

"Robert, I have failed to ask, how old are you?"

"Why, Kate, do you ask now?" He had a little tickled laugh in his answer.

"Robert, it is such a personal question for a lady to ask a gentleman. Now that we are to wed, I feel free to ask the question."

"Well, Kate," he answered her, smiling, "I am twenty-four."

In her own mind, Kate concluded that he was six years her senior and that he should be a good protector. They enjoyed the rest of the morning together.

Fresh water was a daily portioned commodity used for drinking and cooking. Rain water was captured in barrels stationed throughout the ship. After three days at sea, the realization of how hard ship life was beginning to manifest itself in Kate. She had always been sheltered and pampered with much privacy. The two ladies found themselves staying atop the main deck to escape the discomfort of their quarters. The harshness of the wind and sun was giving their milky white skin uncomfortable sunburn and causing their lips to crack and bleed. They had nothing to ease their misery.

Liz had an idea; she told Kate, "Fat gathers around the top of our mutton bowls. Let's save some so that we might grease our lips and skin to ease some of this pain."

The mutton grease certainly did not lend itself to the sweet fragrances of almond butter and rose water which Kate always had in her toiletries.

She told Liz, "I don't think I could kiss Robert even if I wanted to, which I so want to. Liz . . ."

"Yes, Kate."

"Robert asked me to be his wife."

"What was your answer?"

"I said yes, of course."

Liz was not at all surprised that Robert would propose after all they had been through.

"Kate, I am so happy for you. You and Robert will be happy, I am certain."

"Then you will give us your blessing?" asked Kate.

"I most certainly do, Kate." Liz was greasing her lips.

Kate's heart was saddened a bit in realizing that Liz was the only one who could grant them a blessing, something that should have come from her parents. She was very happy that she and Robert were to wed. When, she did not know.

The children were becoming rowdy, running and getting under foot of the sailors at work. Aboard ship, unattended children quickly becomes a hazard; Liz recognized their boredom.

Liz remarked to Kate, "Kate, I think we can do a lot to help the mothers and keep the children occupied at the same time."

"What do you have in mind, Liz?"

"I think we can have lessons, songs, and storytelling for the children. In return, the ladies could do our laundry and keep our bedding fresh."

Kate's eyes brightened, and she became excited with the prospect of fresh bedding. Besides, the days were long and boring, and having something to fill the time would be greatly welcomed.

"Let's think, what we can teach? We have no books or paper or pen," concluded Kate.

"Well, let's think. I know! We can use objects such as sticks or wood chips for adding and take away for a start." Liz reminded Kate of her early schooling.

"I will ask Captain Wallace if he has paper and pens to spare. Surely he would be willing so that we might keep the children occupied and out of danger."

Kate was smiling as she turned to find Captain Wallace.

In the meantime, a mother and three of her children were below deck in their quarters. One of the children, in rough play, knocked the candle off the wall. The candle fell onto one of the bunks that had a straw tick for a mattress.

"Fire, fire, fire in the hold!" was a shout from below. Screaming children bailed out of the hold, behind them a raving mother with a small child on her hip. Flames were ascending high as the cabin filled with smoke.

The mother hollered, "Jacob—where is Jacob?"

One of the sailors went down into the smoke-filled room. Everyone waited with nothing but fear for the child. Out came the sailor with Jacob in his arms; they were both gasping and coughing when they caught a breath of fresh air.

"Bucket brigade, bucket brigade, quick, be quick, I say!" was the command from Captain Wallace. Everyone who could was running with buckets of seawater, trying to spare the fresh water. The fire was extinguished, and everyone settling down realized that this was a very close call. The captain was not a happy seaman. To have such a dangerous thing happen aboard his ship, the call was too close. Fire aboard ship is one of the most dreaded hazards.

A day or two passed as Kate gave the still annoyed captain time to recover from the fire fiasco. "Captain Wallace, sir. If it pleases the captain, might I have a moment of your time?"

"Yes, madam. Be quick with yah. I have no time for nonsense."

The captain appeared to be irritated that a lady would request a moment of his time.

"After the fire two days ago, it has come to my attention that the children need supervision. I am willing to hold a time for learning for the children. You could call it a school."

The captain looked at Kate in her tattered clothing, and he did not realize her status. He did, however, recognize her fine way of speech; it was not as that of common people.

"Yes, yes, anything to corral the little hellions. Tie 'em up if needs be," Captain Wallace spoke in a graveled tone while trying to walk away.

"We are in need of some supplies, such as paper, pen, and ink, if there is any to spare." Kate hurried just a step or two behind him, trying to keep up with his pace.

Captain Wallace quickly turned and got in her face to make sure she understood his position. "Madam, I am not in the business of schooling. I am a sea captain and a mighty fine one at that. I will see what I can do to satisfy your needs. Now be off with yah."

Kate was excited to give Liz the good news. "Liz, the captain is willing to help us with our teaching supplies. I am going to find Robert and tell him of our news."

Kate and Robert found time for each other sometimes throughout most of the days.

"Robert, Liz and I have spoken with Captain Wallace about teaching the children. We need to keep them out of trouble. I have the skills in numbers and reading, and these children have never had an opportunity for study."

The two settled in to eat their boiled potatoes along with hard cheese and flat bread.

"That is a wonderful idea, Kate, for you and Liz to fill your days with something of value. I am most proud of you. How many students do you think you might have?"

"I have taken a count, and there are eighteen children aboard ship."

Robert wanted Kate to know that he supported her as she was in search of ways to fulfill her new and humbling lifestyle.

"Robert," Kate asked while eating her cheese and flat bread for lunch. "I can't imagine how our new life will be. What will this new land be like? Where will we live? What kind of work will we do for a living?"

Kate had never before had to wonder or trouble her mind with such matters.

"Slow down, Kate." Robert laughed, taking her hands in his. "We will work hard, side by side. We have four hands and two good minds, and we will do what is necessary to make our way."

"Robert, I do so love you. I feel protected and safe with you. You give me strength to face all adversities." After eating, they settled in for a short afternoon rest.

Chapter 7

CAPTAIN WALLACE MANAGED TO GIVE the two women some rough paper, one quail pen, and ink. It was enough to make numbers 1 through 10 and a list of the alphabet. They had an idea for a type of chalk. Now they needed to get a cup of flour from the cook; by adding water, it will make a thin white watery paste. Their idea was to use the thin paste to write on boards. Securing the flour from the cook might prove to be more of a challenge than the paper, pen, and ink from the captain.

The mothers were delighted for the children to have the opportunity to gain some form of education. It gave the women time to tidy their quarters and to do the laundry. The women were willing to barter with Liz and Kate for their teaching time with the children in return for laundry.

After chores, Robert and Kate had most of the evenings that they could spend together. There was not much that could be done after night fell. It was unsafe to roam about the ship in the darkness. Oil and candles were in short supply and had proven to be hazardous. When the weather permitted, they searched the heavens for the evening stars and told each other the myths of Zeus and other Greek and Roman gods and their homes on Mount Olympus.

The children gathered each morning after breakfast on the main deck for their studies. Kate discovered she liked the interaction with them. She found herself excited with their learning. She bonded with Jacob. He was a very blond boy with fair skin and sky-blue eyes that danced with excitement. He was very inquisitive and absorbed all she had to teach him. He especially loved to hear about the constellations. Kate spent evenings with him pointing out their locations in the ebony sky. He loved the stories of Robin Hood and Little John and how they supposedly robbed the rich and gave to the poor.

The evenings seemed to bring on a strange behavior in Liz which Kate realized. Liz was constantly hearing the wailing and cries of a female spirit known as a banshee. She said it was following the ship and that she couldn't free herself from it.

"There it is again, Kate." Moaning, Liz was holding her hands over her ears to shut out the cries as she twisted her head back and forth in what was almost a panic attack. "Listen, do you hear it? It's the banshee again, she will not shut up. She just screams constantly. I can't stand it. Someone is going to die, Kate. I know this to be true. The banshee is a sign. Her haunting cries indicate certain death among us."

"There, there, Liz, you are just tired and uncomfortable with all that has happened to us. Our lives have drastically changed with no advanced notice. I myself can't believe we are on a ship going to a strange land."

Liz became more distraught and could not concentrate on teaching, thus leaving most of the duty to Kate.

Jacob had developed a serious cough due to smoke inhalation from the cabin fire. Nothing anyone on board the ship could do eased his distress. Kate didn't relate Liz's behavior and Jacob's illness as one entanglement. Kate sat many hours during the day, trying to comfort Jacob with songs and stories. Jacob's congestion worsened. His high fever caused him to convulse and succumb to his illness. Kate was physically exhausted from the care she, along with others, had given Jacob. Her heart was broken. Never before had she been faced with the loss of someone so endearing to herself.

Jacob's little body was bound and wrapped with white linen fabric stripped from the petticoats of some of the women and then placed on a straight board. Twilight was the chosen time for his eulogy. The anguished cries of his mother could be heard over the churn of the sea.

The captain read Bible verses and gave a short prayer. Kate, with a broken heart and cracking voice, recited an evening star poem. Captain Wallace then commended his little body to the depths of the black waters.

Robert was sensitive to Kate's grief over the death of Jacob. That night, they slept on the top deck, along with others who felt very dismayed over the happenings of the day. Kate and Robert found a place secure from the harsh winds next to the bulkhead wall. Kate confided in him while he held her tightly in his arms.

Kate told Robert how sad she was over Jacob's death. "He was such a sweet little boy with much curiosity." She moved from her thoughts of Jacob to Liz. "Robert, something is wrong with Liz. She is just not herself. She is very agitated and speaks of a banshee following the ship. She is especially aggravated at nightfall. She hears a woman's constant cry and says she can't get it out of her head. It is said banshees are waiting for one to die. Do you suppose this to be true with little Jacob's passing?"

Robert was listening attentively to Kate's concern for Liz as he tried to ease her mind. "Kate, you know Liz is going to a new land with no family. I am sure she has many matters on her mind."

"Robert, she has us as family, and we will always care for her." Kate tightened her arm around Robert's arm, wanting to gain from his wisdom.

"You can be certain of that, Kate," Robert assured her. Yet in the back of his mind, he wondered if Liz was having trouble dealing with the morning of their escape. He dared not tell Kate of the terrible thing Liz had to do to free him. This would always be a lone burden for him to carry, for he did not wish for Kate to feel as heavy-hearted as he did.

The water was low and calm as it slapped the sides of the ship. Robert and Kate snuggled together, trying to keep warm. They fell asleep with the soothing rocking of the vessel.

Several days passed with good sailing. Kate and Liz continued with their classes. Once again, Kate had a hard time keeping Liz focused on their studies.

One morning, the sun's rays skipped across the peaceful blue-green waters casting radiant silver beams on top of the smooth rolling waves; this gave one reason to think it should be a calm day. However, looking to the far west, there was a massive black sky, and the ship was headed directly into its darkness. All of a sudden, the dark gloom manifested itself on all horizons. There was no time to veer around.

The vessel began to toss as the waves rolled with more power. Suddenly, the smooth waves heaved with white caps as the ship hit them head on. The captain and first mate were heard shouting commands, "All hands on deck! A repeat call, all hands on deck. Every one batten down the hatches."

The night crew awakened from their rest and tumbled out of the forecastle to man their stations. All loose items were battened down, and the mizzenmast was ordered to be lowered. The crew tethered themselves to the railing. Orders were given for the women and children to go below deck. Suddenly, it was darker than night for there were no moon or stars.

A gusting, howling wind brought a giant wave higher than the ship, swallowing all in its path as it rolled over itself back into the erupting sea. With great magnitude, the salty seawater rushed over the stern and bulkhead and washed every untied thing from side to side and out to sea, with no regard for life or matter.

Captain Wallace shouted, "God be with thee, every man for himself!"

A flash of lightning briefly revealed the chaos on board. The cracking of thunder echoed across the waters, then reverberated back, not knowing from whence it came. The ship began to groan with creaking sounds as though it were in pain, leaving those on board to wonder if she would survive or surrender to the swelling waters.

Liz and Kate huddled below deck. Each had tied themselves to a supporting post that they might not be thrown about the cabin. Liz felt very agitated. She spoke with wildness in her voice, which Kate had never before heard, sounding even more eerie in the depths of darkness. Kate tried to calm her, thinking it was the storm that had her so unsettled.

"Forgive me, Kate, the banshee, she won't stop wailing."

Liz, in anguish, worked in an uncontrollable manner to untie the straps holding her to the pole. Panic stricken, she fought her way to the top deck. At just that moment, a loud clap of thunder rang out in the night. A second flash of lightning exposed Liz throwing herself across the railing and into the heaving sea. The water engulfed her, taking her under as if it were angry and hungry for revenge. A second wave rolled back over into itself, leaving behind rough, powerful swells and adverse winds.

Just as quickly as it came, the storm subsided, leaving everyone stunned that they had survived. Those aboard, still shaken with the aftermath of the violent storm, gave thanks to God Almighty for what seemed like a reprieve. Captain Wallace, who still feared a storm coming from another direction, did not allow anyone to leave their stations. He was not as yet aware of a hysterical woman jumping to her death. The storm had been so fierce, no one had yelled, "Man overboard!"

As the sun broke through, it parted the blackness that was upon them. The light of the sky was meeting the white caps of the rising sea. It seemed as though the vessel was commanded to push its way through into the sun's rays. The ship wallowed in the deep waters as it heaved up and then down with each towering wave. All those below deck came to the main deck hot and sweaty; they were washed by the ocean spray blown upon them by the crashing of determined waves against the battered ship.

Captain Wallace shouted with great jubilation, "She's a fine vessel, a fine vessel she is!"

He gave orders that the ship be set back on its original course, due west.

Robert had remained on the main deck during the storm, enduring the barrage of waves toppling over the ship. His clothes were dripping wet with seawater as he searched for Kate and Liz. Finding Kate, he asked, "Where is Liz?"

"She broke away from me and went topside. Was she not with you, Robert?"

The worst of their fears were realized when the ship's purser took a head count. Robert was careful not to be among those counted. "We are missing one, presumably overboard." A roll call verified that Liz was missing.

Kate, riddled with grief and sadness, had lost her oldest friend and confidante. She thought that perhaps Liz had been washed out to sea with the last swells, never thinking that she would hurl herself overboard.

"You know, Kate," Robert reminded her, "we talked of Liz's dissatisfaction, about how troubled she seemed to be about something. She just could not deal with the terrible storm. It must have delivered its wrath upon her. More than anything, Liz would want you to be happy." Robert wiped her tears.

"I know, Robert. But my heart is broken," cried Kate.

"She sacrificed everything for our happiness. We must look forward to our new life and the good things it will bring," encouraged Robert.

Robert knew he had an arduous task before him. He searched for one word in the English language to soften the blow of Liz's death. To his dismay, he realized there were none.

Kate continued to cry while trying to compose herself. "I can't believe Liz is gone. Robert, she was all the family I had left. She knew more about me than my parents even dared to know. I only have you, Robert."

Kate clutched him as a fearful and overwhelming thought came that she might someday have to give him up to something unknown.

"Kate, you are all I have as well," he continued to console her.

With Robert's kind words and the gentle rocking of the ship, she drifted off into a restful sleep in his comforting arms.

After assessing the damage to his ship, Captain Wallace called the carpenters on board to do all they could to restore the ship to sea worthiness, using what boards and tar were available. Facing another storm of such magnitude would surely be fatal. He told his first mate, "The old girl might not make it through such a gale the next time around. Should we make it to America, we will be there for some time for major repairs."

Kate returned to teaching the children. This helped her forget the most dreadful experience she had faced in her life. Kate missed Liz terribly; she realized that Liz had always looked after her best interest. She missed little Jacob and his unending questions.

The days were now getting shorter and the sea winds colder on the top deck. Kate kept Liz's few belongings, knowing that she would want her to have them, which gave her some additional warm clothing. Robert, on the other hand, had nothing to keep him warm as the days grew more frigid. Kate gave him Liz's cape and a shirt-blouse that would help extend his clothing.

Captain Wallace announced that they did not have too many days left at sea. He had calculated the days out and took into consideration the bad weather they had encountered.

Chapter 8

"A HOY, LAND, LAND AHOY" WAS the early morning call. Everyone rushed to the railings shouting for joy as they looked forward to embarking upon the new life that awaited them. They also longed for the relief of once again having stability under foot as opposed to the constant roll of tossing waters.

Robert explained to Kate, "Kate, I must go back to the cargo hold for I cannot be among the numbered as we disembark. I will see you on the docks."

He gave Kate a lingering kiss as they parted.

It took Kate one trip below deck to secure her belongings.

The cook offered one last meal before leaving the ship, but not very many passengers took advantage of the thick mush and boiled potatoes. Kate thought, *I cannot do this again. No more mush for me.* She did take several of the potatoes and put them in her pockets.

Clankety-clank-clank, sounded the heavy chains as they lowered the rusty three-forked anchor into the Chesapeake Bay. The first mate shouted orders over the rattling noise to cast ropes and tie off.

Stepping off the gangplank and on to the soil of her new land, Kate drew in a deep breath and exhaled deeply. There was much fear and wonder as to what lay ahead for her and Robert. Her head reeled along with her legs feeling like jam as they adjusted to the firmness of solid ground. The voyage had been most difficult. She had witnessed birth and death and learned the nature, the rage, and the unforgiving violence of the seas. She had given up the throne and her homeland for love, and perhaps the most painful thing of all was leaving behind her parents. Kate realized the unlikelihood of ever returning to Ireland. These last two months had given her a great deal of maturing, along with a sudden surreal feeling of independence. Neither Liz nor Robert was by her side. At the moment, she was alone.

Once again, she went in search of Robert. If he had been successful with this last attempt at being a stowaway, they would truly be free. It was getting late, and Kate had walked the wharf for hours anticipating their reunion. Where could he be? Finally spotting him, she made her way across the dock. Joyously, they embraced, giving each other a well-deserved hug and kiss. Robert apologized that he was so long in meeting up with her. "I had to wait until the purser was satisfied with his passenger count. I came off the ship with the sailors."

It was late afternoon, and the sun was beginning to set. The weather felt mild, but cooler fall temperatures definitely loomed in the air. The maple trees were shedding their red and gold leaves. They tumbled through the brisk air and floated to the ground. The young and impoverished couple had to find refuge for the night. They freely conversed and made a short-term plan.

Robert took control of the situation and suggested, "Kate, first things first. We must find a justice to marry us this night."

Kate swallowed hard. She knew they were to marry; she just had not given thought as to when.

With great concern, Robert continued, "Kate, we have no money or means by which to pay a justice."

Kate answered by reminding him, "But we have three silver goblets that Liz saved for us."

A gasp of excited relief slipped from Robert's breath. Gathering up their few belongings, they walked away from the wharf in search of someone who could direct them to a justice. Following directions, they came upon a two-story house surrounded by a badly damaged picket fence. A sign reading Justice of the Peace swung back and forth in the ocean breeze, giving a metal against metal sound. The lower floor of the house was dark. A dim candlelight shone from the front window of the second floor. Robert stepped up to the front door and knocked with a gentle rap. The sun had already set, and evening grew late as they anxiously waited for an answer.

"Yes, yes, I'm coming, I'm coming!" shouted a sharp voice from the open upstairs window. The justice opened the door. He was an elderly man with white tossed hair, busy brows, and very uneven teeth. He wore an old faded nightshirt.

The justice held an oil lamp light out in front of him. It cast a yellow radiance into the faces of Robert and Kate. Looking quite tense and unsure as they stood before the justice revealed that they were new immigrants just off the ship. The justice was not at all dismayed by their appearance and asked, "Tell me what I might do for you?" Mumbling under his voice, he added, "Be quick about it."

"Could you marry us this night, sir?" Robert asked.

"Come in, come in, and warm yourselves. That I can do," announced the justice, ready for a hard coin. Yawning, he flipped through a stack of untidy papers on top of a desk in search of a Bible; he dug deep, which revealed its occasional use. The justice, a man of few words, delivered a short but meaningful ceremony in an uncaring and hurried tone. Closing the Bible, with a loud slap, he said, "And now I pronounce you married, Mr. and Mrs. Robert McCall. You can kiss your bride."

Robert drew Kate close to him for a not-so-romantic kiss. For his services, they bartered one of the silver goblets. The justice told them of a local tavern and inn for the night. "Ye might find food and ale as well."

The temperature steadily fell throughout the evening.

"Come, Kate, we must hurry, I fear there will not be any rooms available with everyone leaving the ship."

Robert took from Kate the two valises to make it easier for her as they walked briskly along, pulling their capes around them. Kate locked her arm through Robert's so that she could keep up with his long strides. Coming upon the inn, they heard loud singing. Some tavern patrons were whopping it up with songs and brews. Kate and Robert entered the dimly lit tavern. The merriment from the patrons stopped with the entrance of the couple. Pungent odors hit Kate, reminding her of the tight quarters on board the ship. Robert sat down the valises, removed the cape hood from his head, and asked for the innkeeper.

"That would be me, sir." A short stocky man as tall as he was round with a punchy stomach approached them while wiping his hands on a once-white apron.

"What might I do for ye?"

Robert asked, "Do you have a room, sir? We need a room for the night."

There was a low snicker from the onlookers whom Kate thought obviously to be seamen. Kate stood taking in all she saw. Never before had she been in such a tawdry establishment. Kate continued looking around while Robert was in conversation with the innkeeper about accommodations. She reached into her valise and brought out her beautiful needlepoint. It seemed so very long ago that she had created such fine handiwork. Speaking up and surprising Robert, she said, "Sir, might I interest you in this beautiful piece of fine stitching, all the way from Ireland, for a night's stay in your inn?"

The innkeeper was accustomed to wayfaring people who had very little means and accepted it, saying, "Well, pretty little lady, I really have no need for it, but I reckon how that it is late and no one else will be looking for a room at this late hour, I can find a place for it."

The innkeeper gave them one small burning candle that they might find their way to the top of the stairs.

"Mary Katherine McCall—I like it, Robert."

Kate kept repeating it, over and over, as they climbed the stairs to their room. She dismissed from her mind all the formal titles she had always been called. Kate was excited with her new title, Mrs. Robert McCall. But she was saddened that she had no one with whom to share this joyous news.

Reaching the top landing of the dark narrow stairs, they opened the door to the dismal room and stepped inside, waiting for their eyes to adjust to its blackness. Robert, with a hand in front of the flickering candle, found a bedside table on which he could place it. Robert built a fire with four or five small logs to warm the cold room. The floor was covered with a shabby wool rug. Next to the fire hearth were four bricks, which he placed in the fire to heat them. Kate remembered the potatoes she had earlier stuffed in her pockets and placed them on the bricks. Together, they stood by the fire and warmed their hands, hoping somehow the fire would burn hotter. While watching the flames cast dancing shadows on the dark dingy walls, Robert remarked, "Our candle and fire will soon burn out, leaving us to struggle in the dark."

After eating their warm boiled potatoes, they made ready for bed. Mary Katherine went to her valise. Slowly, she shifted things as she searched for a very soft white linen nightgown, which she found in the bottom. The gown was embellished with delicate tatting lace that she herself had hand made. Nervously, she slipped the gown over her head and pulled it down, then slipped out of her clothes beneath the gown, trying to be very modest. She removed her hairpins and loosened the braids, letting her hair fall while brushing through its thickness. The young groom kept his back to Kate, stirring the fire embers ever so often. He was trying to give her some much needed private time. He then wrapped the bricks and placed them in their honeymoon bed to help make it warm and comfortable for his new bride. Turning around, Robert saw Kate in the candlelight. Her hair hung long, down to her waist, and full of unbraided waves. Its red luster captured the iridescent glow of the moonlight. He had never seen her hair long and flowing; he allowed himself to do nothing but focus on her beauty. After brushing through her hair, Kate plaited it back in a single very loose braid. She had long since forgotten the handmaidens who had been at her every beck and call, doing such evening tasks for her.

They climbed into bed. Robert gave Kate a gentle kiss. He turned and snuffed out the candle on the small night table by his side.

Robert woke up the next morning and looked at Kate, marveling at her loveliness. At that moment, he made a promise to himself that he would always make himself worthy of her love and affection.

"Wake up, Kate, wake up," whispered Robert as he moved a long strand of red hair from across her cheeks.

Kate stretched and reached for Robert, drawing him closer to her as she kissed him. "Good morning, my love."

53

"Kate, it is going to be a busy day for us. We have very little and are in need of a great deal. We must get up and look for any available work for the day if we are to eat."

Robert jumped out of bed and stoked the fire to warm the room before Kate rose. Slipping into his clothes, he then once again gave her a sweet kiss. "I will go down and speak with the innkeeper to find out if there is any kind of day labor I might do."

One last time, he again kissed his new bride and closed the door gently behind him.

Kate got out of bed and placed her feet on the floor. Quickly, she drew them back under the warm covers when she realized the floor was cold and she had no house slippers. Shivering, she dressed to escape the chill, brushed her hair, and pulled it up and out of the way for the day. She had no fancy ornaments for adornment. Suddenly, she felt the growl of her hungry stomach for they had only eaten the potatoes from the day before.

Robert returned and helped Kate gather their things while telling her, "The innkeeper told me it might be possible to gain work on the docks. Kate, hurry before the work is taken for the day. Let's hurry, Kate, hurry."

Rushing down the stairs and through the tavern, the innkeeper stopped them. He offered each one a cold biscuit with a slice of fried pork fat. With much gratitude, the newlyweds thanked him for his kindness for their poor man's breakfast.

Quickly, they left the inn for the wharf. Robert asked several sea captains if they had available labor for an able-bodied man who was desperately in need of work. He secured one day's work by convincing a sea captain that he could repair fishing nets. After all, he was a weaver by trade.

Kate couldn't find work. She sat close to Robert on the valises as he worked, eating her cold biscuit. The biscuit was a welcome change to the everyday morning mush provided aboard ship. She found herself fascinated by the surroundings and watched the comings and goings of people doing their day trading.

After a hard day's work, Robert waited in line for his wages. The captain asked him to return the following day because his work displayed such fine quality. The earnings for the day were sufficed to buy a loaf of bread and a small spread of fresh butter with enough remaining for another night's stay at the inn.

Returning to the inn, they realized how tired they were. Robert made a suggestion. "Kate, the innkeeper seemed to have all the information concerning the community. I will ask him where we might find more permanent living quarters."

Leaving Kate in the room, he went downstairs to speak with the busy man about accommodations. Robert interrupted the innkeeper as he was wiping down a table, getting ready for his nightly patrons. "Good sir, might I ask you where one could find more permanent accommodations in this area?"

The innkeeper stopped as he rubbed his bristled chin and answered, "There are several cabins at the end of the street. People use them as they come and go. One might be available."

Returning up the stairs, excited with the information, Robert informed Kate, "While I am at work tomorrow, perhaps you should go and secure a cabin for us."

Kate was reluctant to do this as she thought, *I have never walked on a real street alone in my life. I have always had Liz or Robert nearby.* A sudden realization hit; her life was truly changing almost faster than she could comprehend. She remembered Liz asking, "Is your love strong enough to withstand a lifetime of sacrifices?" and her answer had been an emphatic yes.

In the morning, Robert left before daybreak for the dock. Kate gathered their belongings into the valises, thinking they were not as heavy as they had been when she carried all the silver.

Chapter 9

L EAVING THE INN, KATE WALKED down the street, dodging the mud holes caused by the early morning rain. The horse's hooves, along with wagon wheels, churned up the mud, making it as fine and sticky as a potter's clay. Seeing the horses, Kate remembered Diamond, but quickly, she erased the thought from her mind and returned to the business at hand. After asking several people, she was able to find one cabin vacant.

Kate stepped up on a large flat rock in front of the rough slatted door. It had wide spaces and gaps, letting in unwanted cold air and light. Her eyes took a quick inventory of the one room with its poor furnishings. On one outside wall was a small but adequate fireplace with a heavy cast-iron pot which hung over cooled coals. There was a rough timber bed with rope slating, a table with a low-burned candle, and two chairs, all crudely made. The cabin had only one window, and next to it hung some poorly hinged shelves with two tin plates. It seemed everyone who had used the cabins left a little something behind for the next guest to make life a little more comfortable, for all that had come to this new land were very much in need. Regardless, Kate was very thankful for these humble beginnings.

After work, Robert returned to the inn. The innkeeper told him, "Your wife has been gone all day. She was carrying quite a load for such a wee one."

Robert left and walked down the street toward the cabins in search of Kate. He caught a glimmer of her shimmering hair through the open door.

"Oh, Robert, I did it. I got us a cabin, our first home."

Even for Robert's standards, it was very meager, but he praised her. "You have done well, Kate. I know this must be very hard for you to live so simply. I promise you we will have better one day."

"Robert, I need to help. I have been thinking that I can teach. I am sure there are enough children around here who need schooling. Tomorrow, I will ask around for this purpose."

Robert became very optimistic and told her, "With some hard work and taking care of our earnings, we should be able to manage."

The young couple shared the remainder of the bread purchased the day before along with some water for their evening meal. Kate couldn't help but wish she had some of the peppermint tea she had so often enjoyed in the summer gardens at the palace. She dared not tell her new husband of her wishes in fear of adding to his burdens.

It was time for bed as the candle was all but burned out. They had no bedding to lie on, but Kate was learning to be more resourceful. She suggested to Robert, "Let's use one cape to lie on and the other to cover us with."

Robert responded with a very tired and fading voice, "My dear, that is a grand idea."

Kate promised herself that finding bedding and a few essentials would be her highest priority tomorrow.

"Robert," she whispered while punching him softly.

Robert was very tired and answered with a half-awake yes.

"We still have two silver goblets."

Robert muttered, "Just what are you thinking?"

"Suppose I take one to the mercantile for some needed items."

As he was falling asleep, Robert answered, "Whatever you think, dear."

Later in the night, they found it best to each wear a cape to cut the chill.

Robert was up before daybreak so that he could be in line on the dock for his promised day's work. Before leaving, he built a fire for Kate, knowing she had no experience as how to build a fire. Kate was up as well for sleeping was most uncomfortable. The newlywed's shelves were bare of food. Robert gave Kate a quick kiss as they parted for the day with a hope in their hearts and minds of determination that their tomorrows would be better.

Kate was very excited to go to the mercantile for the things she had in mind. After dressing, she took both goblets with her. She feared leaving them for they were all they had in the world. Kate had never shopped before, and she had a lot of uncertainties about bartering, even though she watched intently her father's dealings. She tried to think on a positive note to build her confidence. "I did secure a cabin for us all on my own." Princess Mary Katherine's shopping needs had been attended to by her ladies-in-waiting or the merchants who came to the castle just as Robert had done. Her stomach tied in knots as she entered the mercantile for the first time in her life.

Stepping into the store, her eyes widened in wonderment as she tried to look for what they needed. They were in need of so many things that she realized she would have to be careful as to what she chose. Her first priorities were bedding. After choosing the bedding, she shopped for soap, a candle, salt, fat meat, tea in a tin can, flour, two tin cups, two tin spoons, and a wooden water bucket. As she was ready to pay for her purchases, she spotted a ball of very fine thread. She had the idea of making tatting lace with the hope of selling it back to the mercantile. She felt sure this would work, and she could gain a fair return on her investment. Using the skills she learned from her father while hiding behind the royal blue drapes, she was again able to barter with one silver goblet. She pushed the last remaining goblet into the corner of her valise.

Kate packed all the small things into the bucket. She carried the bedding in one arm and swung the bucket from the other hand as she walked carefully, trying to dodge mud holes. She forgot her dress's edge, and it soon became thick and heavy with the sticky mud. Struggling with her load, Kate anxiously made her way back to the little cabin, shifting her purchases from one arm to the other.

With the cabin in her view, she caught sight of a number of children running and playing in the dirt yards. Seeing the children reminded her of the children aboard ship and the desire she had to teach. As she approached the cabin, the children ran up to her with great excitement and asked, "Lady, might we help you?"

Caught off guard, Kate replied, "Yes, you most certainly can help. If you would please open the door, that would be very kind." Inside the cabin, she placed everything on the table. Kate turned, startled by a lady standing on the flat rock by the door. She said "Hello." Extending her hand for a handshake, she introduced herself, "I am Mary Katherine McCall."

She realized that this was the first time she had referred herself to anyone by her new name.

"Nice to meet you. I am Sarah Thatcher, and these six children are all mine. Are they a bother to you?"

"Why no, they are not. Actually, they were a great help. Thank you."

"This here is Arianna, she is nine, and she is my biggest help. Nathaniel is seven. Lisa-Jean is five and a half. This is Penelope. She is four. Liam is three, and this little one is Levi. He is one and a half." He sat quite comfortably on her hip. "We have another on the way. At this point, it doesn't matter if it's a girl or a boy." Sarah laughed, a bit short of breath as she shifted Levi to her opposite hip.

Kate stood in amazement. "Well, it certainly is nice to meet you, Sarah, and you too, children. Thank you so much for your help. How long have you been here, Mrs. Thatcher?"

"Please call me Sarah. We arrived in May. My husband, Jonathan, thinks we should stay in the cabin through the winter. With a family this large, it takes time to raise money for fares up the Chesapeake."

That was quite evident to Kate for the children were standing there with no shoes and winter was a few days away. But to Kate, the children seemed to be happy and did not realize the harsh existence that was forced upon them.

Sarah asked Kate, "How long have you been married?"

Kate answered, "We arrived two days ago, so two days. My husband, Robert, is working on the docks."

"Oh well, newlyweds, best wishes to you and your husband," replied Sarah as her mind raced back in time to her own early days of marriage.

"Thank you, Sarah." Kate smiled, feeling so glad to be talking to a woman.

Sarah asked, "Is there anything I can help you with, Kate?"

She knew well that all new brides need help.

Kate replied, "Well, I know nothing about cooking. It would be most appreciated if you could help me in this regard."

"I am sure I can help with that. What are you doing tonight?" asked Sarah.

"Well, I don't know. I only have a little flour, some fat meat, and salt."

"That's a start," assured Sarah. "The children and I go to the forest and gather winter greens, wild onions, and mushrooms when available. You are welcome to come."

"Let me get my bucket."

Sarah, Kate, and the children went to the forest for the afternoon. Sarah reminded Arianna, "You watch after the little ones. Do not let them wander too far from us, for the forest is deep and dark. Wild animals are in abundance, especially bobcats."

After they returned, they cooked their finds at Sarah's cabin. Sarah taught Kate how to clean and cook the greens. She told Kate, "Jonathan will help Robert glean wood from the forest for our cabins. Now that it is getting cooler, it takes quite a bit more firewood."

Robert returned home from the dock. He had fresh fish that was left over from the day's catch. He showed Kate how to gut and scrape the fish, pushing them on sticks and then slow roasting them over the low embers in the fireplace. He was quite surprised that Kate had a few things for their supper.

During the roasting of the fish, Kate excitedly told him, "I met a lady today. Her name is Sarah. She has six children and is soon to have another. The family has the cabin next door. Sarah, the children, and I went to the forest to gather fresh greens and wild onions." Kate changed the subject when the fish released their roasting aromas. "Oh, Robert, they smell so good. I can't wait."

Robert and Kate were very anxious for this meal. It had been sometime since they had anything substantial to eat.

"Thank you, Kate. That was a marvelous supper you helped provide for us."

After filling their stomachs to capacity, they were ready for the day's work to come to an end.

Feeling stronger, Kate, who was quite proud of her day's accomplishments, told Robert, "Sarah is very willing to teach me how to cook. We are going to be all right, aren't we, Robert?"

"Yes, we are, darling," answered Robert.

Kate and Sarah found themselves spending quite a bit of time together as the days went by. Kate learned a lot about cooking. Sarah was curious of Kate and asked, "Kate, you are different from most of the ladies I know. You speak quite well. Well, I mean, so upper class, and you seem to have a greater knowledge about things, like book learning. One would think you to be almost royal with your gentle poise."

"In Ireland, I had the best of teachers." Kate tried to avoid the fact that she was of nobility. "Sarah, I have been thinking that because I have a great deal of education I would like to share with your children, if that is all right with you? You have done so much for me in helping me learn how to cook and clean. I just want to repay you somehow."

"That is a marvelous idea, Kate. Thank you!"

One evening after supper, Robert told Kate, "I was speaking with Jonathan. He told me his family will spend the winter here in the cabin. I think it would be best for us to stay the winter in this cabin while we have a place. It would be most difficult to move this time of the year. I do have some work, and we can save for our fare to move upriver to Philadelphia this spring."

"You know best about these things, Robert" was Kate's answer.

She worked on her lace before the daylight left them. Because the McCalls and Thatchers had decided to stay through the cold season, both Robert and Jonathan realized the need to winterize the cabins with tighter doors and better roofs. Together, the two men shared their knowledge and labor in making the repairs on both cabins. They added more slats to the doors, closing the gaps. Kate, Sarah, and the children collected clay mud from the streets and chinked the cracks in the walls. The two men shingled the roofs with tree bark they stripped from the firewood.

Kate had made several yards of lace. She was able to sell it to Mrs. Morris, the proprietor of the mercantile. Mrs. Morris was a tall thin lady with gray hair tied in a knot resting on top her head. She laughed bigger than life itself as she greeted all who came into the store. She gave Kate the impression that she, along with the innkeeper, knew all the news in the village.

Mrs. Morris told Kate, "Mrs. McCall, I can sell all the lace you can make for me."

This excited Kate. After being so encouraged, she bartered her lace for more thread and necessities from the mercantile. This arrangement with the store added to the couple's income. Robert's hard coins from the dock were placed in a tin can on the little shelf, waiting for enough to purchase their biggest need, which was a rifle and ammunition so he could hunt for wild game.

Teaching the children was a pleasure for Kate. She could see their young minds absorb all she had to impart. Arianna displayed an exceptional eagerness to learn how to read.

Their first Christmas came as the ground was covered with a light dusting of snow. The Thatchers and McCalls spent Christmas Eve together. Robert and Jonathan had killed a deer, which gave the two families meat for two months. Plus, the hide could be traded or used for a variety of things. Kate and Sarah added the finishing touches to the Christmas meal with greens from the forest. Sweet potatoes and butter bought at the mercantile added a delicacy. Kate and Robert splurged and bought each of the children a stick of peppermint candy for a gift.

Kate was feeling a little dizzy and thought it was due to working hard on the Christmas meal. She remarked to Sarah, "I feel so funny today, dizzy like."

Sarah, who had much experience in this area, asked Kate, "So you don't have any idea as to what it might be?" She was playing a kind of teasing game with her. "Well, Kate, I think I know just what might be your reason for feeling dizzy. Think back, when was your last cycle day? Was it in October or November?"

"Well, it was the first of November."

"There you go," beamed Sarah.

"What do you mean, Sarah?"

Sarah looked at Kate with a blank look on her face. "You don't know, do you? You really don't know. Kate, you are going to have a baby!"

Dumbfounded, Kate gasped, "A baby? I am going to have a baby."

"Yes, Kate, a baby," giggled Sarah. "It happens to married people, you know. Let's see. When might this little one arrive? I am counting it to be some time in July."

With this news, Kate had to sit down and fan her face with her apron. She sat there with her hands on her stomach, looking at Sarah. Her face revealed an ever-present state of shock. "When will I know it's a baby in my stomach?"

"Well, Kate, the best I can tell you, the first of March would be my guess," Sarah estimated, standing with her hands stretched across her own hard stomach, reminding herself of her own pregnancy.

Arianna overheard the two talking and shouted out, "Oh no, not another baby!"

Her mother, a bit embarrassed, quickly scolded her, "You must apologize to Mrs. McCall. You should not eavesdrop on grown-ups, Arianna. For heaven's sakes, do not tell Mr. McCall. That is for Kate to do. She wants it to be a surprise."

"I am sorry, Mrs. McCall. I won't tell Mr. McCall," swore Arianna.

"Thank you, Arianna. It will be our secret for just a little while."

The three of them returned to the cooking of the Christmas supper.

The men returned from gathering wood, dragging a small cedar tree. The children were thrilled when their father brought the tree inside the house.

Arianna gleefully hollered, "A tree, we have a tree! Thank you, Pa."

Jonathan placed the tree in a corner and declared, "Boy, it's getting colder out there, and I am willing to bet we have a white Christmas. What do you think, Robert?"

"I think you are right about that." Robert dropped an armload of wood by the fire hearth.

The men, along with Nathaniel, the Thatcher's eldest son, returned from a long afternoon with aching empty stomachs. They asked, smelling the venison and wild onions roasting, "When do we eat?"

Each man gave his wife a quick kiss. Sarah handed the three a hot cup of tea to warm their insides while they waited for the Christmas dinner.

Kate, recovered from her news, elected not to tell Robert just yet. Robert recognized she was a bit giddy, but thought it was the holiday that was making her happy. Whatever the reason, he took great satisfaction to witness the joy in his new bride.

Kate, still giddy, asked, "Robert, would you please go to our cabin and get the table and chairs? Oh yes, and bring the dishes."

Jonathan went with Robert to help carry the load. Jonathan, in passing, remarked, "Boy, your wife sure seems to be feeling the spirit of the season."

"Yes, I noticed that as well, Jonathan."

Sarah asked, "Kate, would you please set the table? Arianna, I would like for you to put that bunch of holly berries in something and place it on the table for decoration. Let's give it a Christmas spirit. I will dish up all the food. Boy, it sure smells delicious."

An exotic fragrance from the cedar tree mixed with the baked sweet potatoes buried in the hot coals had filled the cabin with holiday cheer. Sarah, the hostess, announced, "Well, I think that is everything. We can all sit down."

She placed the potatoes on the table. The adults each sat in a chair. The six children shared two benches, pushing and shoving a little as they each tried to carve out their space. Their excitement built in the hope that Kris Kringle would visit their little cabin this Christmas Eve. Robert, a Methodist class leader in Ireland, led the two families in a prayer of gratitude for their abundance of good friends and food. He then recited an Irish friendship wish.

May there always be
Work for your hands to do.
May your purse always
Hold a coin or two.
May the sun always
Shine on your
Windowpane.
May a rainbow be
Certain to follow each
Rain.
May the hand of a
Friend always be near
You.
May God fill your
Heart with gladness
To cheer you . . .

(Author unknown)

Everyone ate their fill with much appreciation. Getting up from the table, the men thanked their wives for a meal well made. Jonathan got his fiddle, and all gathered around the little tree to decorate and sing familiar Christmas carols.

The Thatchers, from Wales, sang familiar Celtic arrangements. Kate, musically gifted herself, appreciated their vocals. "Your family has beautiful harmony."

Arianna, Nathaniel, and Lisa-Jean made ornaments out of sycamore balls and a holly and red berry garland to hang on the tree. Kate used her tatting lace to tie a white bow, then placed it onto the tree top. Everyone stepped back, admiring their handiwork.

Family bonding was a new experience for Kate in contrast to all the service she took for granted as a member of the royal family. She again thought of her parents, especially now that she carried their grandchild. The fact that she found out about it on such a day as this was special. She wondered, if her parents knew, would they share her excitement? She couldn't wait to be alone with Robert to give him the news.

Walking back to their cabin, Kate and Robert could hear the crunch of snow under their feet. Already four inches deep, it continued falling fast. "I am glad Jonathan, Nathaniel, and I gathered lots of wood today for I fear we are in for a deep snow tonight."

They joyfully counted their blessings. Robert lit the candle and built up the fire to warm their cabin. They hung a heavy quilt over the door to block the cold air. Quickly, they jumped into bed to help fight the chill. Kate knew that she needed to tell Robert he was to be a father. What better day than Christmas Eve to give him the news.

"Robert," Kate whispered, "Christmas Eve is very special, don't you think?"

"Yes, it is, Kate. This is perhaps the best Christmas ever, for I have you, sweetheart."

Kate knew this was a perfect moment to give her husband the news. Very softly and slowly, she began, "Robert," and then very quickly, she let the news roll off her tongue. "Next year at Christmas, there will be three of us."

A few fleeting seconds passed. Robert jumped out of bed and let out a loud yell. He picked Kate up, swung her around, and gave her a loving kiss. "A baby, we are going to have a baby!"

"That's what Sarah told me, and she should know." Kate laughed. "We estimate it to be in July. Come spring, I should still be able to travel up the Chesapeake."

Kate knew how important their future plans were. For this reason, she did not wish to spoil all they had worked and saved for their future.

Next door, Sarah heard Robert yell. "Yep, she told him," she remarked with a smug grin.

Jonathan asked, "Told him what?"

"Kate is going to have a baby in July," confessed Sarah.

"Oh, is that all?" Jonathan was being cynical. Sarah slapped him on the arm with a dish towel for fun.

"Yes, that's all." She reminded him of her condition.

"That is why she was so giddy tonight. Robert and I wondered the reason. Well, it's the first, so I can understand his excitement," reasoned Jonathan, hoping this would soften the conversation with his wife.

The following morning, snow was thick on the ground. Tree branches hung low, weighted down with sparkling white wet snow fall. There was stillness in the air as all outdoor life took refuge. Robert peered out the door and watched a rabbit leap across the yard, leaving deep holes in the virgin snow as it passed by. He was hoping it would get caught in the rabbit snare he had rigged the day before. It certainly would be good to have some fried rabbit or even some good hot stew during these cold days. He went back to bed and snuggled up to Kate as he placed his hand on her stomach. Suddenly, he was in awe of the responsibility fatherhood would bring. He and Kate took the opportunity to sleep in late on Christmas Day. Robert got up and added more wood to the fire. He made each of them a good hot cup of tea. He brought the tea to Kate who was still in bed and confessed, "I can't believe we are going to have a baby."

Kate reminded him, "Well, Sarah says it does happen to married people, you know."

Robert kissed Kate and wished her, "Merry Christmas, sweetheart, I love you."

Kate returned his kiss with love. "Merry Christmas to you, dear."

Several days had passed, and the snow melted, leaving in its wake a deluge of mud, which made housekeeping quite a chore for the women. Robert brought fresh fish home from the wharf. Jonathan reset the traps and, with his musket, hunted for wild game. Both families struggled through the winter, helping each other with their needs.

Chapter 10

ONE LAUNDRY DAY IN MARCH, the wind was blowing hard, contributing to the very cold air. Kate and Sarah worked together, carrying heavy tubs of water from a nearby creek. Keeping the outdoor fire burning to heat the water in the large black cast-iron kettle to boil required a great deal of wood. The abandoned kettle was left for the new cabin dwellers to share. The children, overjoyed to be outside, ran and played hide-and-seek.

Sarah cautioned them, "Children, you be mindful of the fire. Arianna, you watch after the little ones."

No sooner had she said the words than Liam, the three-year-old barefoot boy, chased after the older children. He couldn't keep up. Crying and rubbing his eyes, he backed into the hot embers, which were spread under and around the wash pot. He screamed with agonizing pain. Sarah and Kate rushed to him. His cries were too hard for Sarah to bear. Looking at the bottom of his little feet with loose skin was beyond her endurance. In shock, she fainted, dropping Liam.

Kate realized it was up to her to care for the child. She picked Liam up and ran to a cool tub of water; she submerged his feet and tried to soothe his pain. Kate left Sarah lying on the ground, knowing that she would eventually come to. She screamed for Arianna, who was already on her way as she knew something terrible had occurred. Frantically, Kate screamed, "Go for Mrs. Morris quickly!"

Arianna was unsure of what really happened but only knew it was serious. She ran for Mrs. Morris. She broke through the store doors, not even aware if anyone was in her path. She panted. "Please come quick. It's baby Liam. He's hurt real bad."

Mrs. Morris dropped what she was doing and left the store unattended. She and Arianna rushed through the muddy streets to the cabins. Liam was still crying in anguish, thrashing, about in Kate's arms. He did not allow anyone to look at the burns.

Sarah regained consciousness, although still unable to look at Liam's feet. She tried to console him. With Kate's help, Mrs. Morris got a good look at the burns. She stood back, perplexed, trying to think what to do for the suffering child.

"I'll be back." She turned quickly and ran back to the store. Rushing around in the store, she gathered up things she thought might be useful.

Returning to Liam, she immediately administered a potent dose of paregoric to ease his pain. Sarah and Kate forcibly held him down. They moved Liam into the small dark cabin and placed him on a bed all the while he struggled to free himself. The medication began taking hold. Mrs. Morris could now aid his pitifully burned feet. She handed Sarah six eggs and instructed her, "Whip one of the whites until it is very frothy."

She handed Kate some soft white cotton cloth. "Kate, you tear this into three-inch strips."

Liam drifted into a quiet sleep from the strong dose of medicine. Mrs. Morris worked fast, removing the burned skin. Sarah returned with the egg white. Mrs. Morris spread the beaten white over the burned areas. She separated his toes with thick pieces of cloth so the toes would not fuse together during the healing process. She explained to Sarah, "This must be done often. It is important that you always use freshly boiled white cloths. The cloths must stay wet with the egg whites. You can bathe the feet in cool milk. It soothes the burns and aids in the healing as well." She then wrapped his feet with the cloth strips.

With Liam quieted, everyone could now talk. Mrs. Morris reinstructed Sarah and Kate, "It is important that the feet do not become infected. Keep them clean and apply the egg whites." Gathering her things, she continued, "The protein in the egg whites will promote healing. I am very sure the healing will take quite some time perhaps as much as a month or more." She handed Sarah the little brown corked bottle of paregoric. "He will need this tonight and tomorrow to ease his pain."

"Thank you so much, Mrs. Morris, for your help," sighed Sarah.

"It saddens me to see a little one in so much pain. Keep him quiet and off his feet," advised Mrs. Morris, again making sure they understood its importance. "With proper care, his feet should soon begin to heal."

The paregoric was given to Liam through the night and all the next day to keep him in a semiconscious state.

Two weeks passed. Early one morning, Jonathan knocked on Robert and Kate's door.

"Kate, Kate, Sarah needs you."

Kate sprang up quickly, knowing the time to deliver Sarah's baby had come. Kate found Sarah in the midst of a very hard contraction.

"What can I do, Sarah?"

Sarah bore down with pain as she clutched the bed railing, she cried to Kate, "Something is wrong. This is not like the others."

Kate could see the baby coming. "I can see its foot. Is that right, Sarah?"

"No, Kate, that is not right!" screamed Sarah in agony. "Where is Jonathan? I want Jonathan."

"I am here, Sarah," answered Jonathan with a shaky voice that revealed his fear.

Kate realized that they were in serious trouble. It was more complicated than she could handle.

"Jonathan, do you know of a midwife? I am sure we need one."

Sarah, between contractions, took a sip of water.

Kate wiped Sarah's face and arms with a wet cloth for she was sweating profusely.

"Oh . . . oh . . . here comes another one!" Sarah screamed as she dug her nails into Kate's arms.

Jonathan returned with a midwife. She was a short, stocky little lady with a soft soothing voice named Rachel.

The cabin's single room was separated by a heavy quilt that hung from the rafter. Rachel insisted everyone but Kate remains on the opposite side of the divide.

"Let's see what we have here." Rachel calmly lifted the quilt. "Bring me a light." She rolled her sleeves to free up her hands and arms. "Yes, we do have a bit of trouble. Kate, you hold her arms down. I am going to try and turn the baby so it comes out right."

Sarah passed out with the pain. There was nothing the midwife could do. The perfect baby boy, with the cord wrapped around his neck, was stillborn.

Sarah came to. "Where is my baby?" she screamed, "Jonathan, where is our baby?"

Jonathan knelt by their bed and held Sarah's hand. Chocking back his tears, he explained, "Sarah, he didn't make it. The delivery was too hard for him."

"It's a boy?" Sarah moaned a soft cry and lost consciousness.

Rachel quickly ordered Jonathan out of the room. "She is hemorrhaging! Quick, Kate, give me those cloths. We have to stop this bleeding now!" The two women worked frantically with Sarah most of the morning before they got the bleeding under control.

The loss of Sarah's baby was most disturbing to Kate; it caused a lot of fears to arise in her mind. "Robert, I am so afraid for our baby. What if that happens to us?"

Robert tried to reassure her, "Kate, you are young and healthy. Besides, Sarah has had six babies without a problem. You will be all right. Our baby will be all right, I am sure of it."

Sarah's recovery was slow. She had lost a great deal of blood, which made her body very weak. The death of her baby boy was complicated by a deep depression.

Liam, on the other hand, fared better each day. Sarah cared for him as much as she could from her bed. Kate was experiencing what it was like to care for a large family. She knew now what Sarah meant when she bragged, "Arianna was her biggest help."

Kate's rounded stomach now gave evidence of her pregnancy. While stirring a pot of rabbit stew, she dropped the spoon.

"Sarah, Sarah," she loudly exclaimed, "I feel it! I feel it! My baby, I feel it!"

Sarah gently reminded her, "I told you so. I told you it would be the first of March. Take it from someone who knows. I see your dress will not button much longer, Kate."

"All my dresses, the few I have, are too small. I don't know what to do. I cannot afford new clothes. Do you have any ideas, Sarah?"

"Well, I am thinking we could make you an apron to tie over the top of your dresses, one with a bib."

"I can't sew, Sarah. I would not know where to begin." She rubbed the top of her protruding belly. "I can't afford the material. It's out of the question, Sarah."

Sarah listened to Kate in a motherly way and allowed her to complain about her inadequate feelings regarding her sewing skills. "Kate, you do beautiful, delicate work with a needle. You can do this thing. I will help you."

Kate's eyes brightened. She was delighted with the offer. "Oh, Sarah, thank you. But I can't afford the fabric for the apron."

"Suppose you barter with Mrs. Morris using your tatting in exchange for the sewing goods. You get the material. I will help you cut it out and show you how to assemble it."

Kate bartered with Mrs. Morris for a dark piece of cloth. With Sarah's help, she spent her evenings hand-sewing the apron pieces together with very tiny stitches. Her mind raced back, remembering the hours she had spent as a princess choosing from a beautiful selection of the most exquisite fabrics for a formal gown. She brushed these thoughts away for they were way in the past.

There was no time for schooling with the children. Kate went back to her cabin exhausted every night. There seemed little time for her and Robert, leaving her feeling a little overwhelmed. She hadn't had time to make her lace. Now she had an added reason for the urgency to do her needlework. They needed the income desperately if they were to go up the Chesapeake in a month or two, weather permitting.

The new spring of 1776 reminded Kate that it was just a year ago that she and Robert had met and how their lives had changed. Robert was no longer a businessman working in his weaving craft. Life for her had changed far beyond what she could have ever imagined. She was no longer a woman of great material wealth and social status. Each day, they pushed forward as they kept their goals in mind.

One evening, Robert came home in high spirits. His earnings were now enough to buy the rifle and ammunition they are in such desperate need of. Any further savings would be for passage money up the Chesapeake. This news lifted Kate's spirits. She was looking forward to the future and their new life in the North. Robert shared the extra un-saleable fish from the docks while Jonathan shared his hunt.

Chapter 11

THE TIME HAD ARRIVED FOR the McCalls to make their preparations to move up north. Kate packed their few belongings. Their trip up the Chesapeake Bay would be by way of sailing the two-hundred-mile journey. In her mind, she knew the sail would not be as hazardous as that out on the open seas. Robert cut wood to leave for the next tenants of the little cabin. Kate left a full candle on the table and all the dishes. All in the hopes it would make the little home more comfortable for those who might dwell there next. She decided to leave the water pail with the Thatchers.

On their departing day, both families stood in front of their little makeshift homes. Each couple, along with the children, felt a sad parting, for they had shared so much through the harsh winter. Sarah tearfully hugged Kate, then stood erect with her hands clasped while commanding her in a sweet tone. "You take care of yourselves and that little one. I fear I shall never know if it is a girl or a boy," she lamented while handing her a fresh loaf of round bread.

Tearfully, Kate replied, "Yes, you will, Sarah. We will see you when you move north." She failed to hold back the tears as they rolled down her plump cheeks.

Jonathan and Robert shook hands as men do, each man knowing how much they depended on the help of the other for their very existence.

Kate told Robert, "I would like to go by the mercantile to bid Mrs. Morris a final farewell."

Carrying all the possessions they owned in the world, they entered the store. The bell over the door rang. Mrs. Morris labored in the back, stocking shelves.

"Mrs. Morris," Kate called out, "we are leaving today to go up the Chesapeake. We wanted to say good-bye and thank you for all you have done to help us these last few months."

Mrs. Morris quickly moved around with a sack in her hand. "I want to give you something to help you on your way." She gathered some dried apples, venison jerky, and hard candies to place in the sack.

Kate gave Mrs. Morris a final good-bye hug, expressing genuine thankfulness, and then took the loving gift in her hands. "This will make our journey much easier."

It was the first of May in the year 1776. Again, Kate and Robert were faced with uncertainty, not knowing where they would settle. The only fear Kate had of the trip was perhaps some renegade Indians. She had heard stories about the earlier settlers and their encounters with the Indians. Robert had his new rifle, and this eased her mind to some degree. Kate wondered if she would miss the bay area. Chesapeake Bay bustled with ships coming in and out of the ports after trading with England, France, the West Indies, and Spain. Inflation was on the rise. Work was harder to get as the trade slowed because of the embargoes and the new revolutionary war. Robert and Kate were better financially, even though they had earned a meager income. They had a great deal of gratitude for what they did have.

There was unrest as the colonists tried to establish a republic. Robert had a growing interest in the evolving political issues. As their small ship made its way up the Chesapeake, he found several newcomers to the Americas with the same concerns that he had about governmental issues.

The trip up the bay passed without incident. The young newlyweds found themselves again embarking on a new and uncertain life in the city of Philadelphia, Pennsylvania. Kate immediately recognized that Philadelphia was much more populated than the seaport they had just left. She still harbored fears about her pregnancy and believed the larger city was a better place to deliver a baby as opposed to some western frontier. While walking down the streets in search of lodging, she discussed her fears with Robert, "Robert, I think we should stay here in Philadelphia at least until the baby comes."

Robert was aware of her uneasiness about the pregnancy. "I think perhaps you are right, Kate, it would be best for us to settle here for a while until we find what is available in the area."

Once again, they searched for lodging. Robert asked about where one might find accommodations and was told of a boarding house where a good many immigrants stopped for a short time.

They proceeded to find the last boarding house on the street. Philadelphia hosted a large community with streets branching off one another. Some streets were brick paved and lined with trees and night lanterns. There were millinery shops all along the way.

The boarding house would be the best living arrangements they encountered since leaving Ireland. They found it to be most inviting as they walked up the dirt path lined with rocks. Two large sycamore trees graced each side of the yard providing, much welcomed shade in the hot summers. The yard borders were surrounded by soft pink azaleas and yellow daffodils. The front porch with its rocking chairs, porch swing, and hanging baskets of pink and red geranium flowers lent itself to be a most welcome sight to Kate. For so long, she had had the most uncomfortable of accommodations. Robert and Kate entered through the front door where the owner greeted them.

"Welcome to my boarding house. I am Isabelle Fargo. I assume you are looking for a room." Mrs. Fargo was a stout woman with white hair and soft green eyes. "I have one room available at the top of the stairs if that is acceptable for the missus?"

"It is very nice to meet you, Mrs. Fargo. We are Robert and Kate McCall from Ireland."

After the introductions, they accepted the room. Robert bartered for some of their boarding rent in return for handyman work. Mrs. Fargo wiped her hands on her apron and gave them the key.

"Two meals a day come with the board. Breakfast is always at six-thirty. Usually, it is Virginia ham, eggs, gravy, biscuits, hot cereal, jam, fresh milk, butter, and coffee. Dinner is at six o'clock. It is just me and Lillian, but I call her Lilly. She is my helper here at the house." Mrs. Fargo called out, "Lilly, come meet the new roomers."

Lilly was a very dark, heavy Negro lady in her sixties with graying hair around her face. She walked with a slight hip twist side to side and had a contagious laugh. "It's nice to meet you folks." She reiterated the rules, "Dinner is at six o'clock sharp. I don't likes to be late, so don't youz be late," she added with a chuckle.

"If you have any questions, just come down to the kitchen. Lilly or I will try to help you. Oh yes, before I forget, there are fresh towels in the closet at the end of the hall, just help yourselves."

When they entered the room, Kate said, "It's a real bed with lovely bedding. Come see, Robert. Oh! And it has a tub, Robert."

The room had a curtain dressing screen. Behind the screen was the tub, a washstand with basin, and a pitcher with fresh water.

"That it does, my dear." Robert placed their belongings down. He could sense the excitement in her voice. "Kate, would you like a nice tub bath after the trip?"

"Oh, Robert, a good long warm bath would be magnificent."

This was like a vacation for Kate; she didn't have to cook their meals, clean, or do their laundry. The laundry would be tended by local labor, most likely Lilly, when something in the way of pay could be established. Kate calmly revealed her joy with their new transition to her husband, "Robert, I am just going to concentrate on becoming a mother, if that is all right with you."

"Anything that will make you happy, dear, is all right with me." He leaned over to kiss her. Robert knew a rest would be good for Kate, for she certainly had earned it. "I am going to search for work tomorrow. I think it best for you to stay in the room and rest for the day."

Robert and Kate had the most restful night's sleep since their marriage of seven impoverished months.

Robert was up early. Quietly, he slipped out of their room and left Kate to sleep as long as she liked. He went downstairs to eat breakfast before he left in search of work, at the same time familiarizing himself with the new surroundings.

Kate rested in her soft white nightgown, curled up in bed for most of the day. She was enjoying a nice cool spring breeze as it blew through the open window. She found she seemed to be having a lot of hot flashes these days and wondered why that might be. Outside the window was a very large pear tree with its new spring blossoms. The tree was so close to the house, she could have reached out and picked a pear if it were the season. But they would not be ready until late October or early November. She thought, *It's doubtful that we would be here for that long.* She hoped not. She was longing for a home they could call their own.

While deep in her thoughts, there was a knock on her door. It was Lilly. "Mrs. McCall, Ize's brought you a mid-morning breakfast. Heaven only knows a lady in youz delicate condition needs to eats."

"Why thank you, Lilly, this is very thoughtful and kind of you." Kate remembered the many times in the past that she had received such service and breakfast in bed.

The information list in the room said that dinner was at six p.m. sharp. Kate dressed in her very best dress. It was quite evident that she was late into her pregnancy. She wrapped a knitted shawl around her shoulders and brought it to the front, tying it across her stomach. Robert would be dressed in his best garments to impress prospective employers in his search for work.

When he returned from town, he took Kate downstairs for dinner. She was extremely excited to sit at a formal table once again with nice table linens and silver settings. The menu had listed roasted duck, fried apples, killed lettuce, mashed potatoes, gravy, yeast rolls, and spice cake with caramel sauce. Kate's mouth watered in anticipation of the yeast rolls dripping with fresh butter, for it had been so long since she had enjoyed oven-baked breads.

Mrs. Fargo stood behind her chair at the end of the long dining table and rang a small silver bell, calling everyone to dinner. An arrangement of yellow daffodils, presumably from the front yard, adorned the middle of the table, adding the feeling of a beautiful spring day.

"Boarders, I would like for you to meet our newest guests. This is Mr. and Mrs. Robert McCall. They hail from Ireland. This is Ms. Emily Robinson, she is our schoolteacher."

Ms. Robinson was quite small with dark hair parted in the middle and pulled very close to her head in a tight twisted ball at the neck. She wore one thin wire glass that hung from a silk ribbon pinned to her white dress collar. She spoke with a very high-pitched voice which sounded to Kate as though it came through her nose.

"And meet Dr. Samuel Franklin."

Dr. Franklin stood very tall and appeared unusually thin with graying hair. Kate accessed him as being very tired and in need of one good night's rest.

"Mr. William McDonald from County Antrim, Ireland, is our local lawyer and politician."

Mr. McDonald was perhaps a few years older than Robert and quite a distinguished-looking gentleman with an assertive self-confidence.

Mrs. Fargo directed Kate and Robert to their chairs while the others took their usual places at the table. With a very delicate second ring of the bell, Mrs. Fargo signaled to Lilly that all were seated. Lilly entered the dining room, carrying the main course of the meal which she had prepared with great pride. Mrs. Fargo gave Lilly a compliment as the duck was passed around, "The duck is beautifully roasted and smells wonderful."

Everyone answered in agreement.

"Whys Ize's thanks youz, Mrs. Fargo," answered Lilly with a laugh, "I thoughts that duck never would gets done. Guess it don't wants to gets eat."

Kate found it most interesting to have dinner with such an enlightened group of people. The conversations had begun with trivial small talk, such as the weather. But as the evening progressed, so did the subject matter. Although she thought Mr. Mc Donald seemed to take command of many of the conversations. The discovery of a doctor in the house helped to ease her mind. No one said anything about her condition in mixed company, but Kate felt certain she could speak with the good doctor in private. Perhaps she could make this arrangement for tomorrow. She especially delighted in the conversation with Ms. Robinson as they seemed to have a great deal in common, particularly the literature both had read.

Robert was most taken with William McDonald and the fact that both hailed from Antrim County, Northern Ireland. The common interest they held in current events dominated their conversation. Surprisingly, they shared many of the same views about the current war. The war had officially begun in April after the evacuation of the British from Boston in March, which gave them much to talk about. The two men freely expressed their thoughts of Gen. George Washington and the role he apparently would play on the stage of the war for independence.

Midway through dinner, Mr. McDonald invited Robert, "Come by my office tomorrow. I feel sure I can find work for you."

"Why, thank you, sir. That indeed is very kind of you."

Everyone excused themselves to have coffee in the parlor. Kate's eye quickly caught sight of a harpsichord sitting in the corner of the room between the double windows and a fireplace.

"Oh look, Robert, a harpsichord." She asked everyone, "Please may I play for you? I have not played since leaving Ireland."

The music and songs made for a pleasant evening for the guests. They sang "Sweet William" and "Barbra Allen," both Irish ballads.

Mrs. Fargo joined the group and told Kate, "Mrs. McCall, you can play the harpsichord any time you like. You play quite well, and you certainly have made our evening enjoyable."

"Thank you, Mrs. Fargo. I have very much enjoyed playing. It reminded me of Ireland."

Returning to their room, Kate and Robert had much to talk about, the possibility of a new job for Robert and a doctor in the house for Kate.

Most of all, Robert was surprised with Kate's musical abilities. "Kate, I didn't know you played a musical instrument and quite well, I might add. When money permits, we will buy a harpsichord for our home so you can play and teach our children," he promised as he began undressing for bed.

"I would like that very much, Robert. I enjoyed hearing you sing. You have such a strong singing voice. You are quite good, I might add. I would describe it as baritone. One of the first things I took notice of was your strong voice." While unfolding her nightgown, she changed the subject. "I am so pleased to have a doctor close by. Tomorrow, I will go to his office for a good checkup."

Retiring for the night, Robert touched her belly, hoping to feel a movement. "I can't wait to know if it is a girl or a boy."

"Now that it is so close, shouldn't we choose names?" asked Kate.

"Most definitely." Robert was yawning and very full from the delicious meal that was making him sleepy.

"If it is a boy, I think it should be John Robert, and if a girl, I am thinking Ashley Victoria. What do you think?" Then she realized Robert had fallen asleep. She patted him on the shoulder and pulled the blankets tighter.

Robert accepted the job offered by William to manage his office. Kate rested at home very grateful for this time, as it was so close to her delivery. She was able to do her needlecraft to pass the time. She often found herself downstairs playing the harpsichord in the middle of the afternoons after making sure she was not disturbing the other guests.

Dr. Franklin's office was down Market Street on the corner of Market and Broad Street. It made for Kate a most delightful late spring walk.

"Well, Mrs. McCall, all seems to be on schedule, and you are progressing nicely. You have your date estimated sometime in the middle of July, and I think you are right. I should see you again in two weeks," suggested Doctor Franklin.

As Kate was leaving the doctor's office, she admitted, "I feel so much better after seeing you. Thank you, Dr. Franklin,

While Kate waited for Robert to come home from work, she found the front porch swing to be most relaxing. She swung back and forth and felt the shift of her body weight. This rhythmic motion helped to put her into a nesting frame of mind. Stopping occasionally, she managed to do a few stitches on small baby clothing. She found it much more comfortable to stay at the boarding house rather than familiarizing herself with the new surroundings. When she got bored with sewing and swinging, she left the porch and went to the back kitchen. A breezeway roof separated the kitchen and a small room from the main house. The small room belonged to Lilly. There, she found great solitude after a full day's work.

Kate found Lilly peeling potatoes. "Hello, Lilly, mind if I join you? Can I help you?"

"Why youz don't has to help, but your company would be nice, Mrs. McCall," replied Lilly.

"But I want to and please call me Kate. I am so bored with nothing to do, but wait for Mr. McCall all day."

"Well, pulls up that chair and sets yourself down. There's a knife there on the table. Youz be mindful youz don't cuts yourself. I ain't got no time fer docterin."

Kate moved a chair close to Lilly. The chair was a straight wooden chair that sat very low to the floor. The legs had been worn down through all the many years of use. The sagging chair seat, woven from jute twine, revealed its aged years of service. Kate lowered herself gingerly before falling deep into the hollow of the old chair.

"Now that we are not in mixed company, Mrs. McCall, I mean, Kate, whens youz baby due anyways? Real soon I'm a thinkin?"

"Well, I saw Dr. Franklin and he guessed the middle of July." Kate picked up a potato and the knife and asked Lilly, "Would you mind if I helped some in the kitchen? I am still learning how to cook."

"Why, child, ain't youz never done no cookin?" Lilly dropped the peeled potato into a pot of water.

"Nothing as tasty as you cook, Lilly, I certainly will appreciate all you can teach me."

"Sure, Miss Kate, youz just comes on down to the kitchen anytime. Miss Kate, would youz like a good cool glass of sassafras tea?" asked Lilly as she got up to stretch.

"That would be very nice, Lilly, thank you most kindly." Kate was truly enjoying their conversation.

Robert worked in the office of Mr. McDonald as his assistant. He did the bookkeeping and arranging of appointments. He found this to be interesting and fulfilling as it somewhat related to his own fabric weaving business in Ireland. And it was much easier than working on the fishing and loading docks. He enjoyed the intellectual interaction with his new boss and the various townsmen.

Chapter 12

ONE AFTERNOON IN LATE MAY, Robert came home from work very excited. "Good afternoon, Lilly. Kate, Kate. Where's Kate?"

"Afternoon, Mr. McCall, youz wife is in youz room restin, sir," answered Lilly while shelling early spring peas and enjoying the townsfolk as they passed by the front porch.

Rushing up the stairs, he found Kate lying on the bed. Although he was very excited, he first asked Kate, "Are you all right?"

"Yes, Robert, just tired, but well." Rising on her elbows, she asked, "Why are you so lively this afternoon?"

Robert gave her a kiss. "Kate, I have some good news. William, that is Mr. McDonald, has found out through his business dealings that there is a small abandoned farm just outside of town. He has offered to go to the financer with me and help make payment arrangements. What do you think about this offer?"

"Oh, Robert, you mean a home of our own?"

"Yes, Kate, a home of our own. Tomorrow is Saturday, and weather permitting, perhaps we could borrow Mrs. Fargo's horse and buggy and drive out to see for ourselves if this might be something we can manage. I understand it is one hundred acres, give or take a few. It is a very small farm not far from town. William confided in me a couple lived on the farm, but the wife passed away, and the husband no longer wished to remain." Robert did not tell Kate that the wife had died during childbirth because he knew of Kate's earlier expressed fears.

That evening at dinner, Robert spoke with Mrs. Fargo. "Mr. McDonald has told me about a small farm just outside of town that has been abandoned. He suggested that Kate and I ride out and look at the property. It might be something we would be interested in buying. I thought perhaps we could borrow the horse and buggy for about three hours tomorrow afternoon, if that is all right with you, Mrs. Fargo?"

Buttering a slice of bread, Mrs. Fargo replied, "I know the place well. Of course, you can use the buggy tomorrow. I will have Lilly pack you a lunch, and you can take your time and enjoy a day out."

"We thank you kindly, Mrs. Fargo. I will hitch the horse and buggy myself."

The weather was beautiful as Kate and Robert made the drive to the farm. There was revealing evidence that summer was a few days away by the abundance of wild summer flowers, the golden yellow of black-eyed Susan, white Queen Ann's lace, and the bluish purple hues of bluebells along the dirt road and stretching across the meadows.

It was the first farm after leaving town. Robert expressed to Kate, "This can be a prime property in due time, given the growth of the area."

Rounding the curve, they approached the drive up to the small farmhouse. Morning glory and honeysuckle vines were climbing the sides of the house and the outbuildings. To their right, they saw a young orchard with pear, cherry, plum, and apple trees, the last of the pink and white blossoms falling to the ground. But the dwelling interested Kate the most. The first view of the house featured an outstanding front porch which ran its entire length. Robert helped Kate down from the carriage. Walking down the pebbled path, they could smell the sweet perfume of the honeysuckle. Stepping up on the porch, they knocked down the cobwebs as they entered the open front door. It was apparent that the door had been open for some time because of the abundance of wind-blown leaves and other debris found inside. For some reason, Kate and Robert ignored the rubble that lay in front of them. To the two of them, this was already home, debris and all. The house consisted of three large rooms constructed of tightly chinked logs. The front room, like the porch, ran the full length of the house and featured a large blue granite rock fireplace located in the middle of the room. It backed up to the bedroom located on one end of the house.

Robert said, "Rock on the inside of the house is good." He continued to explain to Kate, "The rock heats up, keeping the inside of the house warm including the bedroom."

Kate's mind took her back to Ireland and reminded her of the enormously large fireplaces in the castle. On the opposite end of the large room was a kitchen. The flooring throughout the house was of wide white oak boards that had been scoured to a smooth finish.

The previous owners had left behind some furnishings; a two-burner potbellied cookstove, a table and four chairs, a rocking chair, and a cast-iron bed. Opening a door just off the kitchen, Robert called, "Kate, come see this. It is quite ingenious."

They discovered a spring room, a feature not found in many houses. The small room had been built over a free flowing spring. The walls were rocked with the same blue granite as the fireplace. The room was quite a bit cooler than the rest of the house.

"Kate, do you have any idea what this means? We will not have to carry water in the winter. It is here in the house. We can keep a lot of our foods cool by putting the crocks in the cold spring water. This alone makes the house worth whatever the price. I think this is a good home. What are your feelings?"

"I love what we see. Do you really think we can work out an agreement with the financer?" asked Kate, as she was getting more excited about the possibility of becoming a landowner.

Leaving the house with lots of enthusiasm, they walked a well-worn path out to a lean-to barn. There they found another surprise, a broken wagon. The rear wheel was in need of repair and lying next to it was a horse plow. The blades needed some rust removed and a little sharpening, but could be returned back to a working piece of equipment. Hanging on the tack room wall was a horse collar and a bridle, both very well-used. Two more buildings, a chicken coop and a smokehouse, were situated off of the barn. They discovered that under the smokehouse was a root cellar.

"Kate, this is just what we need to start our family and new life here in America. Can you believe how much the previous owners left behind? We can make this work."

Robert picked up a handful of loose dirt checking its richness. His mind was reeling with enthusiasm, as he thought of being a landowner and what it would mean for the family. He had missed this feeling of looking forward to a bright future.

It had been a long time since Kate had seen this much excitement in Robert. He was again full of optimism, a quality she very much admired about him.

Riding back to town, they discussed the priorities it would take to become property owners.

"First things first, Kate. We will need a horse. Then we need to repair the wagon in the barn. We have six to eight weeks before our baby comes. Wouldn't it be wonderful to have our baby born in his own home?"

Robert's mind was churning with all these new thoughts. A lot would be needed to establish a real home for his new family.

"So, Robert, you are sure it is a boy," murmured Kate with a chuckle. "I caught that. Born in *his* own home."

Until now, Robert had always been careful not to let Kate know that in his heart, he hoped for a boy.

Kate's head was also spinning with excitement as she realized what would be required to set up housekeeping and preparations for a new baby.

For a brief moment, each sat in deep silence, reflecting their new beginning.

Returning back to the boarding house, the two became very hopeful about the proposition laid before them by Mr. McDonald.

Everyone at the dinner table was aware of the offer to Robert and Kate. Sitting down to dinner, Robert openly engaged Mr. McDonald in a conversation. "Kate and I are happy to accept your proposal to buy the farm. Thank you for assisting us in this matter."

"I think it to be a good opportunity for the both of you, Robert. Monday, you and I will go make the arrangements." Slapping his hands on the table in an orderly fashion, he declared, "Now, that that is settled, let's eat. Lilly, what's for dinner tonight?"

Chapter 13

MRS. FARGO AND KATE WERE sitting on the front porch, enjoying a cool glass of tea, along with some molasses cookies Lilly baked. Mrs. Fargo said with concern, "Kate, I think it would be wise to have Lilly help you in cleaning and making the house ready. You are so close to delivery." She added, "I also have a lot of furniture in the barn that from time to time has been used here in the big house. You and Lilly take what you need to set up your new home."

Kate stopped swinging and looked at Mrs. Fargo in disbelief. "You are so kind, but we couldn't." She shook her head. Really, deep in her heart, she would have loved the furniture but wanted to show some sense of humility or a bit of pride.

"I insist, and that is all there is about the subject," added Mrs. Fargo. "Besides, furniture seems to come and go. I have always lived in this big house. It belonged to my parents. My father was a trader of fine things. That is how he could furnish our home so well. He traveled to Europe on many occasions in search of new markets. I married Mr. Fargo late in life, and we never had children. For that, I am sad. We remained here to care for my aging parents. Lilly came with the house and has always been by my side. I lost Mr. Fargo some years back with the consumption. Enough of that, I am going too far back in time. You need the furniture now, and that is a good thing."

They continued to eat their cookies and enjoyed the coolness of the afternoon. As the two women looked down the street, they saw Robert leading a horse. Kate followed Robert and the horse to the barn. She watched Robert tie the horse in a stall and then give him feed and water. Before Robert offered an explanation, Kate remarked, "What's his name, Robert? He's not as pretty as Diamond. He is big, red, and old."

"I know, Kate," replied Robert, knowing her to be a bit disappointed in his choice of this animal. "His name is John. He is just an old workhorse, but he is what we need now to get us by."

Kate, knowing their finances were meager, asked Robert, "Even if he is old, how can we afford him?"

Robert continued to care for the animal. "It is because he is old. He belonged to a widow in town, and she could not afford to feed him. Mr. Foley, the blacksmith, took him off her hands and made me an affordable deal. Tomorrow, I will arrange with the blacksmith about the repair of the wagon wheel that is left in the barn. We then can begin cleaning and moving before the baby comes." He patted John's rear flank before leaving the stall.

Kate rubbed John's nose and then opened his jaws and looked at his teeth. "He's an *old* horse, Robert," Kate said with much emphasis placed on old.

Robert was now a bit put out that Kate did not seem to be in favor of his decision, and he sharply replied, "Yes, he is old, but he still has a lot of good work years. If we treat him well, he will get us through, you will see."

Kate realized that she had hit a sensitive nerve in Robert. "You know best, and of course, you are right. It is what works with our budget now."

Robert kissed her tenderly, then turned and closed the stable door. Holding hands, they walked back to the boarding house and went through the back door. Mrs. Fargo was in the dining room, preparing for the evening meal.

"Good evening, Mrs. Fargo, I just brought home a horse and put him in the barn. I hope you don't mind that he stay there for a few days. The blacksmith gave me a good deal on the old horse. By the way, I fed your horse while I was there."

"He is an old horse," giggled Kate, she was trying to adjust to the fact of his age while finding humor in Robert's choice.

"That is quite all right, Robert, the barn is large enough for both animals," interrupted Mrs. Fargo, sensing the two had different opinions.

It was decided that Kate and Lilly would begin working in the barn the next day, cleaning and carrying things out to the farm. Lilly was working in a back corner of the barn when something caught her eye.

"Look, Miss Kate, come seez what I has found."

Kate stopped what she was working on and went over to Lilly. "What is it, Lilly?"

"Why, Miss Kate, it is a baby cradle," answered Lilly. "Oh look, a carriage too." Lilly lifted some blankets that had been placed over them to protect them from the dust, all the while exercising her contagious laugh. "Why I has forgotten all about these things. I thought Mrs. Fargo did away with these things a longs time ago. We can clean 'em up likes new, Miss Kate." Kate was a bit confused about the baby things and stated, "I thought Mrs. Fargo had no children."

"Why she didn't, Miss Kate." She was trying very hard to skirt her way around a truly sensitive subject for Kate. "Mrs. Fargo was not young like youz is, Miss Kate, and she just could not deliver her baby. She just did not has the strength likes youz does, Miss Kate. Seeing the concern in Kate's eyes Lilly tried to reassure her, "Youz will be just fine and youz baby will be just fine. I surly does noez that, Miss Kate."

Continuing to work, Lilly tried to change the subject to make it more lighthearted. "Miss Kate, I never hears youz speak about youz family, does youz have any family?"

"Well, Lilly, I am an only child. I came from a very wealthy family in Ireland. My parents do not approve of Robert. They thought that he was not of a high enough station in society. So . . ." Looking for more words, she explained, "We ran away to America."

Kate, like Lilly, tried to avoid the subject and skirt the truth about her nobility. Kate wished to know more of Lilly and asked, "Lilly, how did you come to be with Mrs. Fargo's family?"

To answer Kate's question, Lilly stopped her work and straightened up as she put her hands in her apron pockets. "Oh my goodness sakes,

Miss Kate, Ize's not thought about this story fors a longs time. Ize's was born on a very large tobacco plantation in North Carolina. Mr. Harris and his wife cames down with Mrs. Fargo. She wuzs just a wee baby then. Thez cames to visit the plantation. It was a business trip fer Mr. Harris. There wuz a lots of us slaves who worked the tobacco fields. Ize's wuz eleven then, about old enough to be married off soz Ize's could have more slave babies. Ize's played and tooks care of Mrs. Fargo whiles thez were a visitin. Mr. and Mrs. Harris really tooks a liken to me and the way Ize's managed Isabelle. Ize's suppose thez just could not stand to think Ize's would live the life of a slave to be married off so young. My family and the Harris family faked my death." Lilly, with a slight giggle, laughed to think that they actually succeeded with the plan. "It was told that Ize's had the pox, knowing the big house and the slaves would stay away, leaving my family to cares fer me. Thez had a funeral and all. My Pappy wrapped a sack of straw, making it my size to looks like thez were taking me to the slave cemetery. No one wanted to sees my body cuz thez afered of gitten sick. My Mammy wailed and cried. Her tears were real cuz she knoz that she would never sees me agen. Very early the next morning, my Pappy tooks me out on the road where Ize's waited for the Harris buggy to picks me up. He carried me on his back sos my scent could not be picksed up by the hounds. Pappy was a very large man. He carried heavy cotton bails on his back. Ize's wuz a very long, lanky, and skinny girl then. Ize's remembers him telling me ifen wez gets caught not to run cuz the dogs would tears me apart. That wuz the last time Ize's sees my Pappy. Ize's remembers hearing the hounds chasing something and howz scared Ize's wuz as Ize's waited under the bushes fer the Harris buggy. My Pappy was caught, but he made out likes he wuz in the woods grieving my death. Ize's has stayed with the Harris family alls my life."

Kate, hearing the very stirring life story, asked Lilly, "How did you find out about your Pappy not being chewed up by the dogs?"

"Well, Miss Kate, Mr. Harris on a business trip asked about my Pappy and Mammy, if thez had got sick and died likes Ize's did. They izz both dead now. Ize's suppose it wuz from some mighty hard work thez had to do on that plantation.

90

"Ize's a free woman, Miss Kate. The Harris family and Isabelle that is Mrs. Fargo has always been good to me." With a defensive voice, Lilly continued, "Ize's no slave, Ize's here cuz Ize's wants to be, Miss Kate. The Harrises became my family and Ize's always lived and worked fer my board here at the big house. Ize's given a hard coin bonus at the end of each year so Izs's is paid fer my service. No mam, Ize's no slave. The Harris family saved me from a very hard life on that plantation. Ize's helped to raise Isabelle, Ize's mean Mrs. Fargo." Lilly straightened up and shook her shoulders and said, "Well, that is enough of that story, let's gets back to work."

After a long day in the barn, Kate and Lilly went back to the boarding house to prepare dinner for the guests.

Mrs. Fargo came into the kitchen. "You ladies have been working hard all day. Is there anything I can help you with for tonight's dinner?"

Lilly, being in charge, said, "Yes'm, if you would set our table, it would be greatly appreciated."

"Kate, the baby is going to come real soon. Perhaps you and Mr. McCall, Robert that is, should stay here at the house until the birth, rent free, of course, my invitation."

"Mrs. Fargo, you are too kind. We surely do appreciate your offer. You have already done so much with allowing Lilly to help. I just can't thank you enough for all the furniture you have given us. Robert wants the baby to be born in our own home, and I agree with him."

"I certainly do understand your feelings about that. Lilly and I will miss the two of you, especially your playing the harpsichord for us in the evenings." Mrs. Fargo moved around the table, placing the silver.

This would be the last dinner shared by the McCalls and those at the boarding house. The dinner conversation turned to the events of the war. Mr. McDonald told those at the table the latest war news. He told them of Washington's forces of three thousand that were being weakened by starvation, smallpox, and desertion. The Patriots had retreated to Montreal.

It was the last of June. Kate and Robert had moved to their farm with the help of their new friends. Kate and Lilly had done a wonderful job of making it very homey and appealing. A large round rug of varied colors found in the barn was placed in the center of the sparsely furnished front room. This added to the warmth of the log house. Kate placed the last remaining piece of silver taken from the castle on the mantel. In the silver goblet, she arranged a small gathered bouquet of wildflowers. This was the last of her material things from Ireland. She and Robert never mentioned her nobility, least of all the fact that she was a princess.

It was early morning. Kate wrapped her knitted shawl around her very large belly, then she pulled the door closed behind her. She rode into town with Robert to visit with Dr. Franklin. She was very anxious for this last exam.

"It will be good to spend some time with the ladies today after my visit with the doctor while I wait on you to finish at the office. Do you think you could come by and have lunch with us?"

Robert, always mindful of Kate's condition, drove Old John very carefully, trying to miss the deep ruts in the dirt road that led from the farm. "I feel sure I can do that. I am glad you are not by yourself today. I worry about you all alone while I am in town."

"Well, Kate, it won't be long now, actually any day and you will have your little baby. You need to rest more, you have been doing too much for your condition." Smiling, Dr. Franklin dropped the large horn-like stethoscope from his ears.

The summer day was coming to a close as Robert and Kate were leaving the boarding house.

Helping Kate with her wrap, he graciously thanked the two ladies for a lovely dinner. "Lilly, no one can cook like you do."

Lilly beamed with pride. "Ize's thanks youz, Mr. Robert."

"Now, Kate, you have Robert, come for us as soon as you feel the first signs of labor," encouraged Mrs. Fargo, as she and Lilly bid them good-bye.

It was the first Saturday afternoon in their new home. Robert and Kate were resting on the front porch after a day of hard work. Looking up the road, they spotted a caravan of buggies and wagons driving into their yard. Robert, a little perplexed, jumped from the porch while holding on to a post and landed in the front yard.

"What's this about?" He hollered, "Hello, neighbors!"

Everyone got out and came to the front porch where Kate was sitting.

Ms. Robinson, the teacher, announced, "We wanted to give you a real welcome to our community."

The friendly group had brought a spread of foods of varying kinds for a late picnic supper. A large number of people whom Kate had not been yet acquainted with gathered for the house warming. Robert knew more of the townsfolk because he worked among them. Everyone enjoyed the evening. Entertainment included a fiddle, along with mouth-harp music and dancing. The women brought stock food for a pounding, such as flour, salt, sugar, and general staples to fill Kate's shelves. They also brought baby items. Kate and Robert were taken by surprise and most grateful for such good neighbors.

The ladies, at the invitation of Kate, were invited into the house. Kate proudly showed them their homely accommodations. She opened the baby gifts, nappies, gowns, blankets, and some knitted items. The men gathered off in one corner of the yard under a very old sprawling oak tree to discuss the latest news about the war. The war was beginning to become more of a topic in mixed company. Everyone had great concerns about how close the battles encroached on the town. Robert was kept more informed than Kate concerning the war news. He knew that at some point, he would join Washington's army. He tried to keep his thoughts from Kate at least until after she delivered.

Chapter 14

V ERY EARLY ON A JULY morning, Kate awakened Robert. "Robert, Robert." Kate shook him. "I am having a lot of pain. Go for Lilly and Dr. Franklin. I want Lilly, Robert, I want Lilly."

Kate allowed herself to put Lilly in the place of Liz and relied on Lilly's advice and opinions.

Robert jumped out of bed, half dazed as he clumsily stepped one leg, then the other, into his pants and pulled them up. He stumbled out to the barn all the while he stretched his suspenders over his broad shoulders.

"Now, come on, John. It's no time to get stubborn with me. Not now. It's Kate, we are going to have us a baby today!" he talked to the horse as though he might know the situation.

The sun was rising over the hills just as Robert arrived at the boarding house. He pounded on the door. "Mrs. Fargo, Mrs. Fargo, it's Robert. We need Dr. Franklin, and Kate insisted on Lilly too." Robert ran around to the back kitchen to awaken Lilly. "Lilly, Lilly, get up. Lilly, it's Kate, it's the baby. Hurry."

Kate, meanwhile, was walking the floor at home, holding the bottom of her stomach. She did not realize that it was assisting her contractions to come on faster.

"Let's go in the wagon. It's faster than hitching the buggy," urged Robert, rushing everyone.

Arriving at the house, they found Kate bent double in a hard contraction.

Dr. Franklin advised, "Let's get her into bed so we can see what we have here, a girl or a boy. Kate, the baby is crowning. Give us a good hard push. You can do it!"

Lilly stayed closely by Kate's bedside, while Robert paced back and forth the full length of the front porch, stopping every now and again to listen to the ensuing prognosis.

In a pant, Kate squalled, "You can see its head, not its feet?"

"Yes, Kate, the baby is coming the right way, and everything looks good. I just need you to push," urged the good doctor.

"Ms. Kate," insisted Lilly, "here, holds my hand and do likes the doctor tells yah."

"Oh! Lilly . . . oh, it hurts. Not another one, here . . . comes . . . another one," cried Kate in pain.

"One last push, Kate. We have its shoulders, and everything is just as it should be. Ah! Here it is."

Dr. Franklin held the baby up and gave it one good spank.

Kate rolled her head and looked at the baby while Dr. Franklin held it upside down by its heels. "A girl, we have a girl."

"Is she strong? I hear her crying. Is she all right?" Kate, now free of her pain, dropped exhaustingly off her elbows. Her weakened voice revealed her nervousness about the well-being of their new baby.

"Here, Lilly, you take the baby and clean her up while I finish up here." Dr. Franklin handed Lilly the baby.

Robert broke through the door. "I hear the baby. Is everybody all right?"

Lilly took the baby to clean her up. "Mr. McCall, youz goes to yourzs wife, and I will return with a fresh new baby girl as pink as cherry blossoms," she chuckled. "Mr. Robert, the doctor says youz hasz a fine family."

"Oh, Robert, it's a girl. Is that all right?" muttered Kate, very tired and weak.

"Kate, a girl is just fine. Besides, we can't send her back now, can we? She will be a Papa's girl anyway." Robert gave Kate a kiss on the forehead and said, "You rest, for you have worked very hard this morning. I love you."

Holding the baby close, Kate remembered the name they had chosen. "Robert, I would like to name her Ashley Elizabeth after Liz. Is that all right with you?"

"Ashley Elizabeth it is," confirmed Robert with satisfaction in his voice. He did not tell Kate what a small tribute it was to Liz for her sacrifice.

Lilly smiled in her caring way. "I'll make us some coffee and cook breakfast. We will let Kate and the baby sleep."

Kate's youth and strength had aided her in a fast and easy delivery, which allowed for a quick recovery. Her travel on the ship and the winter months spent with Sarah and her children was the only exposure she ever had with small children. She depended on Lilly to advise her with a newborn.

Kate wrote Sarah and told her that she had given birth to a baby girl and named her Ashley Elizabeth after her dear friend and that all was well. She told Sarah that she and Robert had bought a small farm just outside of Philadelphia. She mailed the letter to Sarah in the care of Mrs. Morris at the millinery.

Kate found housekeeping to be a full-time job. She had to learn how to prepare a chicken. One such thing was wringing a chicken's neck, then scalding and plucking the feathers, then singeing with a low fire to remove the fine feathers, gutting, and finally cutting it up for cooking. She learned to clean the feathers and save them for pillow making.

One evening at suppertime, Kate told Robert, "We need to buy a cow for our milk, butter, and cheese. We have a chicken coop, so we need chickens too and some ducks and some guineas."

"Take it easy, Kate, that is a lot for you to take care of. I am afraid it is too much for you with Ashley as little as she is," reminded Robert. "You know, I still have to work awhile longer in town for Mr. McDonald to pay off the farm and can't be of much help to you."

Kate insisted for she could see the advantage of some farm animals. She had long since resigned herself to the idea that life required much hard physical work.

Getting ready for bed one night, Robert told Kate, "I hear there is going to be a tent revival in town Saturday. I think we should go. It will be fun." Robert knew this would be a fantastic time to hear the latest war news. "They expect about a thousand people. They come from all over. We can pack a picnic supper and even go by and pick up Lilly and Mrs. Fargo if you like."

"I have never been to a tent revival. What is it, Robert?" She put Ashley into the cradle.

"Neither have I, but it sounds interesting, even entertaining," replied Robert. Looking for words to explain, he said, "Well, it is a kind of church meeting where they have a lot of preaching, singing, and getting saved all under a big tent."

"Getting saved? What is that?" Kate asked a little confused. Her religious background had never exposed her to meetings of this nature.

Robert had been a Methodist teacher in Ireland. An explanation should be easy for him, but he searched for the right words. "Well, let's see how I should explain it to you. You take Jesus Christ as your personal savior. As time goes on, I will teach you more about the scriptures."

Kate crawled into bed. Robert blew out the candle. Just then, Ashley cried, and they both laughed.

"I thought she was asleep," whispered Kate as she rolled out of bed.

On Saturday, Robert packed the wagon with the picnic and the baby carriage for the short trip into town. They stopped by the boarding house to pick up the ladies. Driving up to the revival, they saw hundreds of people. Tents had been pitched for acres and acres. The middle of August had brought with it the usual misery of very hot and humid days. All the ladies were fanning and the men were wiping their faces with their handkerchiefs. It was even too hot for the children to run and play their childish games. They were just happy to lie under the shady trees and nap.

The big canvas tent surrounded the wooden makeshift stage and benches. Performing groups from area churches sang gospel songs to encourage a spiritual mood before various ministers brought forth their messages of the last days. This was Kate's first experience in a public gathering of this size.

Suddenly, there was a gentle but welcoming gust of wind which helped to cool the misery of the hot day. It rattled the tops of the large oak, chestnut, and popular trees.

Lilly hissed to Kate and Robert, "Ize's hopes this wind don't bring in a rain to spoil our day, but it sure is good to gets cooled off before the preachen gets started."

The services started. The whole scene amazed Kate with the shouting of amens, hands in the air, and the fainting. She wasn't sure if the fainting was because of the heat or from the high emotions that seemed to infect the crowd. She noticed mostly the women fainted. She felt sure Robert could explain the events of the day. Regardless, she was enjoying herself, particularly the music. Robert and Lilly were more familiar with the gospel songs than she.

Lilly had a lot of black friends throughout the group. The slaves roamed freely among the whites. In fact, race was not an issue between the worshipers. Black and white alike spoke of their concern of the war. There was more talk about the war in various groups among the men. The women seemed to speak of it very little.

Robert leaned against the trunk of a stalwart maple tree and spoke to the men concerning Thomas Paine's views about a republic. He did this with conviction, revealing his passion. "Paine seems to be making the cause his own. In his pamphlet 'Common Sense,' he describes us as colonists as a distinct people with a destiny of our own. Like Paine, I have chosen my destiny. Paine also scorns King George III as The Royal Brute of Britain. I know from a personal encounter, he can be very harsh and unforgiving. Paine also reminds us we are a huge continent an ocean away from the tiny British Isles. In his writings, he reminds us the British have bled us of our wealth and preyed on our liberties." Much like a pastoral sermon, Robert continued, "It is up to each of us how we view this new government and is it worth freeing ourselves of a tyrant. Freedom works! To be free of a tyrant such as Britain's king will allow individuals their God-given rights."

Kate's fears began to grow each time she heard Robert speak in such an unbridled manner.

On the drive home, Robert announced, "Kate, I want you to listen to me. I am going to tell you something I know will not make you happy. General Washington has—" he was unable to finish before Kate interrupted.

"No, Robert, you can't. I don't want you to." Kate feared what he would say next.

"Now, listen to me, Kate. I have been following this war very closely ever since we arrived in America. Our new country declared its independence this past July here in Philadelphia. I must do my part for you and Ashley. It won't be today or tomorrow, but soon. You know the war is moving from Boston and may be upon us in due time. I will make sure that you have all you need for the time I am gone. You will be fine. I must do this thing. I will arrange things with William when I go back to work on Monday."

Kate rode home in silence, trying to digest what Robert had just told her. She realized that he was determined to follow through with his plan.

Arriving home, Robert felt Kate's dissatisfaction with his decision. The evening hours lingered on in silence. Sunday remained a quiet day as Kate continued to deal with the shock. Robert gave Kate time and space; he thought it best not to speak of it this day. Kate's concerns weren't as much for herself and Ashley as it was the fear of Robert never returning to them.

Robert left the house, knowing that Kate was very saddened by his decision. When he arrived at the office, he asked William, "Might I have a moment of your time, sir."

"Certainly, Robert, step into my office," replied Mr. McDonald as he sat behind his desk, packing his tobacco pipe with a sweet-smelling cherry tobacco. He lit the pipe and blew a puff of smoke. He threw his head back to escape the smoky cloud as he asked, "Now what can I do for you? Kate and the baby are all right, aren't they? Sit, sit."

"Oh, yes, sir, they are well, thank you for asking. I wanted to speak to you concerning the war and the plea Washington has put forth for more stable forces. I want to be a part of his forces for my new country and for the future of my family. Therefore, I came to give you my resignation."

"Now, now, not so fast, Robert, are you sure this is what you want to do?" William asked, as he puffed on his pipe and leaned back in his chair.

"I am sure. It is what I need to do." Robert shifted himself into a more comfortable position in his chair. "Will you hold my job for me while I am gone?"

"Robert, I admire your desire. If I could, I myself would join Washington's army, but my fight is here in Philadelphia. It is important that I help set in place the constitution for our good state of Pennsylvania. Robert, these are glorious history-making days." William stopped to think as he gripped the bowl of his pipe and waved his hand. "I'll tell you what I will do while you are in Washington's army. I will make the payments on the farm for you. You can pay me back when you return. Should anything happen and you do not return, I will pay the farm off for Kate and the baby."

Robert was unaware the farm actually belonged to William, which was why he could make such a generous offer and why the payment arrangements had gone so smoothly. "Oh yes, one other thing," William stood to shake Robert's hand in a confirming handshake. "Your job will be here when you return."

"Well! Thank you, William. You are not only a fine employer, but I consider you to be a good friend. It certainly does ease my mind to know my family will be taken care of." Robert, overwhelmed with such generosity, vigorously returned the handshake.

Walking Robert back to his desk, William made another gesture. "I'll tell you what. I am going to write General Washington and tell him he is lucky to have such a fine man as you under his command."

Robert drove Old John and the wagon up to the barn. He deeply dreaded going into the house to face Kate with his plan. Working slowly, he unhitched John. He rehearsed in his mind how he would tell Kate that the arrangements had been made and that he would be leaving as soon as he could make preparations. Going through the door, he immediately noticed there to be a deep quietness about Kate. He could tell she had been crying. With the redness of her face and eyes, it looked as though she had cried all day. Walking up to her, he gently took her into his arms and held her for a time without saying a word. He just pulled her head close to his chest and stroked her hair. "Kate, I must tell you that William and I have come to a mutual understanding about the farm. You and Ashley will be taken care of should I not return. My job will be waiting for me when I do return, and I will return. You must believe that."

Robert lifted her chin, looked her tenderly in the eyes, and wiped away her tears.

"Oh, Robert, if I were only as sure as you are. I could perhaps manage your leaving." It was one of those rare moments when she could breathe his scent, one she would savor. Kate returned to her baking. The evening went by very quietly each in their own deep thoughts.

Robert, with the help of neighbor Charles, cut wood for the house. This was one of the many things that needed to be done in preparation for his leaving. Charles was a very large frontier-looking man with a full beard and large hands. His voice sounded deep and gruff. One might have the impression that chopping wood was an easy task for Charles. They stacked the lean-to at the barn and the entire front porch full of good hard wood.

Kate carried a bucket with a gourd dipper of cold spring water to the hardworking men. The men stopped to drink and refresh themselves. Robert told Kate, while wiping his brow, "This winter, you use the wood at the barn on good days and save the wood on the porch for rainy and snow days." Taking another drink of water, he said, "Boy, this sure is good and cool."

It made him even more grateful for the convenience of the spring inside the house for Kate's sake.

Robert sat down on a tree round and looked across the farm. "Kate, now it is time for those farm animals you want. You know you will have to learn to milk a cow. The cow will need to be milked twice a day. Of course, you know that. I am concerned about the amount of work it will make for you alone."

Kate leaned in to give Robert an appreciative kiss. Turning as she walked away, she hollered back, "Love you, Robert!"

The men continued chopping wood.

Kate was in the house feeding Ashley when she heard a blood-chilling scream. Running to the door, she saw Robert lying on the ground. Quickly, she put Ashley safely in the cradle. Charles was bending over Robert, trying to assist him. Kate reached him, and looking down, she saw Robert's leg gushing blood. "Oh, Robert, Robert . . . oh, Robert, what have you done?"

Beads of perspiration popped out on Robert's forehead; gritting his teeth and looking at his leg, he rocked back and forth on his hips and told Kate, "I came down hard on a block of wood. It bounced, the ax missed, and went right into my leg."

Kate took off her apron to use as a tourniquet. The severity of the cut made her sick to her stomach. She knew she had to hold together to save Robert's life.

"We have to stop the bleeding fast. Charles, quickly get the wagon. Get the wagon. We have to take him into Dr. Franklin."

Kate laid Robert back gently on the ground. She ran back into the house and grabbed Ashley and placed her in the carry basket. Charles and Kate helped Robert into the back of the wagon. Charles knew the age of Old John and ran him as hard as he dared as he drove them in town to Dr. Franklin's office.

Dr. Franklin came out of his office after caring for Robert and looked over the top of his monocle. "Well, Kate, he will be all right, but it is a nasty wound in the fibula. The worst thing is that it chipped the bone. I cleaned it as best as I could and removed some small bone fragments He will be in a lot of pain and most definitely will have to stay off the leg for quite some time. You know, there is a chance of blood poisoning. If that should occur, there is a possibility Robert will lose the leg. You must do as I tell you. Dress the wound morning and night, use this ointment, and for goodness sakes, make him stay off the leg. However, I don't think that will be a problem for a while as it will be too painful. Here is something for pain tonight. I will be out to see him tomorrow. These things can be serious if not taken care of properly."

"Thank you, Dr. Franklin, I will see to it."

Charles helped Kate get Robert home and into bed. Being a good neighbor, Charles offered, "Mrs. McCall, I will finish the wood cutting for the day, and when my days permit, I will chop what Robert has planned for you."

The sedative Dr. Franklin gave Robert helped him rest through the night, but the following day and through the second night was perhaps the most dreadful time of their marriage. Robert became delirious. His temperature spiked in the early morning of the second day. Kate struggled to keep him in bed. He wanted to chase after demons. It was a relief for Kate when Dr. Franklin arrived early that day.

"Kate, you are going to need help for a few days. This is going to get worse before it gets better. On my way back into town, I will see if Mrs. Fargo can spare Lilly to help out for a few days."

Mrs. Fargo drove Lilly out to the farm. "What can we do to help you, Kate? Poor thing, it looks as though you need sleep. I will stay the day with Lilly, and you go to bed for the rest of the afternoon. We will care for Ashley and Robert."

Kate was grateful, but asked, "I very much appreciate your offer, but what will you do about the boarding house dinner this evening?"

Lilly answered that it was easy. "Ize's will makes us a good shepherd's pie. Mrs. Fargo can carries it back with her. Ize's will make one fer here as well. Now youz just take Ashley and goes fer a nap until this evening. We will cares for Robert and Ashley when she wakes up."

Kate and Lilly took turns in caring for Robert. They cleaned and bandaged the leg. After a very long week of agony, Robert's fever broke, and he was able to take in some nourishment.

The accident slowed Robert's plans for joining Washington. He was up and on a crutch and helped Kate as much as he could about the house and caring for Ashley.

Chapter 15

O NE EVENING, NEARING SUPPERTIME, ROBERT and Kate heard the guineas. The guineas always sang loudly when someone approached the house.

"Those obnoxious birds," declared Robert, still hopping on one crutch as he went to the door to see what was causing the commotion. "Well, I'll be, Kate, come see who is here."

Kate rushed to the door. She couldn't imagine who it could be. Stepping out on to the porch, she jumped out into the yard skipping the two front steps. She landed, all the while calling. "The Thatchers, it's the Thatchers! Sarah, oh, Sarah, is it really you? It's so good to see all of you. Please come into the house where it is cooler. I know you must be tired and thirsty."

Everyone in the wagon jumped to the ground, knocked off the dust, and wiped the perspiration from their brows. They were anxious for an offer of something cool to drink. While Kate went into the springhouse for cool water, Sarah saw Ashley in the cradle.

"Kate, she is beautiful with red hair and blue eyes. Now who does she get that from?" Sarah picked up Ashley. "I know you named her Ashley Elizabeth after a dear friend."

"Your home and surrounding land is to be envied, Robert and Kate, you must be doing well for yourselves here in Philadelphia," conveyed Jonathan.

"Timing was more on our side than anything and the help from some good friends." Robert slapped Jonathan on the shoulders, not taking credit for their good fortune. "I see you have two good horses and a wagon. That is not so bad yourselves," praised Robert.

Jonathan explained, "We thought it wiser to buy the team and wagon rather than paying passage on the boat to come north. That's a lot of passage for eight people. We could camp and bring our belongings. Also we could live on the wagon if we had to, and here we are." Quickly, Jonathan changed the subject as he looked about. "I see you are on crutches. What happened?"

"Chopping wood, I suppose I thought my leg was a log." Robert laughed. "It was really bad at first, but it is much better thanks to some mighty good nursing from my good wife and some fine women in the community."

"You are staying the night," insisted Kate. "We will add to supper and draw water for baths. How is that? Then we will work on sleeping arrangements. You are the first out-of-town guests in our new home."

"Nathaniel, you and Arianna help me carry in our bedding from the wagon after I help Kate clear the dishes. I am sure Kate does not have enough blankets for such a large group" were Sarah's orders.

After finishing the chores, everyone settled in for the night.

Kate, Robert, and Ashley were in their bedroom when Kate, filled with excitement, said, "It's so good to see them. I really thought I would never see Sarah again with things as bad as they are with the war and all."

Sitting on the side of the bed while taking off his shoes, Robert agreed and whispered, "Kate, I am thinking maybe they are here for a reason. Don't you think it strange that they come at this time when I am planning to leave soon?"

Kate was gently pulling Ashley's nightgown over her head and, in her own whispering voice, asked, "What are you trying to say, Robert? Are we thinking the same thing?"

Kate and Robert seemed more often than not to be in tune with each other's thoughts.

Robert lay in bed with his ankles crossed and his hands clasped behind his head and said, "I think so. Let's asks them to stay a few days and see how things work out. Perhaps if they are interested, we could make an offer for them to stay on the farm and help you with the work."

Kate got into bed beside Robert and gave him a good night kiss. "I think you have a brilliant idea, Robert, we will see how things are in the morning."

She turned over to go to sleep.

Kate and Robert were awakened by noises in the house. Everyone had gotten up early. Kate nursed Ashley before she went into the kitchen.

Coming from their room, they sang in unison, "Good morning, everyone," and then laughed at their timing.

Sarah began, "We were hoping you could sleep in this morning after we moved in on you last night. I have started breakfast. Jonathan built me a fire in the stove this morning. It's wonderful to have a cookstove, isn't it? I have heard of these little stoves, never thought I would actually cook on one. Unbelievable, isn't it?

"I sent Nathaniel to the chicken coop with a basket for the eggs," added Sarah, continuing to put the biscuits in the Dutch oven.

Arianna was setting the table. The younger children were carrying wood in for the day, one block at a time, and neatly stacking it in the woodbox beside the stove.

"This is so nice to have all this help this morning. Sarah, what can I do to help at this point?" asked Kate, tying on an apron.

Sitting down at the table, Robert blessed the food, giving thanks for once again seeing their good friends and for their bounty.

Passing the biscuits, Robert had a sudden inspiration. Forgoing the plans he and Kate had made the night before, he injected, "Jonathan, Sarah, Kate, and I were talking last night. I'm going to join Washington's army."

There was sudden silence. Everyone stopped what they were doing. Robert recognized that he had the attention of the adults.

"We were thinking that your family might stay here on the farm with Kate while I am gone. You could be our hired help. That is, unless you have something else in mind here in the area."

Jonathan and Sarah looked at each other in complete shock. Jonathan, dismayed, replied, "You have everything, Kate, Ashley, a good job, and this beautiful farm. Why would you even consider such a thing, why?"

"Jonathan, those are the very reasons why. If we fail to fight for our liberties now, we will have none. I do not want my family subjected to the rule of a king."

Robert turned his eyes and searched for Kate's. Looking directly into her eyes, he knew that she knew his reasons. Drawing in a deep breath and with a real conviction in his voice, Robert began in a dissertation fashion that would rival any politician, "It is important while this country is still young to build a free and independent government. That is what will make this nation great. In Ireland, I was a weaver. I once wove a tablecloth for His Majesty. For political reasons, he did not like my creation. He ordered my beheading." Robert pounded his fist on the table which startled everyone. He then continued, "According to Thomas Paine, a monarchy is a foolish and dangerous form of government. However, the Declaration has a different view. It denounces only the reigning king of England, not the institution of the monarchy itself. For these reasons, I want to aid in the weaving of a firm and strong government for my posterity so that they might have justice in all things. Thomas Jefferson believes, and has written right here in Philadelphia, that these self-evident truths of human equality and unalienable rights to life, liberty, and the pursuit of happiness, that these rights have been endowed to all of us by our Creator. I may not be weaving a king's cloth, but I will be adding the threads that will weave a true and strong republic."

"You are right, Robert, I can see you already have a deep and committed love for this land. You have become quite a patriot," added Jonathan as he blew across the steam of his morning coffee. "We don't have any other plans. Actually, we wanted to see if you had any ideas about work. What do you think, Sarah?" asked Jonathan.

"Well, I think working for the McCalls is as good as working for anyone else, so yes, I say yes."

"So yes, it is."

With excitement in his voice, Robert once again slapped Jonathan on the shoulders.

Jonathan reared back in his chair and declared, "Robert, you fight the war with Washington, and I will stay with our families looking after their welfare."

"We are going to have to make some changes here in the house. I am thinking we can add on a bedroom behind the kitchen, one for you and Sarah, with a loft overhead for the children to get us by this winter. Come spring, if all goes well, we can build your family a house on the property. This house will need an additional room at some point, so why not now? That's my idea. Are there any other ideas?"

Robert took a sip of coffee and looked over his cup while waiting for a response.

"It needs to be completed before winter is upon us," added Kate.

"We will all do what is necessary," assured Sarah.

Chapter 16

On August 27, 1776, the British landed an army of twenty-five thousand men on Long Island, New York. The Americans were forced to withdraw after severe defeats in the battles of Long Island and White Plains. Robert kept well informed of Washington's positions during the war and grew anxious to carry through with his plan to join the general as soon as possible.

Late September ushered in cooler days. It was evident that fall was quickly approaching. The trees sported their annual transformation, with gold, red, and orange colors splashed across the landscape. Jonathan, with the help of Charles, cut timber from the property for the additional room. His team of horses proved a great asset in the process of logging the timbers from the woods as well as hoisting the logs in place. Robert, with his leg still mending, participated as much as he could by sizing and trimming the logs.

Kate and Sarah worked hard at keeping enough food for the eleven of them. The women made butter and saved the extra eggs to be bartered in town for salt, sugar, and coffee.

Once again, Arianna, so young herself, skillfully managed the children, keeping them entertained by playing games, and tended to their needs. This was greatly appreciated by both Kate and Sarah.

Everyone fell into bed each night from exhaustion. It was essential they do as much work as possible before winter set in and Robert left for the army.

The farm had a number of large black walnut trees. Robert and Jonathan had spared them because of the nuts, which were a delicacy of the rich townspeople. When cleaned, the walnuts could be bartered for essentials the farm could not produce. The children gathered the bulk of the nuts before the critters could carry them away.

One morning late in the fall, Arianna and Nathaniel were gathering nuts as Jonathan and Charles were nearby logging the last of the necessary timbers for the new room addition. The sharp cold wind whipped through the trees, stinging their cheeks and making them red and chapped. The fierce wind gusts sent the nuts falling to the ground almost faster than the children could gather them. Occasionally, one would hit them on the head or back.

"Hurry, Nathaniel, this wind is too cold and blowing too hard," warned Arianna, struggling with her apron full of nuts as she took them back to the bucket, waiting to be filled.

Nathaniel, whimpering because he was cold, ran his hand under his nose and wiped away the annoying liquid as he tried to pick up his share of nuts.

"Nathaniel, Nathaniel, behind you!" screamed Arianna, dropping her filled apron.

Nathaniel turned to see a bobcat high on a boulder.

"Stand still, Nathaniel!" yelled Arianna.

Overcame with fear, Nathaniel heard none of Arianna's frightening screams. Dropping the nuts, he ran toward her.

"Stand still, Nathaniel. We can't run. The bobcat will chase us," cautioned Arianna, not knowing what to do next.

Suddenly, behind them, they heard a resounding roar that bounced off the gray rock boulders. Turning, they saw a brown bear standing on its back legs. It was swinging its front paws in a fearless waving motion. The bear's mouth revealed teeth that could rip a small animal in half in one instant. The children grabbed each other in a hopeless hug, realizing that they were caught in a deadly situation. Nathaniel began to cry harder, making his hold on Arianna even tighter as he buried his face in her stomach. Arianna froze. She wrapped her arms around Nathaniel, trying to protect him from an attacker bigger than anything she had ever encountered. She could feel her shaking legs getting weaker as though they could no longer support her trembling body. Just at that moment, the bobcat gave an equally loud echoing cry. The bear, monstrous in size to the very small children, dropped on all fours in a mad run. The children, with horror in their souls, clung to each other. Growling and thrusting its head back and forth, the bear bypassed the children, as though they were not there, in its pursuit of the bobcat. Arianna and Nathaniel forgot they were gathering nuts and ran in the opposite direction right into the arms of their father who was on his way with his muzzle-loading rifle. Shaking, stammering, both at the same time, they tried to relate what had just happened. Jonathan hugged them in a comforting embrace.

"It's all right now, you are safe. That was a mother just protecting her cubs over there," explained Jonathan, pointing to the little bears rolling around in the fallen leaves, playfully slapping at one another. "The bobcat really wanted those little cubs. You just happened to be in the way. The mother bear, chasing that darned ole bobcat away, saved you children as well as her cubs. Let's go quietly. She will be back very soon for the cubs, and we don't want to be in her way. She is already angry."

"What about the nuts?" snubbed Arianna. She tried to gain control, knowing their importance to the family income.

"We will get them later after the bear family has gone," Jonathan lovingly told her.

Sarah and Kate heard the fearful cries of the wild animals and came running from inside the house to the far edge of the front yard to see what had happened. At that moment, the children broke away from their father and ran to their mother. They needed the consoling words only a mother could give.

Later in the day, Jonathan and the children returned to recover the gathered walnuts. Once back at the house, the children laid the nuts out individually to dry. The nuts had a thick green outer shell. When dry, the shell turns black and is ready to peel; when the peel is removed, it leaves a very hard black wood shell that surrounds the moist nut. Removing the black outer shell proved to be a nasty process because of an almost tar-like substance. The sticky mess blackened the hands and left the nails shamefully stained. The stain was close to impossible to remove and generally had to wear off. Sarah and Kate were delighted that the children found this chore entertaining.

Finally, the loft room was finished. Two windows, one on each end of the loft, would give the children a good cross breeze during the hot and steamy summers. A stepladder provided access to the room. Lisa-Jean, Penelope, and Liam had fun climbing up and down the ladder, stepping on a few fingers as they went. Levi, the smallest, needed help. Three bunk beds accommodated the six children. Sarah was equally happy, for it had been some time since she and Jonathan had had a room to call their own.

Chapter 17

ROBERT, STILL ON CRUTCHES, RETURNED to work for William. Jonathan, at the supper table, discussed the day's work. "Tomorrow, Robert, I think it would be a good idea to pull out some of the tree stumps. This will clear the land for a good garden and some larger crops this coming season." He scooped potatoes onto Penelope's plate.

Robert agreed, "Well, the farm is not large enough to produce a business profit, but I do think we can make a living for ourselves."

Jonathan asked Robert, "What is the latest scuttlebutt about the city concerning the war?"

Robert had heard the war news from the elite Philadelphians and dove into the subject with great attention to detail. "It is said that Benjamin Franklin has been appointed head of a three-man commission by the Congress to negotiate aid and form a formal alliance with France. Personally, I have my doubts. He is a simple man with a homespun appearance, not at all a nobleman by French standards." Robert stopped to spread butter on a biscuit. "Washington's army is poor and made up of the poorest people fighting for freedom. They have no formal uniforms. They are short on supplies and ammunition. It takes money to fight a war and win. We will see, we will see." He reared back on his chair, holding Ashley in one arm and eating the buttered biscuit from the other hand.

Kate pulled a chair up to the table concerned with the conversation between the two men. "Robert, it frightens me that you speak of the war so often."

"Kate, you know our plans are for me to join Washington as soon as my leg is strong enough, and it is getting stronger every day," replied Robert.

"Who is this Benjamin Franklin anyway?" asked Kate.

Robert, placing Ashley on the floor with the younger children, answered, "You know he publishes the *Pennsylvania Gazette*. He is quite vocal with his opinions. But actually, he is an inventor as well. Mr. McDonald told me he built this stove for the previous owners of this house. It is one of the very few that have been built."

"Well, I certainly am happy to have one of these little stoves to call mine," joshed Kate as she got up to finish clearing the table.

"That goes for me as well," chimed Sarah.

Morning came early on the farm. Crystal frost covered the rooftops as well as the dry brown leaves, which thickly lay across the ground and reminded everyone that winter was in the making. Sarah put breakfast on the table while Kate nursed Ashley. The children were rousted out of bed to do the day's chores. Robert used his crutch less and less these days. He bent over and kissed Kate and gave Ashley a kiss on top her head as he left the house. He hitched old John to the wagon for his drive into the office.

After milking, Jonathan decided this was a good day to clear the north field of all the tree stumps. He gave Sarah a kiss and made ready to leave the house. She handed him a bucket containing cold biscuits spread with butter and drizzled with molasses syrup, along with a glass cork-top jar filled with milk which was wrapped in a towel to keep cool. In the barn, Jonathan hitched one of his team horses to the wagon and loaded a shovel, ax, and pick. He placed his lunch behind the bench seat and propped his loaded rifle on the floor of the wagon in front of him.

Arianna followed him to the barn and pleaded, "Papa, may I come with you?"

Jonathan answered, "I think it best you stay and help your mother today."

Hoping to appease her, he gave her a quick kiss on top of her blonde head. Slapping the back of the horse with the reins, Jonathan drove out to the field. The morning had warmed up, making the ground soft and marshy from the melting heavy frost. Looking across the field, his eyes caught sight of a buck standing as though it were frozen in time at the edge of the uncut woods. Pulling back on the reins to stop the wagon before getting too close and frightening the animal, he slowly reached for his already loaded gun, took aim, and fired.

The much needed meat was brought to the ground. Jonathan was excited that he had made such a good shot, so he drove the wagon as close to the buck as he could. Loading the dead weight into the back of the wagon presented a challenge he didn't think he could muster alone. In the bed of the wagon, he found a pulley and rope used for logging. This assisted him in the almost impossible task facing one lone man to gain leverage for such a heavy load. He estimated the buck weighed two hundred fifty pounds. He felt good about the targeted shot, realizing the fallen buck was a much needed blessing in a household of eleven. Although not what he planned for, it would take the remainder of the day to properly dress out the meat. Arriving back at the barn, he tied a rope around the animal's hind legs and hoisted it to a rafter. He slit it open from top to bottom, allowing it to bleed out. At the house, everyone expressed excitement about the fresh meat and sang their praises to Jonathan for such a marvelous shot.

Sarah gathered kitchen knives, a meat cleaver, tin pans, and a deep wooden tub to help Jonathan butcher the meat. She took a freshly cut roast back to the house to start preparing it for supper that evening. Taking it inside, she said to Kate, "It certainly will be easier to cook this on a stove rather than over an open fire."

Several days passed and Robert was now able to saddle Old John to ride to work. He left the wagon for Kate and Sarah. Jonathan needed his wagon for clearing the land in the north field.

Kate had more time for her needlework in the evening now that Sarah shared in the labor. Her handiwork allowed them to barter for things the farm could not provide.

Kate and Sarah loaded the children into the back of Robert and Kate's wagon along with eggs, walnuts, butter, pot cheese, and lace work to make a trip into town for provisions. They left Jonathan alone to clear the field.

The field had a number of tree stumps that needed to be dug out. Jonathan had removed four of the stumps without any trouble, but the fifth stump was a complete surprise to him. He had swatted yellow jackets once or twice without paying attention to the location of their nest. The fifth stump, hollow and rotten, had made a perfect nesting home for the swarming insects as they prepared for a winter hidden in the ground. Jonathan struck into the stump with the mattock disturbing the hive. The bees swarmed thousands of them, covering his face, neck, and hands and anywhere that was not covered by clothing. He dropped to the ground fighting and flailing all the way. The horse could not escape the wrath of the mighty swarm and reared up, broke loose, and began running wild. It overturned the wagon when breaking free and raced all the way back to the barn, leaving Jonathan facedown in the dirt.

Sarah, Kate, and the children returned home and noticed the horse standing outside the barn, still bridled and looking miserable.

"Something is wrong, Jonathan would never leave his horse out like that," exclaimed Sarah.

"Why is he stomping and rearing so?" asked Kate.

"Arianna, please take the children in the house while Kate and I look for your Pa. Jonathan said he would be in the north field clearing more stumps. I don't see him, Kate."

The two women found Jonathan lying facedown in the freshly turned dirt. They turned him over, and to their horror, his face and eyes were badly swollen. He was in severe pain with body chills and almost in shock.

"Sarah, you stay with Jonathan. I will go back for the wagon. It is still hitched, and we can get him back to the house faster."

Kate ran as fast as she could. They struggled to get Jonathan inside the house to his bed. Sarah began to strip him of his clothes while Kate quickly went to the spring room to soak cloths with cool water before rushing back to Sarah. Sarah applied the cloths to his face.

"I don't know what to do for him, Kate, what should we do? I know it is certainly serious."

"Well, pull the stingers out, at least the ones you can see, and I will make a tobacco poultice. I have seen the stableman do it at the castle stables for my horse, Diamond."

Kate suddenly realized what she had said; she turned her back, rolled her eyes, and left the room. She hoped that Sarah, in her concern for her husband, did not realize her remarks.

Robert, upon returning home, could see that Jonathan's horse was bridled and very agitated standing outside the barn. From inside the house, he could hear a commotion as he ran up on the porch. Rushing inside, he found Sarah and Kate busily attending to Jonathan.

"What happened?"

"Jonathan must have disturbed a nest of yellow jackets in the north field. When we returned from town, we found him facedown in the dirt. I have made him tobacco poultices for the stings."

Kate rushed about, trying to help Sarah in applying them. Robert went to the cabinet in the kitchen and returned with a bottle. "Here give him a brandy tonic. It might help warm him up. I need to go to the barn and care for the horses. Jonathan's horse seems to be stung as well." Robert left, closing the door behind him.

"Whoa, whoa, boy, steady now, steady." He grabbed the horse by the bridle, trying to calm him. After controlling the horse, he looked him over. He spotted a few stings, nothing the horse couldn't recover from. Hitching Jonathan's second horse, he went out to the field to hitch to the wagon. He found the wagon overturned and knew he could not up right it alone. He rode after Charles to give him a hand.

Arriving at Charlie's farm, he found him plowing his field. Waving at Charles to get his attention, he yelled, "Charles, I need your help on my farm. There has been an accident. Jonathan was stung by a swarm of bees, and his horse overturned the wagon. I need your help to right it!"

Charles unhooked his horse from the plow and left the plow in the field. "Robert, let me tell the missus where I am going and I will be right with you."

Together, Robert and Charles burned out the yellow jackets' nest and then righted the wagon. The men pulled the wagon back to the barn after which they assessed the damage.

Kate came out the door with a freshly baked sweet potato pie that she had made that morning before going into town. "Charles, thank you for your help. Please take this pie home to your family."

"Thank you, Kate, it looks delicious. I am sure Alice will appreciate this tonight."

Charles bid Kate and Robert a good-bye.

Jonathan's recovery took a few days before he could return to the fields.

Chapter 18

IT WAS A BEAUTIFUL DECEMBER day. The sun shone brightly, and the air was brisk. The wind dropped the chill factor, making the day seem much colder. Kate and Sarah were taking advantage of the day to wash. They were hanging clothes on the line, stopping ever so often to warm their fingers. The wet clothes made them sting, stiff, and even colder.

"Kate, can I ask you a question? I have thought about this for a while, and I can't seem to find an answer. The day Jonathan was stung, you said, 'Your horse Diamond at the castle.' What did you mean by 'at the castle'?"

"Oh, Sarah." Slowly searching for words, Kate replied, "How should I tell you this? Well . . ." With a long pause, "I will just tell you," swallowing hard, "I am the daughter of King George III," Kate confessed.

Sarah stopped. She almost lost her breath, dropped her hands to her sides, and did a little stomping jump.

"My name is Mary Katherine. Robert calls me Kate for short. I was a princess." Kate continued to hang clothes. "That was a long time ago and means nothing here in America. Remember Robert telling you and Jonathan that he wove a royal tablecloth for the king? My father, the king, was most insulted because it depicted the American eagle. The king called him a traitor and ordered his beheading, so we escaped to America, and here we are. You know the rest."

"Gracious me, that's some story. Kate, someday you would have been queen."

"I am a queen, Sarah. Robert treats me as his queen. Life, at first, was very hard, but we have each other. I chose love over nobility. My parents are in a loveless marriage. I did not want that for my family. Regardless, I still do love and miss them terribly."

Sarah, over her initial shock, continued hanging clothes and said, "I knew you were different, I mean, more refined. Yes, that is how I would describe you. I knew you had a fine education, and now I understand why. A real princess, I know a real princess."

"You are the only person I have shared this with. Robert and I do not speak of it. I am sure he feels bad that it happened so fast, and he perhaps feels it was not fair to me, but I would not change it for the world." Kate brushed her hair back out of her face. "You can tell Jonathan, but please do not mention it in front of Robert. Robert is concerned for my safety. He feels it best that no one knows of my true background. He told me the statue of King George was torn down in New York and the Americans had rituals of killing the king. For this reason, I'd rather no one else knows. Robert and I feel, with the war and the political feelings so high, my life could be in great jeopardy. The fear is that I could be held for ransom and/or forced back to England to face the wrath of my father."

"Oh, Kate, I can't believe it, I really do know nobility, and she is my best friend."

The two finished hanging the laundry, then went into the house to start supper for the family.

December reminded the two families of their first Christmas in America, not knowing that fate would bring them together again for the second year. Kate and Sarah were making plans for their celebration. They were happy that their circumstances had greatly improved for both families. They were grateful to be of service to each other. Each realized that these times required neighbor helping neighbor.

News reached Robert of Washington's retreat across the Delaware River into Pennsylvania on December 7. Washington was able to hold the lines with only three thousand men. Howe pulled back to New York

City, leaving the Hessians to hold the British line on the New Jersey shore of the Delaware River.

Robert came home dreading the news he had for Kate with Christmas so close. He shivered as he entered the house.

"Boy, it's cold out there tonight." He went to Kate and gave her a hello kiss. "What's for supper? It certainly smells good."

After warming his hands at the fireplace, he picked up Ashley and tickled her just to get a giggle from her.

Everyone sat down to supper. Sarah dished up the last of the venison that Jonathan had killed in the fall. Robert sopped the remaining gravy in his plate with a slice of bread. He looked up and said, "Kate, Jonathan, and Sarah, Mr. McDonald has written my letter to General Washington. I am thinking on leaving by the thirteenth to meet up with his forces on the Delaware. News came to me today that Washington has three thousand of his troops on the Philadelphia side of the Delaware River. Howe is making winter quarters in New York City. He has placed the Hessians on the New Jersey side of the Delaware."

Kate dropped her fork. She jumped up and left the table, tearing off her apron as she ran to their room and closed the door hard behind her.

Robert got up from the table and bid, "Excuse me, I knew this would be hard for her." He knocked on the door. "Kate, may I come in?" He could hear her crying. "We need to talk," he spoke very softly.

"Yes," Kate answered with a muffled whimper.

Robert bent over the bed where Kate lay facedown. Turning her over, he brushed the tear-soaked hair from her face and lay next to her. "Kate, sweetheart, you know how I feel. The war is now coming so close to us. I promise you I will be all right. I just want to make sure you and Ashley are safe and that our lives can be all that we want them to be."

The household spent the following days making ready Robert's provisions. He packed dried fruit, a tin of molasses, biscuits, and venison jerky, tying it tight in a four-corner cloth along with a bedroll and his heaviest clothes. He was wearing the only pair of shoes he owned.

Kate was determined that she would not allow him see her cry the day he left. She would reserve the tears when she was alone.

Jonathan and Nathaniel attended to the animals before supper. Kate and Sarah did their usual housekeeping chores, including a special farewell supper for Robert. Kate made southern fried chicken with gravy the way Lilly had taught her. She knew it was Robert's favorite. Hot baked sweet potatoes with lots of fresh butter and cottage cheese were placed on the table. Wintertime had again brought with it the wild winter greens. There were biscuits, walnut loaf bread with butter and honey to sweeten it, along with bread pudding covered with fresh churned cream.

Suppertime was very quiet. No one spoke of the war happenings. Robert was aware of everyone's sensitive feelings concerning his leaving. Thanking the ladies for a marvelous meal, he excused himself from the table.

Kate saw to it that he had the leftovers to add to his already packed food supply for the next day's journey.

Everyone arose early on December 13 to see Robert off. Without waking Ashley, Robert looked in on her as she peacefully slept. He wondered what the future held for them as a family.

He packed Old John with his belongings placing the bedroll, clothes, and food behind his saddle. He hung his rifle and gunpowder alongside. The morning was still dark with a peak of the eastern sunrise shining through the blue-gray clouds that absorbed the rising chimney smoke. The ground was frozen hard from the freezing night's temperatures and caused a crunching sound with every footstep. Everyone stood in a huddle, bouncing and rubbing their hands together trying to keep warm. Robert, with tears in his eyes, shared his good-byes with all, giving Jonathan a firm handshake with a quick hug.

Jonathan assured Robert, "I will take care of Kate and Ashley as though they are my own."

He gave Sarah a hug as well and said, "You take care of my girls and yourself while I am away."

Purposely, he left Kate for last. Kate once again leaned into him as she had done so many times before. Robert gave her a lingering kiss and stroked her face most tenderly. Her body shivered, not with the cold, but with an inward emotion no one else could see or feel. It felt as though her own soul was being wrenched from her body, leaving her lifeless inside. Kate, with all the strength left in her, would not allow herself to cry for Robert's sake. "I love you, Robert McCall. I understand your need to do this thing. May the Almighty go with you and bring you back to me, my love."

Robert mounted Old John and rode out of the yard, not looking back. If he did, he dared to think that he would change his mind. It was approximately a sixteen-mile ride to Trenton where he hoped to meet up with General Washington. On his way, he gathered information from the militia stationed along the Delaware River as to the whereabouts of the general. He was thinking the whole time that this vital information was given too freely which could no doubt enable the enemy.

The morning of December 14, General Washington awoke in the home of Thomas Barclay directly across the river from the opposing General Howe who was dining with his officers in Trenton Falls.

Gen. George Washington was expecting Robert after receiving a letter of recommendation from William McDonald. The army general, standing six foot three inches tall, dressed meticulously in his military uniform. He moved about his office, gathering vital papers, making double use of his precious time while he spoke with Robert.

Robert, for the second time in his life, found himself in the presence of a man with a noble calling. "General, sir, Robert McCall reporting for duty."

"Robert McCall, you hail from Ireland, the letter from William McDonald tells me. He speaks highly of you. He tells me you will be a great asset to my ranks. A man of your standing is most welcome. War is brutal, and the sight of it is sometimes too much for the human soul to bear. The cost of freedom is high especially for a nation so young."

The general's time with Robert was brief and to the point; he planned on moving ten miles up the river "to be near the main body of my small army" were his words. General Washington stopped for a moment and stood with both hands on his hips as he carefully looked at Robert in search of Robert's character and physical stamina.

"I am going to assign you under the command of Gen. Daniel Morgan of the North Carolina Regiment. Your education and business experience will be of great benefit to General Morgan."

Robert was overwhelmed with the high rank given to him by General Washington. He immediately felt the responsibility placed upon him. Was he up to such a high calling?

"General Washington, I don't know what to say, sir. I will do my best to fulfill the trust you have placed in me, sir."

Robert stood erect as he saluted the great general good-bye.

Jonathan, in the meantime, had many concerns about the safety of the family. Word was out that Howe's army and the Hessians were raping, occupying, burning, and plundering everywhere they went. For this reason, he, Sarah, and Kate knew they must have some plan of escape for the family.

Kate knew if Robert, Liz, and she could be so creative as to hide Robert in a potato barrel to cross the Atlantic. Surely, she, Sarah, and Jonathan could devise an equal plan for the family. The three were trying to determine if remaining on or near the farm would be wise for they would definitely lose the horses and livestock and maybe their own lives. If they left in the covered wagon and went further west, they could carry some provisions and perhaps they would be able to save the horses and cows, but could they survive the brutal weather?

All of Philadelphia knew Howe's army was in Trenton and Bordentown. Bordentown was just four miles south of Trenton and twelve miles northwest of Philadelphia. The residents of Bordentown had evacuated their small town of one hundred houses and left it to the foraging parties of the Hessians, Jagers, or British dragoons. The rumors concerning the war's progression revealed that Philadelphia was to be the objective of the advancing British and Hessian forces. The armies seemed to be centered around Trenton and were not moving as fast into Philadelphia as once feared. Kate and the Thatchers decided to remain on the farm in a constant state of vigilance.

Chapter 19

CHRISTMAS WAS A FEW DAYS away, and the weather was bitter cold. Kate and the family had been invited to the boarding house to spend Christmas Eve with Mrs. Fargo and Lilly. Kate happily accepted the invitation. Celebrating her first Christmas in her new home without Robert saddened her.

Kate and Sarah packed provisions, along with a wild turkey that Jonathan had shot. The cooked turkey with dressing and gravy added a lot to the lavish fixings Lilly would no doubt prepare. Sarah made a shortcake, which would be topped with raspberry jam and fresh whipped cream. The children had packed a tin of fully shelled walnuts and tied it with a piece of twine and a sprig of holly berries as a gift for Mrs. Fargo.

The wagon crossed Broad Street on to Market Street with evidence that revealed it was Christmas Eve. Greenery and bright red bows adorned all the public buildings and street lamp posts. The clattering sound of horse's hooves as they met the lightly snow-covered brick pavement could be heard. People were visiting from one house to another. The city parks rang with soft brass band music and carolers. People dressed in heavy coats and scarves wrapped their faces as they gathered around the many musical groups that filled the walkways. Most all the popular street corners were dotted with hot chestnut and apple cider vendors with their warm fires, which made it more alluring to the passersby.

The boarding house looked the most festive with a single candle lighting each front window. Encasing the stained glass front door was a thick garland of cedar and holly with its generous spray of red berries. Neatly tied red bows hung in the corners of the door, along with a holly wreath that was decorated with pine cones and berries, finishing it off with a holiday charm. The fragrance of the freshly cut cedar as it waffled through the blowing snow lent itself to a definite feeling of Christmas.

"Merry Christmas" rang out as all the family took shelter on the long porch of the boarding house.

"Come in, come in out of that weather, and a Merry Christmas to all of you!" greeted Mrs. Fargo.

Lilly, with her joyous laugh, took their coats and wished all a Merry Christmas. "Missie Kate, it sure is good to seez you and that beautiful baby girl. Takes her into the parlor and makes yourselves warm. Ize's be back with some eggnog and cider to helps warm yunz up."

"No, children, you must not touch the tree." Sarah moved quickly to grab the hands of Liam and Levi.

"Jonathan, take the horses behind to the barn and get them out of the weather. This night is not fit for man or beast." Mrs. Fargo chuckled, happy to have the added warmth of the children.

"Nathaniel, go with your Pa. The two of you will make the unbridling go faster," directed Sarah as she helped the small children take off their coats.

The family, along with other invited guests, enjoyed an evening of food, storytelling, and caroling. Kate played the harpsichord. Everyone gathered at the front door as the carolers made their way down the street.

In a few short hours, the winter storm turned into a northeaster, hitting Philadelphia with a vengeance. It became evident that traveling the short journey back to the farm in the late evening was impossible for the family of eleven.

Mrs. Fargo insisted that they stay, saying, "You cannot take these children out in this torturous weather, I won't allow it."

Forced by the conditions, they agreed to stay at the boarding house until the weather ceased. Mrs. Fargo managed to collect six stockings for the children to hang over the fireplace in the parlor. A stocking for

Ashley could wait until the next Christmas. The children became excited to hang them with the prospect of having a late-night visitor.

Lisa-Jean asked Arianna, "Will Kris Kringle find us here?"

Arianna replied with excitement in her voice, "Oh, I am sure he will find us. Perhaps he will leave us some candy, Lisa-Jean."

Lilly later filled the long stretching stockings with cookies, nuts, apples, and a few pieces of hard candies.

The same northeaster hit Trenton on December 24. The howling winds, blowing rain, sleet, hail, and freezing snow covered the frozen ground. Trees were bending to the breaking point with the heavy ice. Icicles hung from the roofs as much as a foot long. Temperatures below freezing caused everything that wasn't sheltered with fire to freeze. Opening the doors on Christmas morning, one would resonate the world to be pure and sterling with the whiteness of the glistening ice and snow.

The Hessian garrisons were worn down due to three consecutive days and nights of relentless and sleepless marches up and down the New Jersey side of the Delaware River. For eight days, the garrisons had been on watch. A combination of weariness and below freezing weather brought to every man a cold damp chill that reached deep down into his bones and caused a darkening of spirit. Their commanders thought surely the Americans would not attack in such ruthless, vengeful weather.

Robert was in much better circumstances than most of the troops for he had moderately warm clothing. He was not yet exhausted from the long exposure to the harsh weather. His horse was old but fresh. Unlike Kate and the family, he awakened to the bitter cold with nothing warm to eat or drink as he chewed on frozen jerky. He stood by an open fire pit, warming first the front side and then the back side before the march began.

After a good breakfast on Christmas morning, Kate and the family decided they would attempt the short trip home. The weather was still impossible, but it was midmorning, making traveling easier than waiting until late in the evening.

Mrs. Fargo stopped Jonathan as he was going out to begin loading the wagon. "Here, take these blankets for the family. You can return them next time you are in town."

Jonathan prepared the wagon by lining the floor bed with the thick blankets. They left the boarding house, unaware of the battles taking place around Trenton, unaware that Robert was among the troops planning to cross the Delaware River in the bitter cold and seemingly defeating weather.

Robert was still greatly impressed with the meeting he had with General Washington much unlike the one he had, had with the king. He recognized that the general possessed a special greatness about him, to Robert, almost a countenance. He was sure that the general could humble a man if in his presence long enough. There was a story about camp that Washington, a man with a deep abiding faith, petitioned the Lord in humble prayer. It was said that the general spent three hours on his knees in the snow, seeking the Lord's blessing upon this young nation and upon those who were fighting for the God-given right of equality and freedom. Isaac Potts was a redcoat who followed and witnessed Washington on his knees as he was looking up to the heavens, asking his Lord for His hand in guidance. Potts went home and told his wife what he had witnessed. He then told her, "We are on the wrong side." This story impressed Robert, deepened his belief and trust in the general, adding to his personal cause and desire for the building of a new republic.

Washington believed the cause to be a righteous one and gave orders for his plan of attack to be carried out during one of the most bitter and cold of nights. Washington's plan for crossing the Delaware on Christmas night was hammered out in great detail. His regiments of about two thousand men were to cross at McConkey's and Johnson's ferries about ten miles upstream from Trenton, in order to attack the town from the north and west. James Ewing's brigade of eight hundred militia from Pennsylvania was to seize and hold the bridge across Aussunpink Creek to block the only exit from the town to the southeast.

A great diversion was to be conducted by one thousand two hundred Philadelphia Associators under John Cadwalader and 600 New England Continentals under Col. Daniel Hitchcock. The brigades were to embark near Bristol, Pennsylvania, and land at Burlington, New Jersey, twelve miles below Trenton.

The family was unaware of the battles that would take place so close to their own community. The ride home for the family was still torturous. The blowing snow and hard sleet made Jonathan's task of keeping the horses and wagon on the frozen dirt road difficult. The wagon would slide sideways on the ice, getting stuck in a number of previously worn ruts. This forced Kate, Sarah, Nathaniel, and Arianna to get out and walk, thus lightening the load for the horses. The four also helped push the wagon, trying to keep their balance while slipping and sliding all the way. In sheer misery, it took most of the day to travel the four miles from town.

When they arrived home, the house was cold for the fires had long died out. Jonathan built a fire in the cookstove as well as one in the fireplace. The children gathered around the welcoming heat to warm themselves. After building the fires, Jonathan led the horses to the barn to bed them for they truly had experienced a day of unbelievably hard work. He did not ask Nathaniel for his help because he knew the child was extremely cold and tired. This night, the children did not have to be coached to bed; they were worn to a frazzle. The exhausted family settled for a deserving night's rest.

Late in the night, Kate was awakened by Ashley. She had a raging fever, coughing, and gasping for air. Kate was frightened; she knocked on Sarah's door, waking her. "Sarah, its Ashley. She can't breathe, and I need your help. I don't know what to do."

Sarah accessed the situation and told Kate, "She has the croup. We need to make a tent with a pan of steaming water with peppermint and put her under the tent. You hold her, walk with her. Pound on her back to help loosen the mucus."

Kate was too gentle in fear of hurting Ashley. Sarah took the baby. "Here, let me show you. Like this, pound under the lungs. It will not hurt her, I promise, I will make the tent." Sarah could see how frightened Kate was. "Trust me, Kate, I have had six children and have been through this, I can't count the times. She will be all right. We have caught it in time, I am sure."

Sarah was moving fast around the room, gathering the necessary things to aid the child. "I am going to make an onion poultice to put on her chest. She will not like it, but we have to do it. I will get Jonathan up to carry in more wood so we can keep the fire going for hot water. When she seems to start choking and can't stop coughing, we will again do the steam tent. It probably will be all through the night. We will need to keep her cooled down with cold towels. We can always take her to Dr. Franklin tomorrow if need be."

Sarah was trying to reassure Kate they had it under control. Kate was filled with anxiety and sat up all through the night holding Ashley upright so she could breathe. She all too well remembered little Jacob and how he struggled to breathe. She quickly brushed these thoughts aside as they made her even more fearful. She was wishing Robert were here so she could draw upon his strength. She missed him so. Little did she know that Robert was equally as anxious with all that was facing him and the men under his command.

Washington's plan began to fall apart when all the brigades failed to start on time. The failure started when the northeaster pounded them with a barrage of rain, sleet, hail, snow, and fierce winds as strong as a tornado, making it impossible for an attack before dawn. Ewing's men were met with a massive ice jam on the river at the point of crossing. But some aspects were right about the meticulous plan. Twenty-five vessels of various descriptions waited at McConkey's Ferry. They began ferrying the men and equipment across the river. Most of the men crossed the river standing in the boats because the boat bottoms were filled with frozen water. The ferries proved to be the most useful for the heavy artillery, ammunition, wagons, and horses. It was a very dark night because a bright moon was hidden by a heavy black cloud cover. A thick fog suddenly appeared and lasted long enough for the crossing, which confused the enemy. "Victory to death" was General Washington's motto.

Washington took Trenton by surprise by braving one of the worst of winter storms.

This was Robert's first military encounter in what truly seemed to be an impossible task to all the brave souls who rode in those frozen boats on that most miserable of nights while crossing the then-vile Delaware River.

Kate and Sarah struggled through the night, trying to keep Ashley comfortable. Dawn came and the weather was still miserable on the morning of the twenty-sixth, but Ashley was now sleeping peacefully for her fever had broken just before dawn.

Sarah told Kate, "She is over the worst, and I think she will be all right. You must sleep while she is sleeping. I will take care of the family this morning. After all, they are mine to care for."

Jonathan battled the storm to get to the barn to attend the animals. This day, he did not allow the children to help him for fear they would be blown away by the fierceness of the wind. Coming through the door with the wind howling behind him, leaving him breathless, he admitted, "Mrs. Fargo is right. This weather is not fit for man or beast."

"Papa, what do you have under your coat?" was a squeal from Arianna. "I hear something."

"Nothing, I don't have anything. I don't hear anything. Do you hear anything, Mama? What do you think I have?" asked Jonathan as he playfully teased the children.

With curiosity and laughter, the children pounced on him with great force and brought him to the floor. Jonathan got to his knees and took off his wet snow-covered coat. Under the coat, he had a very young bird dog.

The excited children cried out with pure joy, "A puppy, we have a puppy."

"Not so fast children, we haven't asked Kate and Mama if we can keep him," Jonathan sided with the children in their plea.

Kate and Sarah looked at the little creature with great pity.

"What do you think, Kate?" asked Sarah.

"Well, he is cute. He looks so hungry. I can see his ribs. One more thing on this farm will not hurt. Every farm and family needs a dog. Don't you think?"

All the children jumped with delight.

Nathaniel asked, "What will we name him?"

Arianna, hopping with excitement, said, "I know, let's call him Rex."

"No! Puppy," shouted Lisa-Jean while jumping up and down.

After the children finished with their discussion as to a suitable name, Jonathan calmly spoke, "Let me tell you how I found him. I went into the barn, and I heard this faint little whimper. I looked over into the far corner of the barn, you know, where we keep all the canning jugs?" At this point, he had the children captivated. "There was this little guy just in the worst predicament."

"What was his trouble, Papa?" asked Nathaniel.

Jonathan continued with his story. "There he was, this cute little puppy, he had his head stuck in one of those canning jugs. What do you think about that?"

"What did you do, Papa?" asked Arianna.

"I am glad you asked that, Arianna. I found me a good rag and wrapped it around the jug and the puppy. Then I got a hammer and gently broke the jug."

"I know what we can call the puppy, let's call him Jug," excitedly, Arianna announced.

"Yeah!" yelled all the children. "Let's call him Jug."

Jonathan, still in a playful mood with the children, placed his hand on the dog's head. "I hereby do dub thee, Sir Jug."

Kate poured a good warm bowl of fresh cream for Sir Jug. The children busied themselves, making Jug a soft cozy bed next to the fireplace.

The weather was too tortuous for outdoor work and forced Jonathan to remain indoors. Later in the day, Jonathan was sitting by the fireplace, sharpening the farm tools; he was in deep thought. He expressed his thoughts to Sarah and Kate, "I am thinking this would be a good time for the three of us to make a survival plan should Philadelphia be threatened with an attack from the opposing forces. I have an idea. It will take a lot of work, but I think it can be done when the weather breaks." Sarah and Kate were interested in his idea. "Well, Kate, you and Robert tell the story of hiding Robert in a potato barrel for the crossing. That got me to thinking. Out in the north field, there are a lot of tree stumps. Suppose we dig a cellar room eight by eight and four foot deep with supporting scaffolding. We can pile the tree stumps that have already been dug up on top and make them look as though they have been piled to burn. The north field is far enough away from the house that I don't think it would be bothered by the enemy."

"I don't know, Jonathan," Sarah said with a frowned forehead. "It sounds terribly hard, and do you really think we can do it?"

"I do. We know we can't stay in the house, and if we try to leave, we won't know who on the road is friend or foe. We know we will lose our animals. That will be the drawback part of the plan." Jonathan left it to the ladies to decide if it was a feasible plan for them.

Sitting down at the table with a cup of coffee, Kate expressed her opinion, "Robert and I didn't have animals except for Old John when we moved here. I would hate to start over, but we will have to no matter what we choose."

Sarah, washing the dishes with the help of Arianna, added to the conversation, "Well, it sounds like a plan to me. You know the British and Hessians will look through the barn and root cellar so we can't hide there. I say let's do it. Do you really think there is time before Philadelphia is attacked?"

"So be it. The ground is frozen way too hard for digging right now. January is the coldest time of the winter, so the local folks tell me. To answer your question, Sarah, I think with the weather as harsh as it is, the troops are going to be moving very slowly. We will have to wait until we have better conditions, hoping the troops will move in another direction," added Jonathan while he cleaned the barrel of his musket.

Chapter 20

ECEMBER 27 WAS STILL A miserably cold day. The news of Washington's surprise attack on Trenton spread throughout all the colonies. Washington met with his war council at the Widow Harris's house near Newton late that night. The council, with much reluctance, decided to demonstrate that Trenton was not an accident. They would implement another surprise attack on New Jersey. Finally, the forces of Washington's army were coming together. The obstinate Pennsylvanians, quarrelsome Yankees, self-governing Jersey men, and the esteemed Virginians, along with the self-determined back country men, were now beginning to unite for a common cause. Word went out to all commanding officers to prepare for forage to cross the Delaware River on December 29.

Again, the horrendous weather slowed the movements of the forces. Food and provisions were scarce. The men longed for home. They were physically worn down, and many were threatening to depart for their time of service expired. Washington asked for volunteers, but not one man stepped forward. Washington turned his horse about and spoke to them, "My brave fellows, you have done all I have asked you to do, and more than could be reasonably expected, but your country is at stake, your wives, your houses, and all that you hold dear. You have worn yourselves out with fatigues and hardships, but we know not how to spare you. If you will consent to stay one month longer, you will render that service to the cause of liberty and to your country, which you probably can never do under any other circumstances."

General Washington offered every Continental soldier who volunteered to stay, a bounty of ten dollars in hard coin. Two hundred able-bodied men stepped forward from his battalion. Word went out to all generals to make the same offer. One half of Washington's army successfully crossed the Delaware, leaving the remainder on the Pennsylvania side. The shortage in the food supply made the division necessary.

In Robert's mind, he may as well have been as far away as Ireland, the place of his birth. Robert had found shelter from the blowing wind and sleet mixed with rain. Not as battle weary as his comrades, he led the fight on the first crossing. Eventually, he too succumbed to fatigue, cold, hunger, and longed for sleep. He wrapped himself in his blankets and rubbed his injured leg, trying to restore warmth to it for it was not as strong as it should be. Almost too tired to eat, he picked up a biscuit filled with salt pork, this being the day's rations. For a fleeting moment, his mind took him back to the dungeon and then to the bottom of the ship. Both times he had been fighting for his freedom. He remembered he had nothing, but his very soul, much less a biscuit filled with fatty salt meat. Once again, he had been called to fight for freedom, but this time on a larger stage. These scenes of battle were of a greater magnitude and demanded all that he had to give and more if it could be found. He hoped his posterity would benefit from his sacrifices. He thought of his lovely Kate and their baby. How he wished he could be with them in their warm little house. Should he not survive this next engagement, would Ashley understand his sacrifice for her and her mother? Deep in his own thoughts and almost on the threshold of falling into a wishful sleep, he was aroused by the abrupt appearance of a fellow soldier.

"May I join you under this wagon? You seem to have found a good place for the night. I am Cpl. Marvin Jones from Virginia."

Awakened, Robert extended the invitation for company and took his arms out from under the wrapped blankets. "Certainly, I am Col. Robert McCall. A corporal from Virginia, you say, make yourself as comfortable as you can. How long have you been with Washington's army?"

Corporal Jones, almost under the wagon, quickly backed up and came to attention, realizing he was now in the presence of a high ranking officer.

"At ease, son, at ease. Sit and tell me more of yourself. First, let me tell you of myself. I am from Philadelphia. I have only been a colonel for two days, so the formalities have not yet found a way into my introductions."

"Well, Colonel McCall, sir. To answer your question, I have been with General Washington since the battle of Long Island. Those British are superior in their fighting and discipline, and I was certainly fortunate to not have fallen into their hands."

"Yes, the British forces have great strength and are not easily defeated. We will succeed, son, of this I am most certain."

Robert once again pulled his covers tightly around his shoulders.

"Corporal, I see by the gold band on your hand that you are married. Do you have any children?"

"I was married. I lost my wife a short time back. She succumbed to the fever. We were married a little short of a year when she died. I carry her wedding band here close to my heart." He took out a little blue string bag he had tied to his undershirt and showed Robert the ring. "For this reason, I do not care to go home." Marvin choked back the tightness in his throat.

"I am sorry for your loss, son. Well, I have a wife and a baby girl in Philadelphia. I am so close, yet so far away from them." Robert, pulling his blankets still tighter, shifted his position, making himself more comfortable on the hard damp ground. "Corporal, you tell your sergeant to come see me. I would like to have you by my side as I learn the miseries of this war."

"Yes, sir, I will most assuredly do that tomorrow." The young corporal placed a log on the fire that he found close by before retiring. The rising red and yellow sparks from the stirred fire lifted high and lit the sky then fell back into the dark night. The two drifted off into a lumbering sleep.

On December 30, 1776, General Washington was making his headquarters at Queen Street in Trenton, New Jersey. He summoned his superior officers to a war council. There, it was determined they would be facing at least six thousand British and German troops with another four thousand on march for backup. It was decided by the council to stand ground in Trenton. It was a place of their choosing and not that of the enemy. The first scrimmage took place on January 1 and lasted most of the morning with the Americans defending themselves very well.

There was a warming in the weather that caused the ground to thaw. The Pennsylvania militia was summoned by Washington in the middle of the night. With much difficulty, they arrived on the New Jersey side just at daylight on January 2. The troops were in agony as they plowed through knee-high mud dragging heavy artillery. They arrived in Trenton about eleven o'clock. Collectively, Washington's forces were now seven thousand men. Their morale was rising regardless of their poor circumstances.

An informant had given word to the British forces that the American army numbered sixteen thousand men. This embellished information was of a great benefit for Washington's cause.

Cornwallis had so many troops that they could not all stay in Princeton. They were well supplied with firearms and food as well as brandy to warm their frozen insides, unlike the Americans led by Washington.

General Washington brilliantly managed a great victory with a series of defensive attacks. The Americans had heavy artillery and won the second battle at Trenton with as few as fifty casualties. The British casualties were estimated to be three hundred and fifty. British bodies were thickly piled atop one another as they fell on the bridge. The red of the British coats, mixed with the red blood flowed over the Assumpink Bridge and spilled into the icy waters below, staining the ice crimson and giving one the sense of being forever frozen in time.

Col. Robert McCall was humbled and amazed as he looked over the stone bridge and realized that was the end of the battle at Trenton. He had survived. Still, the sound of hand-to-hand combat rang in his ears, the clashing of metals, the screams of mutilation echoed as he looked at the dead and those still dying.

Night fell over Trenton, yet the firing of bombs continued until seven in the evening. At last, a silence settled over the night. Men on both sides dropped from sheer exhaustion and hunger. Most had not eaten for more than twenty-four hours.

The next two days were unseasonably warm, but then took a sudden change as the temperature dropped to twenty degrees in a few hours. Once again, the freezing weather added to the misery of the men.

General Washington refused to give up on his fight for independence. His call for another war council went out the night of January 2. The council decided that very night to march on Princeton and Brunswick.

The weather change with below freezing temperatures had turned the ground of furrowed mud into frozen uneven solid sheets of ice. The night sky turned black with the threat of more freezing rain, sleet, and snow. The general's plan was to look as though all troops were settling in. Positioned guards made noise and built campfires that could be seen by the enemy. All the while, other troops were preparing to march. With no shoes for some of the already frozen soldiers, they marched over the snow and ice, which shredded their feet and left behind blood with every step. Some men were making their second nights march in two days.

Chapter 21

KATE AND THE THATCHERS WELCOMED the two warmer days. They needed supplies, so Jonathan decided he and Nathaniel would go into town. Besides, Jonathan was getting cabin fever from being bound in the house with only the women and children.

Everyone in town spoke about the battles in Trenton and how the Americans, led by Gen. George Washington, had surprised the British and Hessians with their single concentrated rifle fire upon the solid British columns.

Jonathan could not help but wonder about Robert and his circumstances. He and Nathaniel visited the office of William McDonald. After cordial greetings, Jonathan asked, "I am in hopes you can give me some firsthand information about the war and if you have heard anything concerning Robert. I am hoping to carry home some encouraging news for Kate."

"Jonathan, I am sad to say I have no further information to add to what you have heard about town. If I should hear anything concerning Robert, I certainly will inform Kate immediately. Please give Kate my best."

William went about the business of running his office.

"Thank you for your time, Mr. McDonald. Say good-bye to Mr. McDonald, Nathaniel."

"Good day, sir."

"Good day, son," answered William.

Jonathan wanted to teach Nathaniel to watch the sky and feel the weather change. He pointed, "See, we should start for home. We are losing daylight with the dark storm clouds forming. The darker it gets, the colder it will become."

Kate and Sarah used the day for washing. This time they washed inside by heating the wash water on top of the cookstove while, in turn, it heated the house.

Kate remarked to Sarah, "It sure is good not having to go out in the bitter cold to carry water for the wash."

They strung lines behind the stove to aid in the drying. The clothes would surely freeze if hung on the outside line.

Kate was unaware of Robert's participation in the battle of Trenton or that he was again headed for another slaughtering battle to take Princeton on this the morning of January 3, 1777. The air was clear, the sky was blue. The battle commenced in an open snow-covered field and orchard. The blue of the clear sky turned gray, then yellow, from the rising smoke that followed the firing of musket rifles. Four-pound long-barreled cannons also left behind the lingering smell of sulfur. Men from both sides fell in battle. The blood flowed and merged, becoming one bloody red stream on a canvas of frozen ice, painting a gruesome paisley picture.

Robert charged with his bayonet fixed. He was trying to keep the men in his regiment centered in their thoughts. The British were charging with fixed bayonets. The brightness of their red uniforms with the shining of brass buttons and gold braids in the glimmer of sunlight blinded him to everything else before him. He dared not look the opposing soldiers in the face. He couldn't bear to remember their eyes as his bayonet pierced the very life from their bodies. He would never forget the feel of that fatal puncturing wound as he withdrew his weapon. A flashback in time made him remember Liz and wonder if this is how she had felt when she took the life of the palace guard. He better understood the driving factor for ending her life. He could feel the nausea rising within himself as he looked left and then right, taking in the repulsive sight of young and old men lying in their own blood. Some dead, others with such horrendous injuries, that it left them trashing about mindless of their own whereabouts.

The British fought with form, skill, and discipline. Their formal training as professional soldiers matched their elaborate uniforms. They had the mind-set that war was a nobleman's vocation and brought with it the pursuit of honor. The Americans were farmers, artisans, shop owners, and manufactures with no training, just the will to be free of oppression.

The battles of Trenton and Princeton baffled the British who had devised a strategy of carefully planned advances. They had manufactured an illusion of invincibility, which was spoiled by Washington.

Robert and many of his comrades saw Washington as fearless. As their commander, he rode out into the middle of the battle to instruct the advancement of his troops, shouting, "It is a fine fox chase, my boys!"

The general himself chased after the enemy.

On January 3, 1777, Washington's Continentals caught the British troops completely by surprise and forced a quick surrender on the outskirts of Princeton, New Jersey.

Chapter 22

THE HARSH WINTER OF 1777 faded. The early green grass gave notice that spring had arrived. The fruit trees in the small orchard had an abundance of full blossoms, hinting that it would yield a good harvest.

Kate had been over to the boarding house, gathering cuttings of plants to place around her new home. Lilly helped her cut a starting of azaleas. They dug iris and daffodil bulbs, along with roots of English ivy. Kate wished she could tell Lilly of the beauty and lushness of the castle gardens and how she especially missed her afternoon teas with the queen.

It was good once again to open the windows and doors, allowing the fresh crisp spring air to flow through the house.

This year they could plant a large and much valued garden. Sarah, Kate, and Nathaniel, along with Sir Jug, were out in the plowed garden planting with the hopes of a fruitful bounty.

"Stop that, Jug, stop it now" was Nathaniel's command. Jug was digging in the fresh dirt, uprooting what Nathaniel had planted. Arianna was in the house with the remainder of the children. Jonathan was working to clear more fields.

Kate stopped to wipe the dust from her eyes. She looked down the dirt road to see someone approaching on horseback. As the rider got closer, she couldn't believe what she thought she was seeing. It looked as though it might be Robert, but that was not Robert's horse. The rider was so haggard-looking, had long stringy hair, and a most unmanaged beard. It is Robert.

He hollered, "Kate, Kate, it's me!"

Dropping the hoe, she ran, tears streaming down her cheeks; her eyes so full she could barely see to reach him. Robert jumped from the horse with his arms wide open, waiting for her leap. They embraced with much joy in their reunion, neither uttering a word, just that long-awaited familiar embrace, one that conquers all emotion. Both with dusty, dirty faces gave each other a heavenly kiss.

Sarah yelled out to Nathaniel, "Go fetch your Pa, Nathaniel, tell him Robert is home!"

Kate was still holding on to Robert. "Let's go inside. You must see Ashley. You won't recognize her, Robert, she has grown so and is standing, holding on to things. Soon, she should be walking. She tries to keep up with the other children. They carry her too much, so she doesn't try to walk."

Jonathan and Nathaniel bound in with big wide grins of welcome on their faces, taking off their hats and wiping the dust from their brows. Sir Jug brushed by them anxious for attention from the newcomer. "It's good to have you home, Robert." Jonathan gave him the usual slap on his back. "You are very tired, I am sure, by the looks of it. These last few months have been hard on you." Jonathan pulled a chair out from under the table for Robert. "You just rest this evening, Nathaniel and I will water and feed your horse. I am sure he is tired as well."

"It is really good to see you and Nathaniel too." Robert sat down.

"Who might this critter be?" asked Robert as he tried to control Sir Jug who was all over him, smelling him up one side, then down the other.

"Oh, this is Sir Jug, we found him at Christmas." Nathaniel, rescuing Robert, called, "Come on, Jug, let's go feed."

Kate quickly got Robert a cool glass of water.

Robert asked, "Why the name, Sir Jug? That's an odd name for a dog."

Kate told Robert how the puppy came by his name.

"It looks as though you have done well with keeping things up here on the farm," he said while taking in all that was around him and holding Ashley.

Ashley reached out and called, "Mama."

She struggled, trying to free herself. Her expression revealed she was not sure who he might be.

Robert handed Ashley over to Arianna. "I must look very scary to her. All I want now is a good hot bath and fresh clothes. Perhaps when I am cleaned up, she will like me better."

Kate and Sarah busied themselves in the kitchen and prepared a homecoming supper of Robert's favorite food: fried chicken with gravy and biscuits.

Robert bit into his chicken, "This is so good. It has been some time since I have had a meal such as this. We were lucky to get a cold biscuit and a slice of salt meat."

"Are you home for good? Please say yes," pleaded Kate while piling his plate with more mashed potatoes.

"I am afraid not." He shook his head. "General Morgan has given me a month's leave. Then I am to report back to my post. General Washington has appointed me to the office of colonel on the recommendation of William. I requested the furlough time to help here on the farm and to see if things were going well for all of you. Besides, I needed to see my girls." Robert leaned in to give Kate a tender kiss while reaching for her hand.

"What happened to Old John?" asked Nathaniel with a mouth full of potatoes and gravy.

Sarah quickly corrected him, "Nathaniel, not with your mouth full."

Robert looked down in search of just the right words. "Well, he was old to begin with and just could not keep up with the pace. It was too much for him. I woke up one morning and Old John was dead. He died in the night. War is a horrible, miserable thing. Dying is all around, engulfing both man and beast." Robert stopped in thought. Dare he tell them the horrors he had witnessed? "Kate, I hesitate to tell you of the terrible things that one man can inflict upon another."

"Robert, I want to know. I am already full of fear, knowing will not make it any worse."

Robert, still reluctant to share, caught his lower lip between his teeth. "This is hard. I fought in three battles and am lucky to be alive. I don't know what saved me except it be by the grace of God. Men left the battlefield without legs or arms. Some blinded and those are the fortunate ones. Most days, we had very little rations. The weather was so miserable, we could barely stay warm let alone stay dry. It was equally hard to keep our rifles and ammunition dry enough to fire. Marching in the snow and ice was the most arduous. I saw men with their feet turned black, they were so frozen. Some men's feet were sliced to the bone and left bloody footprints on the ice because they had no shoes. Moving the heavy artillery over the rough terrain through the deep snow and ice left our bodies so tired we could fall asleep anywhere under any condition. A lot of men froze to death from giving into sleep." Robert stopped and drew in a deep breath, releasing a sigh and exhaling very slowly. Should he raise their hopes, dare he tell them his thoughts of the war ending soon? He continued, "The high-ranking British officers who are long-serving and have been trained in modern methods of warfare have concluded that the Americans can win this perilous war. Washington himself is confident we will not be defeated. General Washington is superior to any British general in my mind by the way he conducts his strategies. He keeps the British generals off balance." Stopping suddenly and shaking his head, his face relaxed. "That's enough, I don't want to talk about it anymore. I am at home and that is what is important now."

Everyone sat in stunned silence by what they had just heard.

Kate abruptly jumped up and asked, "Does anyone care for more coffee?"

Sarah quickly began removing dishes from the table and was overtaken by a shiver. "This war makes my blood run cold," she attested. Stacking dishes, she realized how grateful she was that Jonathan was in a safer situation, that she did not have to raise their family alone.

Kate tried to bury deep in her mind the horrors she had just heard from her very tired and war-worn husband. She held a silent prayer of gratitude in her heart that Robert had been spared.

After good baths for everyone, they settled for the night. When in bed, Robert held Kate, stroking her soft red hair, and told her, "It is so good to be home with you and Ashley. It is so good to be in a real bed again."

His heart saddened as he felt the hard calluses and new blisters on her once soft hands. Hands as small and delicate as hers should not be subjected to such harshness. He knew the work she had done was for sheer survival. Kissing the back of her hand, he placed it on his chest as he drifted off to sleep.

It was a beautiful spring day. Even the birds were rightfully happy as they fluttered about from tree top to tree top singing their happy song. The weather was warming and inviting. Everyone wanted to spend more time outside after being confined to the indoors throughout a brutal winter.

At the breakfast table, Robert told everyone that the word around the camps warned that the British were planning to overtake Philadelphia. "I don't know when or how, but we must be prepared for it. That is the real reason I came home."

The thought of everyone's safety was greatly bearing down on him.

Jonathan told Robert, "We have a rough plan, but we are not certain it will work. You tell us what you think of it." He described their thoughts.

"Jonathan, I think the plan is as good as any I myself could devise. I say we get started today. It will take some time to dig out that much space and to haul all the tree stumps needed, but we can do it before I leave again."

For days, the two couples dug and carried away the dirt, spreading it over the already cleared field. Robert and Jonathan built the supporting scaffolding for the tree stumps. A tripod and pulley was necessary to hoist the stumps to the top of the scaffolding. These were things they already had from the building of the added room. Between the scaffolding and the stumps, they spread a layer of oil-soaked canvas to shed the rain. They also dug a two-foot trench around the room to catch the rain runoff should it come. The two men built rough benches to place around the dirt walls as well as a ladder to raise and lower. The overall plan was to make the heaped stumps appear as natural as possible and ready for burning.

Sarah had an idea. "Robert, the root cellar under the smokehouse. I am sure the British will search it for food."

"Yes! You are right, Sarah. They leave no building unturned. Do you have something in mind?"

"Well, shouldn't we build a similar cellar in the woods? If it is hidden well, we could stash our food there, safe from the redcoats."

"Yes, I think you are right. We should do that. It is a grand idea, Sarah."

Robert turned to Jonathan. "I am worried about this being a plowed field. I am afraid when you come to take shelter, your footprints might be detected. I am thinking we should plant a corn field. That way you could walk through the field and your trail would not be as noticed."

"Yes, I think you are right, Robert. It will take us a week to plow the field fresh and plant."

When the two were away from the ladies, Jonathan had another question, "What should we do about the animals?"

"Turn the horses out, and tie Sophie the cow deep in the woods. Chances are, they will not find them. I think we should dismantle the wagon and store it in a couple of places, a wheel here, an axle, there and so forth. Your wagon is the better one, let's save it. You can use my old wagon for chores. Let's pray Washington can stand his ground and save Philadelphia from the British. If not, God help us all." He took a deep breath and then sighed. "The aftermath that Cornwallis's brigades leave in the wake of their raids is terrible. They plunder, ravage, and rape all of young women everywhere they go. It is important that we protect our wives, children, and Arianna at all costs. I do not want to speak of this in front of the women."

Kate and Sarah prepared a canvas sack with provisions along with gunpowder and flint for the musket. It was placed by the door ready to go at a moment's notice. Kate took the silver goblet from the fireplace and wrapped it in a cloth. She stood in deep thought as she rubbed the goblet. "I need to find a good burying place for this."

The family was blessed with plenty of good working days, which made it possible for them to accomplish their goals. Time shortened for Robert.

At supper one evening, as the adults were again going over their plans for the escape to the hideaway, Kate had deep concerns. "I truly worry about Mrs. Fargo and Lilly being alone. They are up in age. What will they do should Philadelphia be overrun by the enemy? We could make room for two more in the hideaway, couldn't we? They could help with the children."

Robert sopped up the last bite on his plate then turned to Kate, "Kate, I think there is something in what you are saying. You are going to need to know when the British troops are in the city. Mrs. Fargo and Lilly could ride out and tell you. They could stay here on the farm until it becomes safe again."

Kate poured Robert a full glass of cool milk. "Yes, I think we should ask them if it is something they would do."

"Tomorrow, you and I will ride into town to discuss the idea with the ladies. I also would like to see William one more time before I leave for my post."

Robert leaned back in his straight chair and rubbed his full stomach.

Midmorning the next day, Robert and Kate drove to the boarding house to visit with Mrs. Fargo and Lilly. The house remained just as it was the first time Kate and Robert saw it, with all its blooming plants, the welcoming rocking chairs with soft cushions, and the swings on either end of the porch. Baskets full of lush green Boston ferns with long leafy vines flowing in the breeze, hung between the porch columns. The front door stayed open, allowing the seasonal breeze to flow uninterrupted down through the long hallway and out the open back door, creating a cooling draft.

The ladies were sitting on the porch, cleaning young spring lettuce. "Well, look who is here."

Mrs. Fargo got up and stood on the edge of the front steps to welcome them. "Robert, it is so good to see you. You look well, son. How are you doing?" The words ran together without giving Robert any response time. "Come in, come in. Lilly, get us something cool to drink."

Robert got down from the wagon and tied the horse to the front post beyond the gate. Kate handed Ashley to Robert. Robert extended his hand and allowed her to steady herself as she stepped on the hub of the front wheel, lowering herself, then straightening her petticoats and dress. She moved her wind-blown hair up under her bonnet and brushed the dust from her face.

"Mrs. Fargo, Lilly," greeted Robert, gently bowing, taking Mrs. Fargo's hand. "It is good to see you both. I am doing well thank you. It is good to be home with Kate and Ashley. Both of you ladies look wonderful."

Lilly returned with the tea tray and placed it on the small table in front of a group of chairs. Mrs. Fargo, Robert, and Kate sat on the porch. Kate and Mrs. Fargo were fanning as afternoon temperatures rose. Lilly cared for Ashley by walking her around and showing her the flowers.

Robert began, "Mrs. Fargo, as you know, I am in Washington's army. The word throughout the army is that the British forces are gearing to take over the city of Philadelphia. I don't know when this might take place, but I am assuming it to be soon. I am most concerned for the safety of Kate and the family on the farm. We are mindful of you and Lilly as well. The British and Hessians can be very brutal with the citizens. I am sure you have heard of their unbridled behavior. They plunder and destroy what they don't take. For this reason, I would advise you to bury or hide your valuables."

Kate interrupted, "Mrs. Fargo, we have a plan. On the farm, we have dug a shelter away from the house for all the family. We thought perhaps you and Lilly could join us, if we are invaded by the enemy. They surely will come into town first. The two of you could drive out to the farm as quickly as you can get away. Do you think you can manage to do this?"

Mrs. Fargo poured a second glass of tea for Robert. "I am so grateful that you would think of us. Of course, we will do as you say. Do you really think that the British will attempt to take over our city, Robert?"

With an emphatic reply, he said, "Oh, yes, ma'am I do. Philadelphia is a major city for the British because it is the capitol of the new government. Cornwallis is ruthless. His forces are equally as cruel. He is determined to have this advancement to his credit."

Robert got up to leave, reminding Kate their time was short and that they had planned to see William before leaving town.

"You and Lilly come to the farm day or night. It doesn't matter as long as you can be safe," encouraged Kate as she gave Mrs. Fargo and Lilly a hug.

Robert again gave them a slight bow. "I bid you ladies a most pleasant afternoon."

Robert and Kate dropped by the office of William. William greeted them with much enthusiasm and bid them to sit down. "Well, Robert, tell me all about the war and how things are progressing for General Washington."

Sitting in front of William's desk, Robert was very forthright with William. "Sir, I again want to thank you for your letter to General Washington in my behalf. He immediately made me a colonel under the command of Gen. Daniel Morgan. You of course know General Washington is a fine officer. He aches for the forces and the conditions they have to endure. Also, I would like to say, I am humbled and grateful for the care you have given to the farm."

"Robert, it is the least I can do as a needed service to our young nation. My thanks to you and Kate for your sacrifices." William tickled Ashley under the chin. He reached into his pocket and brought out two hard coins and gave them to Robert. "Go by the emporium and buy yourself some new shoes and a heavy coat for this winter."

"Thank you, sir, this is greatly appreciated. William, I just want to make sure that you are aware of the campaign Cornwallis and Howe want to launch on Philadelphia. I don't know when or how, but I wanted you to know so that you might make some preparations and not be caught off guard."

"Robert, I assure you that I am well aware of Cornwallis's threats against our fair city. I will tell you this much, I have informants. General Washington himself has created a system of secret intelligence with a high degree of autonomy. That is all I will say."

"Yes, sir, I am aware intelligence is extremely vital to Washington's strategies. I am glad you are informed of this important aspect of the war."

"Robert, this is another reason I stay close in the city and keep my office open." He walked the couple to the door.

"I must tell you, William, I am certainly learning war is a frightening and inhumane thing. If we succeed in becoming a self-governing nation, it will be very interesting looking forward how well history will protect and record our efforts."

Robert put his hand around Kate's back to guide her to the door.

"Good day, sir, and thank you."

"I pray that God will go with you, Robert."

Kate and Robert left William's office, grateful for such a friend.

On the ride home, Robert told Kate, "Tomorrow, I must leave. Of course, you know this. The time has come and gone so fast. I do feel better knowing we have made some preparations for your safety. Leaving you and Ashley again is so difficult. Maybe I can come home between assignments."

"I suppose, I can be an officer's wife. It is not easy. I miss you so desperately I can hardly bear it most days. If it were not for Ashley, I could easily die from being without you."

"Kate, I know this is not what we had hoped our lives would be. You have endured so much and never seem to complain, and for this, I am truly grateful. I thank God every day you are my chosen love. I have promised Him that I will always do my very best to care for you and Ashley. My dearest, I am assured He will care for all of us if we are but faithful and rely on His help." Robert put his arm around Kate and drew her closer to him on the wagon seat.

Robert's time was up, and he left to join his regiment. Kate, once again, was left to adjust to life without him.

Chapter 23

IN THE SUMMER OF 1777, the British general Howe had hoped to seize a seaport and the surrounding countryside. But instead of the seaport, he centered his thoughts on Philadelphia.

In August, he approached the capital city by sea, disembarked on the Maryland shore, and headed for Philadelphia fifty miles away.

Washington knew he must defend the city of the newly formed republic.

The battle of Brandywine Creek, Pennsylvania, began on another hot humid day; it was September 11, 1777.

"Run, run with all your might!" shouted Robert, turning his horse around as he tried to bring up the rear of his lagging brigade. "This way, pull that gun, push up this hill." He pointed with his saber in a commanding voice.

The lush tall green grass was equally as slick as the ice they had previously battled on and made it almost impossible to climb the fifty-degree incline. Robert was in the middle of a raging battle, his own home perhaps four miles away. Once again, all around him, men and their horses were falling under enemy fire. Suddenly, Robert's horse was spooked by the firing of cannons and rifles; it reared and became hard to control. Robert tried to stay mounted. He pulled back on the reins but to no avail. He was thrown. To his good fortune, he landed in a clump of trees and bushes, which gave him some safe ground cover.

While assessing his fall, he heard a mournful sound coming from under the bushes. Looking to his right, he saw a very young soldier who was mortally wounded, delirious, and begging for help. Forever engraved in Robert's memory would be the vivid image of a massive wound that exposed the insides of this young soldier covered in blood as he lay dying. He tried to give him aid, lifting his head to give him a drink of water to moisten his drying mouth. He dared not to move the soldier because of the extent of his injuries. Robert was trying to keep the soldier conscious by talking to him. "Young fellow, what is your name?"

The boy tried desperately to answer and reached to pull Robert closer. His voice was so weakened Robert could not understand his words. His wounds were so severe that there was nothing Robert could do. He died a few minutes later in Robert's arms. The only comfort Robert had was to know that he had not died alone nor was his death in vain.

Some of the American forces who were lacking in disciplined training broke line and ran. Only those forces under Gen. George Washington and Gen. Nathaniel Green remained and fought until darkness fell.

Washington's forces, with great resolve, were determined to defeat the British and Hessian troops. The British troops were directed by General Cornwallis and led into battle by Sir William Howe at Brandywine Creek. Disaster fell upon the American troops, and they were beaten by Howe's army. Washington failed to defend Philadelphia and retreated for Valley Forge, twenty miles northwest of Philadelphia, to settle and regroup his army for a long hard winter. The battle at Brandywine had delayed Howe's army. The delay prevented Howe from merging with Bourgogne en route south from Canada.

Robert knew the importance of remaining with his troops. He followed the example of Washington who went into battle with his forces and lived among them, eating the same food when available and feeling the same suffering. But Robert also knew all too well the dangers facing his family because of losing the battle to defend Philadelphia.

Kate and the family were unaware that Robert fought in the battle at Brandywine and that he was so close to home. She did not know of the sick feeling that lay in the pit of his stomach because of the defeat.

There was plenty to do. In fact, more than enough with preserving the abundance of garden vegetables, especially countless stalks of corn, from the large field along with the summer fruit crops. Sarah and Kate started very early in the mornings, gathering the ripened vegetables and fruit. They spent the remainder of the day preserving and storing the bounty. They filled the hideaway cellar with the bulk of dried food. They sparingly placed food in the house cellar.

It was an unusually hot day on September 27, 1777. The sun shone brightly and the air was humid. Not a hint of a breeze could be felt or seen through the tree tops. Mrs. Fargo and Lilly were sitting on the front porch resting and watching passersby. They were enjoying a refreshing glass of tea after finishing the inside work.

"Look, Lilly, do you see all that commotion on the street in front of the bakery? I wonder what is taking place!" asked Mrs. Fargo.

"Yes'um, Isabelle, Ize's surely do," said Lilly standing up stretching, looking over the white porch banisters to get a better view down the street.

"Why looks, Isabelle, here comes Mr. William he sure is in a mighty big hurry and itz too early ferz him to bez coming home this times of the day. I wonders whats is wrongs with him?"

William greeted the two ladies as he leaped and skipped the steps landing on the porch. With a great urgency in his voice, gasping for breath and clutching his chest, he blasted, "The Redcoats have entered the city, ladies." He stopped to draw in another breath. "I suggest you go inside and lock your doors."

Lilly and Mrs. Fargo went to the kitchen and started gathering their already packed escape bags. Suddenly, there was a crash. It was obvious from the sound that the front door glass had been shattered, and instantly, a second sound as the door was being slammed violently against the wall. The two women dropped what they had in their hands at the sudden frightening sounds. Two British soldiers forced their way into the house with fixed bayonets. William came down the stairs from his room to address the commotion. Just as he stepped off of the last step onto the polished wooden floor, one of the soldiers thrust the butt of his rifle into William's stomach, bringing him to his knees.

Mrs. Fargo rushed to his aid, "Oh, Willi—" she was not able to ask the question before the forceful young man grabbed her by the shoulders and pushed her backward.

"Old lady, leave him be. This house and its contents now belong to the army of His Majesty, King George III. How many people are here in the house? Answer my question and be quick with yah."

With a very weak and frightened voice, Mrs. Fargo answered, "Three, there are three of us at present."

"Who might she be?" he stood in an attacking stance and pointed his musket at Lilly as though she were less than human.

"She is my housekeeper and cook," Mrs. Fargo answered as she gathered strength in her voice.

"Very well, we are in need of food. Lots of food," commanded the redcoat. He was a young fellow, just following orders. He must have seen his share of battles for he had a very prominent scar from the corner of his right eye, etching across his face and down under his chin. Along with his disfigurement came a cocky attitude. Mrs. Fargo perceived him to be a very bitter young man driven into a war not of his choosing in a foreign land, for a no good apparent reason, except that of being a conqueror for the king.

At that moment, the room suddenly became full of loud redcoat soldiers roughly moving about, rummaging and throwing things as they wildly scavenged through the household furnishings. The crushing of very old family glassware could be heard as it hit the floor before flying in all directions. In the corner stood a family secretary made by Mrs. Fargo's father. The drawers from the century-old desk were thrown to the floor with papers scattering. One redcoat saw the family Bible on a side table, and with malice, he ripped its cover, tearing out a good number of pages. Window dressings were yanked from the rods and thrown to the floor. The butt of one soldier's rifle was used to drag across the fire mantel, forcing the brass candlesticks to the floor. The commanding officer ordered his troops, "I will take this place for my command post. See to it."

In a very ill-bred tone to a lady, one of the soldiers asked, "Do you have any weapons, gunpowder?"

Once again, Mrs. Fargo was shoved backward into the staircase as he passed her on his way to the second floor.

"Sir, I do not have anything of the kind," answered Mrs. Fargo, and with a condescending voice, she added, "If you want food, we must go to the kitchen behind the house. Come, Lilly, let's fix these polite gentlemen some food."

She pushing Lilly in front of her through the back door of the main house and slamming the screen door as they went out to the kitchen. Speaking very softly under her breath, she whispered, "We must hurry, Lilly, we have to go to the farm and warn Kate and the Thatchers." She handed Lilly the emergency bags. "Go out to the barn and hitch the buggy, I will follow after you have had time. I will make noise here in the kitchen to distract them. We must get to the barn before they do. We will just leave the house, and they can have it. We are not going to cook for those rascals."

"Yes, ma'am, Dear Lord Jesus be with us." Praying, crying, and running at the same time, she fled the main house.

The redcoats, zealous in turning the house upside down, confiscated anything to their liking. Mrs. Fargo drew her body tight as she heard the continuing sound of breaking glass and the overturning of furniture. Much of the furniture pieces were from her parents and held special memories of days gone by. She and Lilly slipped out to the barn unnoticed and drove away in the buggy. Driving down Chestnut and turning on to Broad Street and then Market Street, the two could see mayhem everywhere. The city was overrun by the redcoats, carrying fixed bayonets with the metal gleaming in the sunlight. The invaders shouted as they ran in and out of stores and shops. Some were so hungry, they were eating loaves of bread and cheese as they ravaged the city. People fled from the streets as British soldiers shouted orders, "Off the streets, go back to your homes, you barbarians! This city belongs to His Majesty, King George III."

Lilly and Mrs. Fargo arrived at the farm in a very emotional state. Kate, carrying Ashley, met them as they drove into the yard. She knew what their abrupt appearance must mean and shouted, "Jonathan, it's the ladies!"

Out of breath and flustered, Mrs. Fargo dropped the horse reins and clutched her chest; she managed to say, "They are here, they are here. Hundreds of them! Quick, get the children."

"The town is just swarming with those jackals. The redcoats they's in all the stores takin everything and anything they's wants. We could hears em ordering everyone back to they's homes, get off the streets. Oh, what in the world isz we gonna do, Miss Kate?" shrieked Lilly, climbing down from the buggy.

Philadelphia was under siege. The family hurriedly prepared their escape to the hideout.

"We are a little ways from town. Perhaps we have a bit of time. They obviously approached from the northeast of the city," calculated Jonathan as he dropped an armful of wood in the woodbox. "I think it best if we go to the hideout while it is still light. Gather the children. We will take our supper with us. Don't forget the emergency packs, the rifle, and water. I am sure we will have to stay the night, perhaps tomorrow as well."

"I will gather the blankets!" yelled Sarah while dragging Liam with one hand and balancing Levi on her hip. "Nathaniel, you help Mama carry the blankets." Sarah began to pull them from the beds.

Arianna took charge of Lisa-Jean and Penelope.

Now, late in the afternoon, the sun was going down behind the rolling hills, projecting metallic rays of red and gold through the thick tree tops.

Sophie's heavy udder sagged as she waited to be milked. The chickens scattered off their nests clucking as they paraded around the coup. They stretched their necks and shook their feathers front to back, communicating in their clucking musical fashion their day's work well done. The horses had been stalled in the barn for the night. Supper awaited its trip to the table. Would their lives ever be the same after this night?

Chapter 24

"SARAH, YOU AND KATE TAKE the children and the ladies to the hideaway. I am going to the barn to get the horses and tie them out in the woods past the cellar with Sophie. I will quickly milk Sophie so the children can drink the milk tonight. Don't worry, horses are creatures of habit. If they break loose and are not caught, they will return to the barn in due time," ordered Jonathan while gathering his ax, small tools, a bucket, and the stool.

The family and the ladies headed for the hideaway.

Sarah hollered back to Jonathan as he hastened toward the barn, "Don't forget to remove the cow bell, Jonathan! Do you hear me?"

"All right, Sarah, I hear you!" shouted Jonathan.

Sir Jug followed Jonathan as though he looked forward to an evening of entertainment. Returning from the woods, Jonathan went down the ladder into the semi-dark hole in the ground so he could help the others. Kate and Sarah dropped the provisions. Sarah carefully handed Jonathan his fiddle. The ladies, along with the children, lowered themselves into the darkening hole.

Jonathan was still giving orders. "We must be quick arranging our things because the daylight hours are quickly passing. It would not be wise for us to have a light, it might be seen from the house."

Everyone gathered in the hideaway and found a place to settle. Sarah and Kate knew they had to keep the children comfortable and, most of all, quiet. Sarah softly whispered to the children, "It is important for you children to stay quiet. Remember how we play hide-and-seek? Well, we are playing a big game of hide-and-seek with Papa, Mama, Kate, and our grandmas. We must be very quiet so the men in the red coats can't find us."

"Well, at least we have a warm supper tonight," murmured Kate.

Everyone took some bread and dipped into the cast-iron vessel to eat. Each of the five adults took a child closely, reassuring them that all would be well if they remained quiet. They waited for the enemy who would invade their comfortable world, wondering what new challenges would be in their future.

After an hour of being very bored and uncomfortable, Arianna, folding her arms, muttered, "Will this night ever end?"

The other children chimed in, "Yeah, we are tired. This is no fun."

Sarah, trying to console the children, tenderly whispered, "We will be safer here tonight, children. I feel sure we can go back to our house tomorrow."

The night was very long. The rough dwelling, with no windows or doors, resulted in humid stale air. Jonathan folded back the canvas for a fresh breeze. There had been no signs of movement around the house or outbuildings throughout the night. Daylight came with the sun breaking through the gray clouds. After a very difficult night with very little sleep, Jonathan told Sarah, "I am going to have to milk Sophie again. The children can use the milk today. There hasn't been anyone about the house. I feel it would be safe enough to return after the milking."

"Do be careful, Jonathan," cautioned Sarah, knowing he was risking all, leaving them to milk Sophie.

About midday, there was the thundering sound of many horses coming down the dirt road kicking up a cloud of dust. Then suddenly, from around the bend emerged a perfect formation of disciplined scarlet redcoats. Their brass buttons and metal bayonets reflected the high noon sun, signaling their unwelcomed approach to the house.

The guineas were loud and beside themselves with the invasion of redcoats as they came up to the front of the house.

"Dismount!" the lieutenant hollered in a distinct and commanding order. The soldiers quickly followed orders by dismounting, with their bayonets fixed, and scattering in twos. A pair broke the door open and entered the house. Others scouted around the outside buildings, turning over and kicking anything in their path.

The family could hear them shouting, "No one here!"

"This place has nothing, but a little food," remarked one rather disappointedly.

Another shouted, "They have been gone for a while, the fire embers are cold!"

"Jug, be quiet. Be quiet," pleaded Nathaniel while trying to hold him.

"Let him go, son," cautioned his father. "We can't let him give our hiding place away."

The dog broke free from the family and raced back to the house, barking all the way at the invaders. He grabbed one of the soldiers by the pant leg. Just at that moment, another soldier hit him in the head with the butt of his rifle, rendering him unconscious. Satisfied that the house was vacant, they took the preserved food from the smokehouse and cellar. They loaded Robert and Kate's old wagon with the already cut firewood from the outside lean-to. The ruthless soldiers were able to catch a few chickens, tying their legs together and hanging them across the backs of the horses. The intruders left, shouting, "Long live the king!"

Immediately, there was a sigh of great relief by the adults from the safe place. Arianna and Nathaniel's intense fear revealed their grasp of what could have been.

Jonathan was now a bit more at ease. "I think it is safe enough to go back to the house tonight. They got what they came for. We should wait for a time to be sure they are gone."

It was around sunset when they gathered their necessary things, but left some in the event they would have to return. They climbed out of the hideaway and walked back to the house. Everyone was tired, hot, and thirsty. The past twenty-four hours had been very uncomfortable.

The children called and called for Sir Jug. Finally, they heard his soft cries from under the front porch. Nathaniel picked him up and carried him inside. He laid him down near the hearth. The children gathered around.

"Poor Jug. Mama, will he be all right?" they asked.

"We will see, children. He is hurt pretty bad. We will have to take good care of him. Let him rest now. We will clean his wounds after things get orderly."

Sarah was frazzled as she picked up the overturned chairs. Jonathan unloaded his arms, not wanting to seem too alarmed. "I think it would be wise for us to stand guard through the night. Perhaps we should take two-hour shifts. I am going to the woods to get Sophie and the horses. I will leave the gun with you. Sarah, it's loaded, so be very careful."

Kate, Sarah, and the two older ladies set to work putting the house back in order. The kitchen furnishings had been turned over and the cutlery thrown about. The beds were torn apart, the feathers and straw strewn throughout the rooms.

Jonathan found his horses loyally standing by Sophie. He led them all to the barn. After returning to the house, he told Mrs. Fargo, "Your horse was not with my horses. I think it broke loose and went back to the boarding house."

"Well, Jonathan, the horse is important, but what is more important is we have survived this time." Mrs. Fargo had an idea that she suggested to Sarah and Kate. "You do know that smallpox is everywhere among the British and American soldiers? There is a sign we can place at the road leading into the house. A red flag warns of smallpox. What do you think?"

"We'll do anything that will help to discourage the British. I think it is a good idea, Mrs. Fargo," said Sarah. I don't know how long it will work, but it is worth a try."

Several days went by without an incident. The red flag seemed to be working. The family cautiously continued with their regular daily chores. Sir Jug was recovering from his trauma with the tender nursing care of the children.

Jonathan carried the smallpox plan a bit further by digging and mounding two shallow graves under the big oak tree and tying red ribbons on the two wooden crosses.

Chapter 25

CTOBER 4: WASHINGTON'S SECOND ATTEMPT to recover Germantown by defeating the British and regaining Philadelphia failed. This defeat forced him back to Valley Forge.

The hot muggy days had suddenly turned cooler, and a cold front had moved in behind it. Soon, it would be winter.

Robert's troops had been severely hit by the enemy. Among them was a very young soldier, not much older than sixteen, Robert guessed. His leg had been shattered by gunfire and had become infected with gangrene. His agony was almost more than those around could bear. Robert was especially drawn to this young soldier because of his age and because he knew the threat of the infected leg. Robert knew Dr. Franklin could be found somewhere among the army troops. He went in search of the doctor's whereabouts. Dr. Franklin came at Robert's request to attend to the wounded soldier.

"Doctor, is it possible to save this young man's leg?"

"Colonel McCall, if we can save his life at this point, it will be a miracle. I am afraid the gangrene has advanced to such a stage that we must amputate above the infection, and that will be well above the knee. I will need plenty of hot boiling water and as many white cloths as you can find. Also, if you can, muster up some liquor. We must give him as much as he can stand, and we need some to pour on the wound. Strap him down. Get a few men who will be willing to help restrain him and keep a stick in his mouth. How old is this boy?"

"Sixteen is my guess," replied the colonel.

"Well, that's a shame. May the Almighty attend to him."

Dr. Franklin searched through his tools and laid them out in order on a cloth, placed on a makeshift table. The doctor handed some of them to a soldier who was standing by to help.

"Here, put these in the fire. We will need them to cauterize the stump when the leg has been removed. It's good for him that the day is cold but hard on my hands when I do the delicate work of tying off." Dr. Franklin held out his hands. "Pour some of that whiskey over my hands before I begin this thankless task."

The young soldier, even in his delirium, was aware that he was soon to lose his leg. He began screaming, "Not my leg, O, God, please help me, not my leg!"

The screams could be heard echoing throughout the camp, but it was a familiar sound all too often heard, and it fell on already hardened ears.

Robert sat at a desk in General Washington's headquarters, preparing to write a letter to the parents of the young soldier. Just then, a light knock sounded on the door, and as it opened, Cpl. Marvin Jones entered. "Colonel, sir, I trust the colonel would care for a cup of hot tea this evening."

A cup of hot tea was a rare thing for Robert. If he hadn't been in the officer's headquarters for the evening, he would not have had such a luxury.

"Thank you, most kindly, Corporal, I assure you I would welcome a good cup of tea at this moment. This is perhaps my most difficult task to send these sad letters to so many families, telling them of their loss. Many are to wives with young children." He dipped the quill pin in the dark ink. Robert tried to put into words his deep and heartfelt remorse for their loss. As he began, the sound of the pen could be heard as it scratched across the paper. "It is with deep regret that I must inform you of the death of your son. Your nation will forever be grateful for your sacrifice and that of your brave son. He served his nation with unwavering pride and honor."

In the back of his mind, he asked himself this question, "Will this newly found nation forever remain grateful?"

He thought of all the too many fearless soldiers who had cemented the dreams of many for a more independent nation, with the sacrifice of their young blood.

Back on the farm, Jonathan decided he would go into town for some overdue supplies and catch up on the war news. "Mrs. Fargo, I need to hitch your buggy for the drive into town."

The buggy was the only mode of transportation on the farm except for horseback until Robert could help Jonathan assemble his wagon.

"Of course, Jonathan, the buggy belongs to all of us." Mrs. Fargo asked, "If possible, would you please drive by the boarding house and see what might be taking place there. There is no need to go inside."

Nathaniel begged, "Pa, may I please come with you? Please may I?"

"Me too, Pa, me too," pleaded Arianna.

"Sorry, not this time, children, it will be too dangerous in town. We need to make sure it is safe before you go."

The city's residents, those who had remained and not left for the backwoods, were quiet. There were no children on the streets. The redcoats stalked up and down the streets and in and out of the shops and houses asking what business residents were about. Jonathan saw a group of redcoat solders enjoying a game of kickball in the city park.

He could not buy any provisions for they were too costly. The redcoats had taken all they wanted and not paid the merchants, which generated extremely inflated prices on all the remaining goods.

While in town, Jonathan visited with William.

"Jonathan, tell Kate that Washington's troops have moved over to Valley Forge. They tried to recover the city on two occasions, but to no avail," explained William, while in search of something as he shuffled through papers piled high on his desk. It was evident to Jonathan that William was in a hurry and he quickly changed the subject. He did however take the time to ask, "How are Mrs. Fargo and Lilly? They are at the farm, aren't they?"

"The family is well," answered Jonathan, watching out the window as though he expected a redcoat to enter at any moment. Jonathan repeated a second time, revealing his nervousness, "Yes, the ladies are with us and doing well. Mrs. Fargo would like to know about the boarding house. I promised I would check for her."

"The structure is there, but the redcoats have taken up residency because of its size." William reached into his breast pocket and took out his pocket watch. He checked the time, as though he had an appointment of sorts. "It is my understanding that the house is occupied by the high officers in Howe's army. They seem to be living it up. There is music and whisky drinking every night I am told."

Putting on his coat and hat, Jonathan asked, "The family and I, especially Mrs. Fargo and Lilly, would like to inquire of Dr. Franklin and Miss Robinson as well. Where might they be now that the boarding house is in the hands of the British?"

Checking his watch for the second time, William said, "After the second attempt by Washington to defend the city, Dr. Franklin went with the troops. There were so many in need of his help. As for Ms. Robinson, she has gone back to New York to be with her family. I haven't heard from either one at present. I am living here in the office and have been since the redcoats took over."

"Well, William, it has been good to see you again. Thank you for your time." Shaking William's hand, not wanting to invade his time. "I must start for home for the ladies will be in constant fear until I return."

"As you leave, remember, you can't be too careful. You have not been in town for some time, and there is no telling what the redcoats are up to." He cautioned him for the second time. "Be extremely careful, Jonathan." William led him to the door.

The evening grew late and the sun was on its way down giving way to the brisk air, as winter loomed around the corner. Jonathan left William's office. Just as he was untying his horse, a drunken redcoat approached him. Staggering and with blundering speech, the redcoat asked while finger punching Jonathan in the chest, "Just what is your busineth on His Majethshes's strihs this night?"

Nervously, Jonathan realized the drunken condition of the soldier, his breath revealed he had an abundance of hard liquor. Jonathan replied calmly, "Just locked up the office and headed for home. Can I help you?

It's getting colder, don't you think? The missus will be unhappy if I am late again this evening."

He hoped the small talk would satisfy the redcoat. Climbing into the buggy, he tipped his hat and drove away, daring not to look back. The soldier stumbled and steadied himself against a street lamp and shouted, "Long live the king!"

Giving the soldier a high hand wave, Jonathan pulled his collar up around his neck and ears trying to ward off the night chill and thought, *That was close.* As he rounded the bend he could see the dimly lit house with the rising gray chimney smoke, and with relief, he sighed, "Everything appears quite normal."

Sarah met him at the door. "Thank goodness you are home, I was so worried."

She took his coat and hung it on the wooden peg, just inside the door. Jonathan placed his gun in the rack above the door and moved close to the fire. "Town is quite different. The redcoats are all over. They are in all the shops and homes. William is now living in his office. By the way, Mrs. Fargo, the house is standing, but it is totally occupied by the British army. It does not look as inviting as in the past."

Sarah asked, "Were you able to get the provisions?"

Jonathan, sitting by the fireplace to warm himself, shook his head. "Sorry, Sarah, things were just too expensive. I could not buy one thing on our list. Philadelphia has depleted its resources with the influx of Hessian and British soldiers taking as they please, without payment. The shop owners have no money left to purchase from Britain and France.

"Kate, William said to tell you that Robert is in Valley Forge with General Washington and his forces. Washington's army tried twice to defend Philadelphia, but were defeated. I inquired about the doctor. He has gone with the troops who are in need of his services, and as for Ms. Robinson, she has returned to her family in upper New York."

Chapter 26

F ALLING FROM THE TREES WERE the last dried brown leaves that fluttered to the ground, covering up the dying summer grass. The backdrop of a thunderous winter sky, seen through bare tree limbs, left a feeling of despair, giving one the feeling of hopelessness for the future.

Meals were becoming more and more conservative as provisions were depleting. Lilly, with her slave background, had been taught to cook by taking what seemed to be nothing and making something of it, leaving no waste.

The women were in the kitchen preparing supper when Kate announced, "Ladies." She stopped midsentence to collect her words. "I have something to tell you. I am going to have another baby. I estimate it to be in April." She then took her hands out of the bread dough and wiped them on her apron, watching for their reaction. She continued, "It saddens me that Robert won't be here. I can't even give him the news." She choked up, trying to fight back the oncoming tears.

Sarah, feeling for Kate, put her arms around her to comfort her, saying, "A baby. This house can use another baby. After all, Ashley is walking now and is on her way to becoming a big girl. Kate, Robert will be home soon, of this I feel sure, just try to be strong and take care of yourself for him and for Ashley."

Kate turned back to kneading her bread dough. "I am so thankful we are all together. I do not think I could manage this all alone."

Jonathan prepared to go to the barn for the evening milking. Sir Jug stood with wagging tail ready to follow him, knowing that he would get the first squirt of milk. Before leaving the house, Jonathan loaded the rifle ready for firing, to be on the side of caution. In the barn, he leaned the gun upright against the wall. "Jug, what is wrong with you, boy? Don't annoy Sophie."

He pulled the stool up and sat down, all the while slapping Sophie on her rear, steadying her, and letting her know he was there to relieve her heaviness. Sophie decided she was going to be a bit obnoxious as she attempted various ways to put her foot in the milk bucket, thus knocking it over. Jonathan, for the second time, put the milk bucket under Sophie. With an attitude, she swung her tail around with the purpose of trying to slap his face. Jonathan repositioned himself once again on the milk stool. "Now, Sophie, I have had just about enough of your shenanigans."

Just as he reached for Sophie's udders, Jug started barking uncontrollably, backing up, growling, snarling, and showing his teeth. "What is it, boy?"

Turning around, Jonathan almost fell off the stool. He saw a Hessian soldier in a very dirty uniform standing behind him. He had no weapon in his hand. Jonathan, thinking quickly, rolled off the stool and over to the rifle, grabbing it before the soldier could make a lunge. Bounding to his feet and pointing the rifle at the soldier, he demanded, "What do you want here?"

The soldier spoke very little English; he pointed to Sophie and then to his mouth, indicating he was hungry. Jonathan determined him to be a German soldier, and he certainly did not want to take him back to the house. Nor did he have the heart to kill an unarmed man, much less one who was hungry, unless provoked. Jonathan continued to point the rifle, forcing the intruder over to the door. He then pointed out to the graves and put his hand up to his forehead and, pointing toward the house, indicated there were sick people there. He was hoping the soldier would leave because of the illness. The soldier, with wildness in his eyes, drew a knife hidden under his belt. He lunged at Jonathan, forcing him to fire his loaded rifle. The Hessian soldier, holding his stomach, fell to the ground, first on his knees and then forward facedown, taking in his last breath. Jonathan was very shaken by the whole ordeal and could not believe how quickly it had all come about. Why had this man wanted to force his own death? Jonathan realized, at that moment, that he had been brought unwillingly into this war, defending what was his. He was even more saddened that he was compelled to place in the ground the body of a poor soul whose name was unknown, knowing that he was some mother's son; surely he was loved by someone. Jonathan's mind was reeling with thoughts, for which he had no answers. Perhaps there was something on this soldier's person that would give a clue to his identity. Turning the dead soldier over with the warm blood still flowing from his mortally wounded body, he searched his pockets and found a letter. The letter proved to be written in German. It was obvious the letter had been read many times. Jonathan folded the letter in its same folds and put it in his own pocket for a later time.

The loud blast of the gunfire had been heard by all those in the house. Sarah quickly sat down a bowl of food. Her heart leapt in beats as though it was going to leave her body. "I must go check on Jonathan." Sarah barreled out the door.

"Oh, do be careful, please, Sarah," pleaded the ladies with worry in their voices.

Sarah ran from the house to the barn, her heart felt as though it was in her throat. Approaching the barn, she saw no evidence of an intrusion, as she searched for Jonathan. Very cautiously, she opened the door and saw the soldier lying in a pool of blood.

Jug was standing over the intruder as though he was unsure of what had taken place. Frantically, her eyes searched for her husband, but she did not see him. It was obvious something terrible had taken place. Full of fear, she continued in her search. "Jug, where is Jonathan?" As though she expected the dog to answer her. "Had he been taken away by other soldiers?" At that moment, coming from behind the barn, she heard what sounded like digging, a shovel striking the ground then the sound of falling dirt. Quietly, she picked up the ax next to a pile of farm tools.

"Come, Jug," called Sarah. Carefully, she slipped around the corner of the barn. There she saw Jonathan, his face ashen white as though it had been his blood soaking the dirt on the barn floor. Looking up, he saw Sarah and dropped the shovel to open his arms for her.

"Come here, Sarah," with perplexity and sadness in his voice.

Sarah dropped the ax and walked into his arms. He wrapped them around her and they embraced for a moment. Backing away, she asked, "Jonathan, what happened here?"

"I must bury him, Sarah." He picked up the shovel and continued to dig. "He just wanted to die, Sarah, he just wanted to die." He shook his head in disbelief.

Sarah could see the despondency in her husband. He was extremely upset at what obviously had taken place. She and Jonathan wrapped the enemy soldier's body in some old dirty sack material and lowered him into the freshly dug grave. Together, they covered him with the fresh earth. Standing side by side and holding hands, they reverently said a humble prayer and committed his body to the ground.

"Sarah, we must rake over the grave and leave it unmarked as though it were not here."

As he raked across the ground, spreading the fresh dirt, a bewildering thought entered Jonathan's mind. How many young men were forced to leave this world, with their death forever unmarked as this grave, because of this wretched and unforgiving war?

"We will talk about it later, Sarah, I just can't now."

Jonathan was shaking as he picked up his tools. Together, they went inside the barn and cleaned up the blood-soaked ground where the soldier had fallen.

Sarah finished the milking chore for Jonathan while he sparingly fed the livestock. Feed was becoming as rationed as all their other provisions.

Walking slowly back to the house, Jonathan stopped. "Sarah, I understand better now what Robert meant when he said, 'War is misery for all.' May God bless Robert if this is what he faces each and every day. Was this young man so miserable he was willing to leave this life behind?"

Upon returning to the house, Jonathan went to their room and closed the door. Jug stood outside, wagging his tail and realizing that he would not be allowed in the room. He then lay in front of the door and put his paws under the bottom open space to let Jonathan know of his presence even though he had been shut out.

Sarah told the ladies what had happened at the barn, being careful not to allow her children to hear the details of the tragedy. Jonathan chose not to come to the supper table that evening. He needed time alone in the wake of the loss of another human life by his hands.

Chapter 27

HOWE HAD SECURED A PERIMETER north of Philadelphia. The day was December 17, 1777. Washington had gathered his forces at Valley Forge, a village on the Schuylkill River, twenty miles northwest of Philadelphia. The site had been chosen because of the broad river and the commanding hills that surrounded the valley. General Washington made his headquarters in a stone house on the river. His troops numbered eleven thousand, and their provisions were meager. Because of the refugees from Philadelphia, there was a shortage of food for the villagers. Washington refused to allow his troops to commandeer the village's supplies. One-fifth of the army had deserted because of their lack of food and clothing.

Robert, along with other officers, directed his troops to dig trenches in an area of about 750 acres. They built the most scant of huts using wood from the surrounding forest. The weather was bleak and miserable, with the usual bitter cold ice and snow. The half-frozen men wrapped in blankets or anything that would warm their stiff bodies. They hovered in the trenches and makeshift shelters trying to find refuge from the brutal blowing wind, snow, and rains.

Keeping up the morale of the army proved to be a hardship in itself. The army felt deserted by their own countrymen who had fallen short of furnishing supplies and money to support the war effort. What food did reach them was rancid. The clothing they received was thread rotten and in bad repair.

Robert witnessed the death of 2,500 soldiers because of diseases, mostly brought about by the lack of food and warm clothing. Among them was Corporal Jones. Robert was by his side as he drew shortened, hard, and labored breaths brought on by consumption. With a very weak voice between tormenting coughs, the weakened dying soldier reached into his breast pocket and took out a tiny blue string bag. He then removed the ring from his left hand and placed both the bag and rings in Robert's hand.

"Please take these for you and your wife. I have no further need of them."

Robert was saddened by the loss of such a fine young man. He gently closed the eyelids of the soldier, then pulled the worn blanket over his face. Once again, the war had wrenched Robert's heart. Robert raised his head, even more repulsed by the blowing winds that carried the stink of decaying flesh. In the days that followed, burying the dead alone was an overwhelming experience.

Robert sat in a trench with several half-frozen soldiers huddled together around a small fire as they shared their feelings about the war. They told of their disappointment in Congress and how it had let them down. They wondered if it was worth all their sacrifices. Would their posterity hear of and appreciate their endurance of this inhumane treatment that had befallen them and their enemy?

Robert himself had despairing moments for he was away for the second approaching Christmas. Moving about the camp, he tried to raise the morale of his troops. He told them, "Men, we have the opportunity to build our own government. If we succeed and win this war, we can free ourselves of tyranny and oppression. Believe me, in my meetings with the war generals, I witness sincere concern. General Washington has the determination to win this war, and he knows and feels your suffering and pain. Why do you think he puts himself in the middle of combat? He has a wife, home, and family just as we have, and he wants for them the same as we do, a better government, a true and free republic." Robert continued to tell them, "I missed my baby girl Ashley's first birthday and

Christmas, now I am going to miss another Christmas. I miss the sweet tenderness and support of my beautiful wife."

Thinking about it, he felt guilty at having taken Kate from a life of such prominence to that of being placed in some of the poorest of circumstances. He thought that should he even survive this hell on earth that surrounded him, death, men starving, freezing, and in mortal pain, for the lack of medicine to ease their suffering, could he ever make a good life for her and Ashley? He was unaware that there soon would be another child born in such uncertain times.

Winter complicated life on the farm as well. The days were shorter and colder.

Recounting the winter of 1776, Jonathan had been able to trap wild game, trying to spare the ammunition. They were better off than most of the townspeople, for they had stored and preserved an abundance of garden and fruit crops. The fallen tree trimmings that remained in the woods, from the new room addition, supplied enough wood for the winter fires. The flour from the grist meal was gone. The last had been used to make ginger cookies for the children. Lilly was teaching Sarah and Kate how to stone grind corn for they had plenty of that. It was hard work and took a great deal of time. She taught them how to make corn fritters for bread and corn meal mush for breakfast. Kate remembered the mush aboard ship and thought she would pass on the mush.

Once again, it was Christmas Eve, but festive decorations of the past were very sparse in the once busy city. The redcoats abandoned the main streets and had forcibly taken shelter in the homes of the town's people. The parks and street corners were void of the carolers and venders. The boarding house was dismal. It lacked the festive lighting and the beautiful green garlands with red bows, adorning the windows and the once beautiful stained-glass door. The only thing that remained the same was the extremely cold days, and freezing nights, and the frozen ground, slick with ice.

On the farm, no one spoke much about Christmas. Little could be given to the children except the sharing of stories, fiddle music, songs, and the ginger cookies for Christmas morning. Jonathan once again brought a cedar tree to the house on Christmas Eve for the children to decorate. They appreciated the simple pleasures that were theirs. Thus far, they had escaped the wrath of the redcoats. The little house had an abundance of gratitude for their safety, warmth, and ample food.

Kate felt a little melancholy. She missed Robert while thinking about their good times and how much she loved him. Rubbing her stomach, she wondered if this time it would be a son for Robert? She couldn't help but think that their days of courting had been much easier than these hardships they now endured. She asked Jonathan, "Do you think perhaps William has heard anything concerning the war? It has been since October that you last spoke with him."

Crouched with ragged subdued troops on Christmas Eve, Robert huddled miserably in his shelter under a tarp, covering a foxhole. He was grateful he was not pushing man and beast through turbulent snow and ice storms as he had done the previous Christmas. Someone remembered it was Christmas and began to play "Hark the Herald Angels Sing" on a harmonica. Poor in spirit with much fatigue in their voices, the troops joined in with soft singing. The singing spread throughout the camp and with much more vigor across the fields and throughout the foxholes, sounding out a harmonious round.

January 1778 left waves of mud, and March brought with it a blasting of blizzards and fierce winds. What little food they had was now gone. The men foraged through the forest for hickory nuts and fauna. An occasional trapped rabbit provided a welcomed treat. Smallpox, typhus, and dysentery took its toll. Washington's army had dwindled to approximately three thousand able-bodied men.

With a break in the weather, the army emerged out of the trenches. In February, Baron von Steuben had taken over the drilling and restructuring of Washington's army, which made a marked improvement in efficiency and morale.

There was still a sharp chillness in the air, but April brought with it the hope for new beginnings. The brutal weather seemed to be behind them. The days were getting longer and the skies were a brighter blue, with white fluffy cumulus clouds, the kind you want to study and find a picture likeness.

With a reprieve in the weather and the arrival of much needed supplies for the broken army, Robert gained great encouragement by the improvement in the new emerging forces. As a high ranking officer, it would be most unwise for him to cross the barriers of the British perimeters around Philadelphia. However, he still had great concern for his family and friends and worried for their safety.

Gardens had been planted on the little farm with the hope the new crop would yield as plentiful as the previous year. Much of the land of Philadelphia had been foraged and ravaged. The homes had been vandalized, their furnishings and outbuildings had been destroyed, and then burned by the British to keep warm. Still very fearful of the redcoats, the family stayed on high alert.

Kate woke up early in the morning in pain. "Lilly, Lilly, I think I am in labor, can you help?"

Lilly and Mrs. Fargo shared Kate's room. "Why yes, Miss Kate, I is here." After checking Kate, Lilly laughed her contagious laugh. "I thinks we is goen to have us a baby this very day."

The rest of the household was up and about, being awakened by the commotions birthing brings. Mrs. Fargo took Ashley out to the kitchen to keep her entertained by the other children while she prepared breakfast. Mrs. Fargo told them, "We are going to have us a new baby today."

Sarah stepped into Kate's room to see how far the labor had progressed. "I will get a basin with hot water and towels and also a warm blanket for the baby."

"Some string too," called Lilly. "Miss Kate, you sure is made for haven babies, this baby is comen fast."

"Oh, Lilly, here comes another one."

Kate held Sarah's hands with her knees drawn to her chest while pushing hard with a loud groan.

"It's comen, Miss Kate, one more push and here it is," laughed Lilly.

"What is it, Lilly?" Kate asked, as she dropped her shoulders back onto the pillow, catching her breath. She rolled her head while searching for a glimpse of the new baby. Lilly cut the cord, then held the baby upside down and gave it a smack on the rear. Out came a cry and a deep breath from a very wet pink baby. Lilly handed the child to Sarah to clean up before giving it to Kate.

"What does you think it is, Miss Kate?" teased Lilly. "It's another girl, Miss Kate, youz haz another girl," replied Lilly, happy that all seemed well with the new arrival. She went about attending to Kate, humming a Negro spiritual. Sarah placed the baby in Kate's arms.

"She looks just like Ashley, don't you think?" Kate held the baby to her breast. "She is good and strong." The baby latched on. "I am going to name her Mary Margaret after my mother. I am glad now that it is not a boy, so that when Robert comes home, he can be here for the birth of a son."

Holding the baby, Kate drifted into a well-deserved sleep. Sarah took Mary from Kate's arms, wrapped her tightly, and put her in a freshly made cradle, while Lilly cleaned up the evidence of the new birth.

June 1778, the weather was hot and humid and the days grew longer. Disease, brought by the Hessian and British armies, was rampant throughout the city of Philadelphia. The family had escaped the epidemic by remaining on the farm and not going into town.

On June 18, the British retreated from Philadelphia, removing a large part of their forces under the orders of Sir Henry Clinton. Clinton had replaced Gen. William Howe as commander of the British army.

On June 28, the continental army broke camp. Some of Washington's troops had been sent into Philadelphia to harass the remaining British troops. Washington and the remainder of his forces were in pursuit of the British, following them to New York, confronting them at the Monmouth Courthouse.

The family was aware of the British leaving Philadelphia. The boarding house was free of its unwanted winter guests. Mrs. Fargo and Lilly packed to go back to their house.

"We are going to miss all of you. You kept us safe and shared with us all you had, and for that, we are truly grateful," Mrs. Fargo expressed with arms outstretched for a hug from the children.

"Children, give the grandmas a hug and tell them they will be missed," coached Sarah.

Knowing the boarding house would be barren of any foods and staples, Kate and Sarah packed a basket, along with what bedding they could spare.

"We will see you soon and we will miss all of you terribly," choked Kate with a lump in her throat.

Jonathan drove them back to the house in the buggy, using one of his horses. Approaching the house, Mrs. Fargo gasped and silently cried, "Oh, Jonathan, it looks so bad, but at least it is still standing. The porch furniture is gone. My beautiful porch is destroyed."

The porch floor boarding, except for a small section in front of the door, was missing. Obviously, it had been used for firewood.

Jonathan helped the ladies down from the buggy. "Allow me to go inside first just to make sure it is safe for you. The two of you wait here on the porch."

The door was standing open as Jonathan entered. Looking around, he saw that all the nice furniture was missing or heavily damaged. He went upstairs and checked all the rooms. Stepping out onto the porch, he bid the ladies to come in. "It is safe. No one is here. Let's make certain you have beds for tonight."

Lilly went throughout the house and gathered bedding from various rooms. "Missy, we needs to launder this before wez can sleep on it. What is left of our nice quilts are so soiled. Thanks goodness, Missy, Sarah and Kate thoughts of bedding for us."

"Yes, yes," whimpered Mrs. Fargo, still in shock from what she was seeing and saddened by what she was not seeing. She was taking a mental inventory of what was missing. "We will have to start over, Lilly, it is just so bad. Our sweet home is gone, Lilly, it is gone." Mrs. Fargo wiped away the tears that filled her eyes.

Lilly was being positive, "We isz home, Missy. Wez will clean it up and wez can fix it back, youz will see."

Jonathan came through the back after checking the surrounding property and extended an invitation. "If the house is too destroyed, come back to the farm, and we will make repairs a little at a time for you."

"Thank you, Jonathan, that is most kind of you, we appreciate it, but we will stay and make do. We will be all right," murmured Mrs. Fargo.

Upon leaving, Jonathan told them, "I will stop by and tell William that you are home, I am sure he would like to know. Once again, are you sure you will be all right?"

"Oh yes, we will be quite all right, I am sure." Mrs. Fargo walked Jonathan to the front door.

"We will check on you soon." Jonathan closed the door behind him. The door now had a heavy quilt hanging to replace the once beautiful stained glass.

Chapter 28

O NCE AGAIN, ROBERT SURPRISED KATE and the family. He tied his horse some yards away from the house. Seeing the two fake graves, he almost lost his composure, giving him a wavering feeling of not wanting to go inside. Stepping up on the end of the porch, he saw Sarah. Putting his hand up to his mouth, he motioned for all to be quiet.

Jug was unsure of Robert's presence and barked continuously.

Sarah pointed into the house and whispered, "Kate is in her bedroom."

Robert breathed a sigh of relief.

"Quiet, Jug, be quiet. Come here," commanded Sarah.

Robert quietly slipped up on Kate; he found her bent over the cradle, cooing and baby-talking to Mary while changing her nappies. Robert put his arms around her. Kate turned in his arms, lifeless with shock. Robert carried her over to the bed and gently laid her down. "Kate, Kate, it's me."

Softly, he slapped her cheeks and wrists to revive her.

Kate came to. "Oh, Robert, it's you. It truly is you. They embraced with a lingering kiss. Kate, still a bit weak from the fainting, pointed to the other side of the room. "Now I have a surprise for you." Taking him by the hand, she led him over to the cradle. Picking Mary up, she handed her to Robert. "I want you to meet your new daughter. This is Mary Margaret McCall, Mary, this is your father. Mary was born April 18."

Robert was taken by surprise. "Wow, I have missed a lot. She looks like Ashley, and she is beautiful." He cradled her close in his arms. Turning around, looking about the room, he asked, "Where is Ashley?"

"You passed her in the front room with the other children. She has grown so much. She is a big girl now." Kate gently reminded him that he had been gone for some time.

"Well, Robert, Ashley will be two in July." Kate put Mary back into the cradle. "Let's find Ashley."

They went into the kitchen and met the rest of the family. Kate picked Ashley up and kissed her. "Ashley, this is your Pa." She thought Pa would be better understood by Ashley because the other children called Jonathan, Pa. There were a lot of times that Ashley called Jonathan Pa.

Robert lifted her from Kate's arms to hold her for a bit. Ashley was still very uncomfortable in his arms, revealing that she had no interest in this strange man. He kissed her on the top of her head and let her down to play with Liam and Penelope.

Arriving back at the farm, Jonathan saw a horse tied some distance from the house. He was a bit concerned, but as he approached the house, he saw the military paraphernalia, which lead him to believe it to be Robert. Nevertheless, he opened the door with great caution his rifle ready for defense. He could hear a joyous reunion taking place.

"Good, Robert, I am so glad it is you. Welcome home." Jonathan smiled as he hung his rifle in the gun rack.

"Everyone seems well. I can't tell all of you how worried I have been," expressed Robert, sitting at the table. Kate gave him a good cool glass of water followed by a glass of fresh cold milk. "So much has taken place: the adverse weather, starvation, sickness, and the battles with the British army. It all has been so horrific. How on earth did all of you manage?"

Jonathan answered, "The ladies came and warned us and we followed the plan. We only had to stay in the shelter one night and day. The British did come the next day, but they took only the cut wood, food, and most of the chickens. We were able to hide the animals in the woods. They tore up the house pretty good. More than anything else, we think they were in search of guns and ammunition."

"Yah, and they hit Sir Jug in the head with a gun," interrupted Nathaniel.

"Is Sir Jug all right?" inquired Robert.

"Oh, he is a tough little guy," laughed Kate.

"The two graves out front, are they Lilly and Mrs. Fargo's?" asked Robert drinking the last of his milk.

"Oh, no," interjected Sarah. "We just hung a red cloth at the road to scare the redcoats. That seemed to work, so then Jonathan dug the false graves. He was just returning from taking the ladies to the boarding house just as you arrived. The two of them have been with us since the British invaded Philadelphia in October."

"Robert, you look so thin," noticed Kate as she walked behind him, rubbing the top of his shoulders and feeling the protrusion of his bone structure.

Robert muttered, "I ate a lot of roasted rabbit."

"Sorry, Robert, we have rabbit again tonight. We know fried chicken is your favorite, but we have been trying to build up our brood after so many were taken by the redcoats. Lilly taught Kate and I many ways to cook rabbit," laughed Sarah, as she stood stirring the string beans.

Kate suggested, "Robert, let me draw water and heat it while the stove is hot, so you can take a good relaxing bath."

"I certainly am looking forward to that. Let me help you." They carried water from the spring room to heat. Then all sat down for supper.

"Goodness, that was a wonderful meal. It has been a long time since I have had a meal like this," complimented Robert as he got up from the table to carry the bathwater to his and Kate's room.

Sarah insisted, "Robert, you and Kate spend the evening together, and our family will care for the children." Jonathan agreed to the evening plan offered by Sarah.

After Robert's good bath, he and Kate carried a quilt with them as they took a long walk around the property, talking and enjoying the peaceful summer evening. Stopping, Robert whispered, "Listen to that."

Kate, holding on to him and not wanting to let go, asked, "What? Listen to what?"

"It's the crickets and the frogs, one chants and the other croaks in a rhapsody. It is so good just to hear peace, as opposed to the firing of guns and cannons, the sadness of death, and the misery of pain."

Kate knew Robert needed to speak of the war. She listened, but deep down wanted to change the subject. "This evening walk reminds me of my eighteenth birthday when we declared our love, remember? The night is so beautiful, the sky is clear, and the stars sparkle like diamonds under light. Look at them, Robert. I come here to this field often to get away from the house. I sit in solitude just thinking of you. It is so quiet, sometimes a rabbit races by, but mostly quiet. There are thousands of dandelions with their white tops. I pick one for you and one for me. I blow the tops off and make a dandelion wish and then I watch the wind capture and carry the little furry things away. My prayer is, please, God, don't let our lives be carried away in the wind like the tops of the dandelions."

"Oh, Kate, I love you and our girls so much. I know these times are hard for you and that you live in fear and I know you have that right. Dandelions come back every season. I will be back, this I promise."

The darkness was lighted by millions of fireflies, as they looked over the hill down into the meadow below. Robert reached out and caught a firefly, cupping it in his hand. Opening his hand slightly, he said, "Here, I want to show you something. Look in my hand and see it light up."

"Robert, that one little fly gives off so much light," replied Kate.

Robert continued to cup his hand, imprisoning the tiny bright bug. "I know, Kate, that is kind of like me and the army. I am just one little man among many, but I feel I can help light the way for my family and my new country. You and I are much like these little fireflies. Separately, we give off a spark of light, but together, we can cast a beam."

Kate spread the quilt out in the tall grass. "Robert, you have such a great love for this new land of ours. I pray all your efforts are rewarded. I missed so much as a child, doing childish things. I want our girls to have normal life experiences, the little things like this make life real. Most of all, I want my husband here with me to show them these things. I didn't send word to you about the pregnancy because I didn't want you to worry about me. You have your safety and men to worry about, and I understand that."

"Kate, it is so wonderful to be with you this night. You are more beautiful to me than ever, even when you were eighteen in your elegant green gown. You have truly grown into a woman. It is obvious you have a very strong constitution. There have been days I have been in doubt if I would return for even this short time. It seemed as if this day would never come. I promise, I will return to you and the girls. I feel God is with us during these trying times."

Chapter 29

J UNE ROLLED TOWARD JULY. THE gardens were again producing a good yield. The vegetables were ready to be harvested, and the hard work of preservation lay ahead for the two women. The temperature was slowly rising, making for a hot summer. The humidity was creeping in and brought with it a sweltering feeling one could not escape.

The British had not returned to Philadelphia. The children could once again play outdoors without fear. The hot late June days brought with them a harmless insect known as June bugs. The children enjoyed their large iridescent emerald green wings. Nathaniel, barefoot and covered in dirt from head to toe, revealed a good day of hard work and play, as he had fun with such a bug. He had tied a four-foot string to a back leg of one bug. He then turned the bug free to fly. While extending his arm out as far as it would go, he held on to the other end of the string. Turning in circles, the June bug made a buzzing sound, flying up and then diving down, as it flew within the perimeter of the string. Sir Jug chased after the bug. When the June bug flew up, Jug was on his way down. Jug, as hard as he tried, was unable to coordinate the capture of the bug.

Lisa-Jean played with the two of them. She excitedly watched the whole show. Her big brother impressed her, all-knowing to do such an ingenious thing. She encouraged him, "Fly the bug again, Thaniel, fly it again," failing to pronounce his name fully.

With the warm weather, Philadelphia slowly tried to restore the parks and streets to their original beauty. Funds were low for such city needs. Hard coin was scarce. High inflation resulted in greater bartering as the town's people tried to return to a simple style of provident living.

Many of the colonial troops made Philadelphia their home.

"How many would return to the ranks?" Robert questioned himself, for so many came and went as they pleased. *Perhaps*, he thought, *with the new intense training of the troops by Baron Von Steuben, more would remain to exhibit their new skills.* Not much time was left for Robert and his men to stay in Philadelphia, as they prepared to meet General Washington and the rest of the Continental army in New York.

Robert and Jonathan were reassembling the good wagon. Robert commented, "I am saddened to leave my family, it is not an easy thing to do. You have done well by them, Jonathan, and I am thankful for the care you have given them."

"It has been difficult, but everyone pulled their weight, even down to the children," replied Jonathan, who was glad to have this one-on-one time with Robert. "May I ask you a personal question, Robert?"

"Certainly, Jonathan, you can ask anything," answered Robert as he slapped grease on the axle of the last wheel.

Jonathan told Robert of the killing of the young Hessian soldier in the barn. "How do you forget about the killing of another human being, Robert?"

Hoisting the wheel onto the axle, Robert stopped and looked at Jonathan. He saw the sincerity of the question, even though he was taken aback by it. He stopped and wiped the sticky grease off his hands. "Jonathan, I don't think you will ever forget, it will always remain with you. This is one of the many questions my men have for me after a siege. War is a nasty thing, it pits good against evil. We did not ask for this, but we are forced to defend what is ours. You did not start your day with the intent to harm another person. The way I look at peace is there are two choices: one is persuasion, and the second is force. You had no time to persuade this young man. His choice was by force. It sounds as though the young soldier wanted to meet his maker for whatever his reason. Just know this, you were on the side of right. You had to defend yourself because our families depended on you. Time will heal, but you will never forget, Jonathan, you will never forget."

The day came for Robert to leave. He stood over the beds of his sleeping children, just watching them as they quietly rested. He thought that they had not a care in the world and that it was well that the innocence of childhood protected them from knowing of this ravaging war. Deep down, he had a hidden fear. The one thing that haunted him the most was, if they would ever know him? Would the war take him from them and their mother? He once again thought that their mother had the right to be as frightened as she was.

It was a repeat of two times before. Very early in the morning, the family prepared for Robert's departure. Heavy fog filled the air as the clouds hung low over the fields, forcing the chimney smoke to the ground, and releasing with it the smell of burning wood. Kate packed as much food as would keep, along with fresh clean clothes. Standing with a heavy heart, she realized that she was a veteran herself, companionless for however long, she did not know. This time, regardless, she was left with two children, Ashley, who had only spent the first six months of her young life with her father, and Mary, who had only spent a matter of days.

"Robert, I will wait for you. You must come home to us."

As Robert caressed Kate, his hand in her soft hair, holding her head close to his chest. He resolved to carry this moment with him. Breathing deep, Robert captured her sweet smell, felt her softness, and believed in her endearing love. "Kate, you are a small delicate woman, but you have more tenacity than my entire corps."

Listening to Robert's heart as it beat assured her that for that fleeting moment in time he was alive and that his love belonged to her. She too had a silent inward fear of death as the war raged on. Kate looked up into his face and remembered the first time she saw the depth and the brightness of his deep blue eyes as the two were entangled in the palace draperies. Now she could only see how thin his face had become, the brightness had faded from his eyes, leaving in its place a tiredness no man as young as he should carry.

With the desire to give Kate hope, Robert said, "France has taken a new interest in the war. In February, Benjamin Franklin successfully secured funding from the French. The colonists will win this war, and it will come to an end."

"I pray, with all my heart, that you are right and that you will not be away from us as long this time, my love," Kate replied with tears welling up in her eyes.

Giving each other a lasting kiss, they parted. As in times past, the early morning fog was hanging low to the ground, Kate could scarcely see Robert as he reached the bend in the road that would take the only love in her life out of her sight. Robert could not bear to look over his shoulder. He was grateful for the fog as he struck his horse with a swift lash, making the animal bound into a full gallop.

Two children certainly demanded a lot of Kate's time. The preservation of the food was a big priority for both she and Sarah. Jonathan felt safer to hunt in the woods. Everything had a season, and summer was best for fishing and turkey and quail hunting. Elk and deer hunting was best left for fall and winter, simply for the preservation of large amounts of meats.

It had been months since all the family had gone into town. Once again, they felt free to go with their farm goods, butter, eggs, and fresh summer vegetables in exchange for coffee, sugar, and the most needed of all, salt. After making their trades, they stopped by to see how the ladies were faring.

"Oh my goodness," sighed Kate, putting her hand up to her face, "how different the house looks."

The porch had yet to be repaired. Going up to the front door, they were greeted with great enthusiasm by Mrs. Fargo and Lilly.

"Come in, please, come in. It is so good to see all of you," beamed Mrs. Fargo. The ladies gave the children giant hugs and kisses. Lilly and Mrs. Fargo cleaned up most of the inside of the boarding house, but much of the furniture needed to be repaired and replaced before the house could be restored to fully functioning.

Kate handed Lilly a basket. "We felt sure you could use some fresh vegetables."

Jonathan chimed in, "Well, ladies, you certainly have done a lot with the house since last I was here."

"I have a gentleman coming in the next day or two to make repairs on the porch before someone falls through," exclaimed Mrs. Fargo. "Then we can dress it up a bit to look more like home. Kate, for some reason beyond my thinking, the rascals did not destroy the harpsichord. They certainly destroyed everything else. William said it was used to amuse the British. I think because it survived, it deserves a good home. I want you to have it for your family. No one here will ever appreciate it as much as you."

"No, Mrs. Fargo, I couldn't. That is too much to give away." Kate was very much surprised.

"But I insist. You and your family did so much for us for months. Load it up, Jonathan," insisted Mrs. Fargo, waving her hand in the motion of taking it from the house.

"Only if you promise that you and Lilly will come to our house for every Christmas hereafter." Kate gave Mrs. Fargo a warm appreciative hug.

Jonathan and Nathaniel loaded the harpsichord in the wagon, making seating tight for the children. Kate handed Mary to Arianna to hold as she climbed up to the wagon seat with the help of Jonathan. Sarah gave Jonathan her hand as he steadied her balance for the climb up next to him. Arianna gave Mary back to Kate to hold. There was joyous laughter and singing on their short trip home, for it had been a long time since the family had had such a day of enjoyment.

By late afternoon, the children were picking on and teasing one another. They also expressed their hunger and the desire for supper. When the wagon rounded the curve, leading to the front yard, it was evident something was out of order. The guineas were in an uproar as they ran about the yard with their loud honking, singing sound. Jug stood outside the barn door, barking frantically.

The war had forced a lot of rogues to travel in search of shelter and food. Jonathan cautiously approached the house. "There is something wrong. The animals are too disturbed. Everyone, stay in the wagon while I check the house and buildings."

Climbing down from the wagon, Jonathan tied the horses to the porch post and reached for his gun. He went inside the house to make sure there were no intruders. Coming out the door, he gave the nod that the house was safe. Then he struck out for the barn, calling back to Sarah. "Take the children in the house while I search the outbuildings."

Sarah, Kate, and the children waited very quietly in the wagon before following his orders, not knowing what he might encounter.

With his eyes scanning the surroundings, Jonathan tried to quietly open the barn door. All the while, Jug continued to bark. The door made a scraping sound as the bottom planks slid across the dirt. With caution, he entered the structure pointing the gun with his finger on the trigger. His mind raced. He recalled somewhat the same situation just months before. "Is anyone here? Come out now, I say!"

At that moment, a woman came from behind the feed bins; she was followed by a second woman and then a third.

Still pointing the gun, Jonathan asked in a deep manly voice, "Who are you and what are you doing here?"

The older woman, looking very tired and weary, stepped forward. She had a very strong German accent, which revealed that she was a new immigrant.

"My name is Violet Kaiser, and this is my daughter, Adeline. This is Olivia Kaiser, my daughter-in-law. Sir, we mean you no harm, we are very hungry and have no shelter." Violet continued to talk using hand gestures because of her broken English. "All our men have been killed in the war, and we have been forced to leave our home. I don't feel so good, sir." She slumped over slowly and slid to the floor.

The other ladies rushed to her and began rubbing her face and slapping her wrists, trying to revive her.

Jonathan stepped to the barn door and called out, "Sarah, you, and Kate come here."

Jumping off the wagon, Sarah gave Arianna orders to care for the children, "Take them inside the house and stay there."

Arianna reached for Mary, carrying her in one arm; she then took Ashley by the hand to help her up the steps. "Nathaniel, you bring Liam

190

and Levi with you. Lisa-Jean, you take Penelope's hand and follow me. Come along now all of you, do as Ma says."

Sarah and Kate rushed to the barn, not knowing what the problem might be. Sarah entered the barn. "What is it, Jonathan? Who are these women? What do they want?"

Violet still lay in the dirt of the barn floor.

"These women are telling me they are homeless and very hungry. I suppose that is what this one needs." He pointed to Violet. "The lady on the floor is Violet Kaiser, her daughter, Adeline, and daughter-in-law, Olivia Kaiser."

Kate immediately took charge. "Let's get her up and get them to the house."

Kate, with Sarah's help, took Violet by the arms, balancing her as they walked her to the house. Adeline and Olivia followed.

Jonathan walked with them back to the wagon, relieved that the situation was manageable. "Sarah, ask Nathaniel to come outside and help me unload the harpsichord so we can move it into the house."

Sarah had just reached the front porch and hollered, "Nathaniel, your Pa needs you!"

"Yes, Pa, what do you need?' Nathaniel came out the front door, eating a cold biscuit.

"Son, I am going to back the wagon up to the porch so we can unload this harpsichord. It would be easier if the wagon is even with the porch. That way we won't have to lift it, just slide it as far as we can." Jonathan gave the horses the direction. "Back, back, whoa." Kate, where do you want us to put this thing?" asked Jonathan.

Kate, helping Olivia and Adeline, answered over her shoulders, "Over in the corner between the windows, as long as it is not too close to the fireplace."

Jonathan instructed the boy, "Come, son, we need to put the horses up and milk Sophie."

Jonathan knew Sarah and Kate would ask enough questions of the three strange women. Kate, while pouring warm water in the basin for Violet to freshen up, introduced herself and Sarah to the three ladies. "I am Kate McCall. These two children are mine. This is Ashley and this is Mary. My husband, Robert, is a colonel in Washington's army. This is our farm. This is Sarah Thatcher and her children, Arianna the oldest, Nathaniel is helping his pa, Jonathan," she continued, "Lisa-Jean, Penelope, Liam, and the baby, Levi." She named them in order of their age. "The family lives here and helps on the farm."

Kate asked the women, "Tell us about yourselves and how you came about being in this area."

Olivia, knowing Violet was still too weak for much conversation, explained, "We are from Brandywine. Our men, Violet's husband, my father-in-law, and her son, my husband, were killed in the Brandywine battle." She paused with deep pain in her voice as she spoke of their losses. She took in a deep breath and continued, as her voice quivered. "We were unable to stay in our house because the enemy soldiers took possession. We slipped away in the middle of the night. Without our men, we could no longer make our payments to the lenders. We tried following the troops, going to Valley Forge, doing laundry, cooking, and caring for the wounded."

Violet softly interrupted, "Adeline is only sixteen. It was not a safe environment for her. We had to keep her very close to us."

Olivia continued saying, "Food and provisions became scarce for even the soldiers. Violet became too weak for the conditions. When spring came, we moved on. We decided it would be best to come to Philadelphia because the British had moved on. We thought perhaps, we could find some domestic work. We came through the city, but could not find shelter, so we came a little farther south and found your place. Violet could no longer travel without food, so we took refuge in your barn. We will do most anything for some food and a good safe night's rest in your barn.

Kate remembered the time that Liz, Robert, and herself were much in the same situation with gnawing pangs of hunger and the overwhelming fear of being discovered. Nodding to Sarah, Kate offered, "Of course, you can stay the night. We will find you something to eat and draw water for some good baths. Tomorrow when you have rested, we will talk about what can be done to help your situation."

All three chimed as one, "We thank you most kindly."

Violet, still with a weak voice, added, "We will stay out of your way. The barn will be sufficient for our needs."

Kate kindly insisted, "That won't be necessary. There is an extra bed in my room for you, Violet. Olivia, you and Adeline can stay here in the front room. We will make pallets on the floor for you."

Sarah was dishing up stew from the night before and gave them some bread and milk.

Olivia broke a slice of bread. "Mrs. McCall, did I understand you to say your husband was Col. Robert McCall?"

"Yes, that is right. He serves with General Washington. He has been in Valley Forge this past winter. Why, have you met my husband?" asked Kate while carrying water to make ready for baths.

"Why, yes, ma'am, we do know him. A kind, fine gentleman he is. Looks after his soldiers real well he does," answered Olivia while eating the stew and bread.

"This is very good stew," declared Adeline, "and the milk is so good. It has been a very long time since I have had milk."

Together, Sarah and Kate found enough clothes for the three visitors.

"Tomorrow, we will wash your clothes," insisted Kate.

Chapter 30

ONCE AGAIN, THE LITTLE HOUSE was full of women, leaving Jonathan and Nathaniel with very little man space. After a good breakfast, the two went about doing the outside chores and leaving the house to the women.

Nathaniel asked Jonathan, "Pa, how long will these women stay? Will it be like Mrs. Fargo and Ms. Lilly?"

"Son, I don't think it will be that long. Mrs. Fargo and Lilly are like family to all of us. For now, these ladies need our help. Everyone needs to do whatever they can to help lighten the burdens of those in need during these hard times." Jonathan, while pitching hay into the livestock, called to Nathaniel. "Son, what if we go fishing after we finish with our chores? With three more mouths to feed in the house, we can use a good catch. We will feed the animals, milk, and carry in a lot of wood for the day and then we can go. The house will belong to all the ladies for the day, and we won't be in their way. Does this sound like a good idea to you?"

Nathaniel went about raking up the loose hay. He stopped and put his hand on his hip and in a matter-of-fact fashion blurted out, "Yeah, Pa, fishing is a good idea." Mimicking his Pa, he added, "We will leave the house to all the women. Pa, how many women do we have anyway?"

Jonathan couldn't help but laugh silently to himself as he answered the boy, "Well, let's see, we have five. I suppose you could say six with Arianna. She is almost a woman now. I would say we are two lucky men."

All the women were in the house when Kate expressed her idea to Sarah. "I think tomorrow would be a good day to make soap if the weather permits." She dressed the girls for the day. "With Olivia and Adeline, it will go a lot faster. Violet is still too weak for such a day of hard work."

"Yes, we should do that. Perhaps we should make some extra to barter in town and take a couple of bars to give Lilly. I am sure she could use it at the boarding house." Sarah agreed with Kate on the plan for the next day.

Sarah asked Jonathan, "Would you and Nathaniel bring in a lot of wood for we need it to make soap tomorrow? We will need an outside fire most of the day to bring the tallow and ash to a boil."

"The boy and I had plans to go fishing this afternoon for our supper tonight. We will bring up as much wood as we have time for. If it is not enough, we will get up early in the morning and chop more. I hate to break the promise to the boy. He is looking forward to the fishing." Jonathan leaned in to kiss Sarah as though it were for approval or maybe permission.

Sarah rolled her eyes. "I know what you are doing. You and Nathaniel need some father-and-son time. But you are right, fish would be a good change."

Jonathan and Nathaniel packed a lunch for an afternoon of father-and-son time.

"This looks like a good spot, son. The bank and edge of the water has a lot of debris. That makes good hiding places for fish." Jonathan stood the poles alongside a large elm tree. "Let's dig here in this damp ground. We should find some rich red fishing worms. I will dig, and you pick up the worms and put them in this tin."

"Boy, Pa, this is the life, isn't it?" Nathaniel baited his hook on the end of a six-foot cane pole. He then stepped back and took a good full swing, casting it out across the swift-flowing mountain stream. "What kind of fish are in here, Pa?"

Jonathan, making himself comfortable on the bank after casting in his line, answered, "Well, let's think. There are trout, sun perch, and sometimes bass. I would like to catch a good mess of trout. Now that would be some good eating. Little sun perch have too many bones, besides they are small and harder to clean. Son, you are right, I think it is good to be working and having fun at the same time."

Jonathan and Nathaniel leaned back against the elm tree, taking shelter from the afternoon sun and all the while watching the corks float on top the water, bobbing up and down and becoming more and more hypnotized by their movements. Jug found himself a shady cool spot under the wagon. The afternoon was sweltering hot, and the fish had dived down to deeper cooler water. Father and son making themselves comfortable, along with the heat and the serenity of the day, found a quiet nap too hard to resist.

Jonathan was awakened to a loud yelp from Nathaniel. Looking over, he saw the boy holding his foot and screaming. He also caught the glimpse of a snake in a fast slither down the incline back into the foliage. Immediately, Jonathan grabbed the boy by his leg, ripping open his already too short pants leg. Reaching and undoing his belt, he quickly tightened a tourniquet just above the ankle midcalf on Nathaniel's leg.

"Hold still, son, this will hurt just a bit, but I have to do it."

Pulling his hunting knife from its holster, he made eight small but deep incisions around the puncture wounds, then sucked as much of the venom from the incisions as he could, spitting each time, so as not to swallow it himself. Nathaniel's screams were now reduced to a soft cry as he tried to be brave for his pa.

Leaving the fishing gear, Jonathan lifted Nathaniel and placed him in the back of the wagon, then drove the horses as fast as they would go. He forgot to call for Jug, but the dog raced alongside the wagon back to the house.

"You are going to be all right, son, hang on till we get home to your mother. She will know what to do."

"Oh, Pa, oh, Pa, I don't feel good. I am getting sick." Nathaniel rolled in the back of the wagon.

Jonathan, slapping the horses with the reins, trying to speed them up at the same time, looked back at Nathaniel and cautioned him, "Son, lie still, don't move about, we are almost home."

Sarah and all the women were in the yard under the shade of the oak tree gathering the essentials for their soap making when they heard the horses at a wild gallop down the road.

Sarah dropped an arm load of wood and screamed loudly, "Kate! Kate! Come quick, something is terribly wrong. Jonathan would never drive the horses so fast if something were not wrong."

Kate and Sarah ran up to the wagon as Jonathan yelled, "Whoa, horses, whoooa. It's Nathaniel. Snake bite. Get him inside fast!"

Jonathan jumped from the wagon and ran to the back. He scooped the boy up, and he carried him into the house, placing him on his and Sarah's bed.

Jonathan was feeling guilty. "I should have told him to be mindful of the snakes. It is a hot day, and snakes like to lie in the sun to warm themselves."

Sarah cried out, "What kind of snake, Jonathan?" Sarah repeated the question with great fear in her voice. "What kind of snake?"

Violet, who was slowly regaining her strength, interrupted, "I helped treat a lot of soldiers with snake bites, maybe I can help."

Very calmly, Violet asked Jonathan, "What kind of snake bit him?"

"I am sure it was a queen snake. I saw it as it made its way down through the grass. It had a white stripe on its belly," described Jonathan, completely out of breath. "They don't usually bite. We were napping. I suppose the snake was close and he rolled over on it."

"First, we must keep him very quiet. Then we need to continue sucking the wound around the swelling every few minutes for another two hours so we can draw the venom." Violet checked his forehead for a rising temperature. "You did good, Jonathan, with the incisions around the bites. We will treat the wounds by washing them out and cleaning them often. He will be very sick for several days. Queen snakes are not poisonous, if that is what it was. We will know in a short time." In Violet's thoughts, if it is a poisonous snake, it would be fatal and soon. "We will need plenty of wet rags to wipe him down. We need to keep him as cool as we can. I am sure he will have a high fever coming on."

"It's entirely my fault," confessed Jonathan, feeling upset with himself for falling asleep. "If only I had told him we needed to be mindful of the snakes so close to the water's edge."

"He will be all right, Jonathan, just sick for a few days," reassured Violet. "I am sure it was not a poisonous snake. The boy is too conscious. You folks go on about your business, and I will care for the child. Jonathan, you go back and catch us a good bunch of fish. I had my mouth all set for a good fish supper." Violet stayed with Nathaniel while everyone returned to their chores.

Jonathan caught a good mess of trout, which he cleaned for the evening meal.

Sarah and Kate fried up the fish along with fresh garden vegetables, corn bread, and cold milk. Olivia turned out the first yield of soap that had been left to cool, cutting it into small blocks.

Nathaniel was restless. Violet tried to keep him as quiet as possible; she told Sarah, "His leg is beginning to swell and be painful. We need to apply a potato poultice to draw the poison."

Sarah checked on him frequently. "Violet, I am just not accustomed to anyone beside myself attending my children. I am certainly grateful for your help because I have never cared for anyone with a snake bite." Sarah left Violet with Nathaniel and went to the kitchen.

"How is Nathaniel?" inquired Kate.

"He seems to be resting now that the poultice has been on for a while. Violet seems to know what she is doing in caring for him. I am certainly grateful for her experience."

"I am so glad that he will recover, Sarah. I am finding out no one worries like a mother worries." The two went about their kitchen chores, Kate suggested, "Now that we have made the soap for the winter, perhaps we should make our candles while we have the extra help."

"We need to spend the day collecting bayberry leaves and bark to boil for wax. It most likely will take us as much as two days to get enough for the amount of candles we need to make," answered Sarah who had much more experience than Kate in such things.

Jonathan started his evening chores early. "Without Nathaniel's help, it will take me longer," he told Sarah as he gave her a quick kiss before going out the door. He was beginning to realize how much the boy did in the evening.

Kate, Sarah, Olivia, and Adeline went in search of the bayberry trees, collecting berries, bark, and leaves. They were back and forth between the woods and the house for two days. Arianna stayed at home with Violet to tend to the other six children.

Nathaniel had survived the worst of the bite. His leg was still swollen, and he had to stay off it.

Violet told the children stories of when she was a little girl in her homeland, Germany. "Nathaniel, you remind me so very much of my own son, Hans. He was Olivia's husband. He was a hard worker like you and helped his pa. Together, they made a good team, just as you and your Pa. I do so miss that pair."

The candles were made for the winter and some extra to barter in town. Nathaniel continued progressing very well with Violet's constant care.

Jonathan hitched one of the horses to the buggy for Kate, Sarah, Violet, and Olivia to drive into town to sell the soap, candles, and the last of the garden vegetables. There were no extra eggs, butter, or cheeses for barter because of the size of the household.

On the way into town, away from the family, Kate's interest in the war peaked. "Violet, Olivia, I know you must have seen a lot concerning the war. Can you please tell me of some of your experiences as you traveled with the troops?"

"Kate, I am not sure how much you really want to hear with your man in the army. It was real bad," stressed Violet.

"Yes, please do continue," pleaded Kate. "I would like to know a woman's opinion of this war."

"There were a lot of women like the three of us who lost everything. Some were very fine women who followed their officer husbands. Others were not so fine, they sought to pleasure the soldiers. We were ordered to cook, clean, and nurse," related Olivia. "The worst thing was that after combat, we had to glean the battlefields and strip the dead of clothing and possessions. The exposure was too much for Adeline and the children who were forced to follow their mothers. We went as far as

Saratoga with the forces. We were there when the British, under General Burgoyne surrendered to General Gates."

"Life was very difficult for us. We are so grateful for all that you and your families have done to aid us," murmured Violet.

"Oh, good," interrupted Kate, dropping the subject while driving up to the boarding house. "The porch and front door have been repaired. The porch is not as inviting as it once was, but perhaps a season or two will return it to its original comfort."

"Come in, ladies. It certainly is good to see you this warm day. How have you both been? How is the family?" Mrs. Fargo invited them into the parlor.

"We have been well, thank you. Nathaniel was fishing with his Pa when he was bitten by a snake, but he is recovering very nicely thanks to Violet." Kate turned to Violet and Olivia to make introductions. "Mrs. Fargo, I would like to introduce you to Violet Kaiser and her daughter-in-law, Olivia. Violet has a sixteen-year-old daughter, Adeline, who has stayed on the farm helping Arianna with the other children. The ladies have been with us now for several weeks. They are from Brandywine and are looking for domestic work here in Philadelphia. We have all worked very hard, making soap and candles. I felt sure you could use a few bars and some candles along with the last of the summer vegetables."

Mrs. Fargo took the basket of provisions to the kitchen, telling the guests, "I will return with something cool for all of you. Please make yourselves comfortable."

Mrs. Fargo returned to her guests.

Kate continued the conversation while removing her bonnet, "Violet and Olivia lost their husbands in the Brandywine battle. They both met Robert in Valley Forge."

Mrs. Fargo poured the sassafras tea and looked up with a thoughtful idea. "Well, you are looking for work. Lilly has been my domestic help for forty years, but she is slowing down. This house needs a lot of work to restore it well enough to be a boarding house again. I am sure if you have been good help for Kate on the farm, you would do good work for me. Is this something that would interest you?"

Violet and Olivia looked at each other in complete shock and answered with an emphatic "Yes, we can. Assuredly, yes."

Passing the tea glasses, Mrs. Fargo continued, "I can give the three of you room and board. The attic room is very large, and I think it would be quite sufficient for all of you. During your free time, you are welcome do handy work for extra provisions. I must tell you that we do have two guests, William McDonald, who has been with me for many years. We also have Dr. Samuel Franklin when he returns. At present, Dr. Franklin is serving with the troops at Valley Forge and New York, along with Robert."

Taking a drink from her tea glass, Olivia remembered the doctor. "We know Dr. Franklin. We helped him quite often as he performed surgery. Like Colonel McCall, he is a very fine gentleman."

"It has been a pleasure to visit with you both this afternoon." Kate got up and placed her glass on the serving tray. "I would like a short visit with William, and then we must start for home before it gets too late to rescue Adeline from the children."

Mrs. Fargo walked the ladies to the door. "Violet, you and your girls come anytime to begin work. Lilly and I will be very happy for your help."

Olivia extended her hand to Mrs. Fargo. "It has been a pleasure to meet you this afternoon. We appreciate the opportunity to work for you. If it is convenient for Jonathan to drive us in tomorrow, we will be here before noon."

Driving up to William's office, Kate brought the horses to a halt. She climbed down from the buggy and invited the ladies to visit with her and William.

"Hello, William, it is good to see you this afternoon. I just wanted to check with you about the status of the war and what might be the next move for Washington. First, William, I would like to introduce you to Violet Kaiser and her daughter-in-law, Olivia. Ladies, this is William Mc Donald."

William bowed slightly. "It is my pleasure to make your acquaintance, ladies." He kissed the top of their hands.

"Violet and Olivia are currently staying with us on the farm. They have been with us for several weeks. Both have become widows because of the war. You will be seeing them at the boarding house for Mrs. Fargo has employed them to work for her. She says the work is beginning to be too much for her and Lilly. We don't want to take much of your time, William."

"As for your question, Kate, I do know that, Washington is outside New York City. The word is that he will be moving his forces soon. I don't know what will be his next strategy."

"I understand that you are back at the boarding house. I am sure we will see you there. It has been nice seeing you this afternoon. We bid you a good day," said Kate as she and the ladies walked to the door.

William escorted the women to the door. "Have a pleasant evening, ladies, and give Jonathan my best."

On the ride home, Sarah was teasing Olivia. "I think William was well taken by you Olivia. Don't you think so, Kate?"

"Now that you mention it, I did notice his looking at Olivia whenever the opportunity permitted as he was speaking with me," chuckled Kate.

Olivia's cheeks turned a flush pink. "He is strikingly handsome and tall. He seems to be a very interesting gentleman."

"Yes, he is," agreed Kate. "He likes to talk and can speak on many subjects. I am sure you will see him quite often now that you are going to be living at the boarding house."

Kate asked, "Violet, didn't you think William was spellbound by Olivia?"

"I think Olivia was equally as spellbound," murmured Violet, her gentle smile letting Olivia know she approved.

As they arrived at home and before Kate was able to pull rein on the horses, the children came running out the door and down the steps in hopes that they would receive a treat from town.

Sarah told them, "We do have a small treat for after supper."

Violet told Adeline, "We must gather our few belongings before we retire for the night. We will be leaving the farm tomorrow. Olivia and I have been offered work in the city."

After supper, Sarah gave each of the older children a small piece of hard horehound candy. Adeline, Arianna, and Nathaniel could enjoy the sweet but bitter candy. However, Lisa-Jean, Penelope, and the boys had one lick from the candy. They were not in the least interested in the unusual flavor of the treat as they all pushed the unwanted flavor from their mouths, allowing it to run down their chins. Sarah wiped away the sticky candy mess and confirmed, "It looks as though peppermint is this family's favorite."

Jonathan knew this would be the last evening the ladies would be with them. He remembered the letter from the Hessian soldier and was reminded of that dreadful day. "Violet, I have a letter from a young Hessian soldier that has come into my possession. Would you be so kind as to read it to me? For quite some time, I have wondered of its contents."

Violet placed her and Adeline's belongings next to the door, ready for loading the next morning. "I would be happy to read it for you, Jonathan."

Jonathan went into his and Sarah's bedroom and brought out the stained letter. He handed it to Violet. He and Violet sat on the front porch to read the letter before dark.

"Let's see what we have here," continued Violet. "The letter comes from Frankfurt, Germany. It's an old letter. Someone has written it for a young woman named Helga. It was to be sent to this young soldier in the event that she should die, for she has been stricken with the plague. The soldier's name is Ralf Stockhausen. Helga tells Ralf of her everlasting love for him."

"Thank you, Violet, this explains a lot to me and helps to put my mind at rest." Jonathan refolded the letter and put it back into his shirt pocket. Having the young soldier's name and circumstances revealed made it easier for Jonathan to bring that dreadful day to a close.

Getting up very early, Violet, Olivia, and Adeline helped with the morning chores before leaving for the boarding house. They said their good-byes to the family.

"Kate, we will forever be grateful to you and the Thatcher family for the kindness you have shown to us. You saved our lives and our good names. I am not sure we could have gone on any longer without your help. God bless you for your service to us."

"Violet, we are grateful you were here to nurse Nathaniel. We needed you as well, thank you." Sarah exchanged her mutual appreciation.

Jonathan drove the three ladies to the boarding house. Returning home, he discussed his thoughts with Sarah. "I thought perhaps it would be a good day for Nathaniel and I to try our luck at fishing again before it gets too cold. With the help the ladies gave me this morning, we are caught up on the chores for the day. This time, we are going to trout fish standing in the stream."

Packing a small lunch and fishing gear, Jonathan and Nathaniel struck out for the afternoon. Standing in the cold water and looking up at the treetops, Nathaniel called to his Pa, "Look, Pa, look at the trees. They are so tall, the limbs look like a roof over the water."

"Yes, son, they do. We call that a canopy." Jonathan dropped his line in the swift-moving water.

"Boy, Pa, this water is cold." Nathaniel stood in his bare feet with water up to his knees. "Pa, I got a fish!" hollered Nathaniel, giving his line and pole a quick hard jerk.

"Hold it tight, son. I am coming, don't let it get away." Jonathan crossed the water.

At that moment, dropping from the sky with a sudden swishing sound, a very large bird swooped down and snatched the fish, breaking the line and leaving the empty pole in Nathaniel's hand. With one flap of its enormous wings, the giant bird was gone as quickly as it appeared.

"Pa, Pa, did you see that?" an excited Nathaniel yelled. "It got my fish!" Nathaniel had a thrill in his voice. "What kind of bird was that?"

Jonathan chose to take this time as a teaching moment for the boy. "Well, son, that was a mighty bird known as a bald eagle."

With curiosity, Nathaniel asked, "Why is it called bald, Pa?"

"Did you see the snow-white feathers on its head? The white feathers against the dark feathers of his body makes one think he is bald, that he has no feathers to cover his head," answered Jonathan as he helped Nathaniel rebait his hook. "The Indians use the feathers of the eagle in their very best dress. They also tell many tales about the great bird because of its strength and the wide spread of its wings as it soars through the skies. Eagles are birds with stout legs and very strong feet with sharp talons. The bird has a long life and a magnificent look. It lives high in the tops of mighty mountains, giving it boundless freedoms." Jonathan floated both arms in a movement, imitating the eagle, all the while explaining. "With his strong wings, the bird sweeps into the valleys below and then upward into never-ending spaces beyond. These things represent freedom to me." Jonathan did not know in the distant future for those very reasons, the bird would become a national emblem and treasure. Continuing in lighthearted fun, Jonathan teased, "You know son, they eat a lot of small rodents like mice and squirrels, and there is one thing we know they really like."

"What's that, Pa?" Nathaniel hung on his Pa's every word.

Jonathan laughed while smiling. "I think he really liked your supper."

The boy looked at his father in puzzlement.

Jonathan laughed at his son's blank expression. "Your fish, boy, your fish."

"Oh yeah," chuckled Nathaniel, catching on to his father's joke.

The evening came on, bringing with it a welcomed coolness and the slight hint that fall was just around the corner. With an ample amount of fish, the two gathered their gear, called for Jug, and the three then headed for home.

Chapter 31

FALL CAME EARLY IN THE year of 1778. The wind blew, stirring the leaves as they fell to the ground. The family was gathering gourds and orange pumpkins, along with apples and pears. Many trips were made to the woods to gather chestnuts and walnuts. Arianna and Nathaniel were able to help by wrapping the apples and pears, along with the pumpkins, which were to be stored in the cellar for the coming winter.

Jonathan sawed and cut wood for the winter. Nathaniel carried and stacked the wood, filling the front porch and the barn lean-to, as Robert had done in the past.

This year, the little house was well prepared for the harsh winter of 1778–79.

Jonathan hunted deer and elk for winter food and taught Nathaniel to shoot and hunt. Kate and Sarah were again making ready for Christmas with the hopes that it would be better than the Christmas of 1777.

November came with a hard frosts, light rains, and sharp winds.

Kate and Sarah bundled up tightly, as they journeyed into town for trading. This year, for bartering, they had baked pumpkin and walnut breads. They had hopes of trading these things, along with their regular farm foods for some wool yarn.

"Come in, come in, ladies. Come in out of that wind and rain," invited Mrs. Fargo as she opened the door for the two. "Warm yourselves by the fire." She then called, "Lilly, please get these ladies some hot cider to help warm them."

"Yes, ma'am, I surely will do that."

Laughing, Lilly walked back to the kitchen, exhibiting her pleasure in having visitors. Kate took notice that Lilly seemed to be moving slower. Her contagious laughter seemed to be less explosive.

Violet and Adeline heard the chatter and laughter and, recognizing the voices, came to the parlor.

"It's so good to see the both of you. How are things on the farm?" asked Violet.

"We are all well, thank you. We are trying to gather a few things for the children's Christmas in the hopes we can make it better than last," answered Kate.

Sarah looked around and asked, "Where is Olivia?"

Adeline quickly answered with a giggle, "Olivia and Mr. McDonald are at his office. Olivia works in his office now. They like each other a lot."

"Now, Adeline, not so fast. Watch what you say," reminded her mother.

"Is that so?" Kate said with a bit of surprise in her voice. "I am glad to hear that, I mean that she has work."

"Adeline is right. They do seem to really enjoy each other's company." Mrs. Fargo passed the hot cider.

"Well, it appears the employment arrangements are working out nicely between all of you," implied Kate.

The ladies finished up their cider, thanking Mrs. Fargo and Lilly.

"We would like for the family to come for Christmas Eve this year. I am sure all the festivities in town will resume as they have in past years," Mrs. Fargo reminded the ladies as they were leaving.

Wrapping their head scarves tightly, Kate and Sarah agreed they would love to spend Christmas Eve in town.

Kate added, "We extend an invitation for everyone here in the house to spend Christmas day with us on the farm." She gave Mrs. Fargo a good-bye hug.

"Sarah, I should stop by William's office for a short visit to see if there is any word from Robert," exclaimed Kate as she climbed up to the buggy seat. "We can't stay long, this wind is fierce."

The wind caught the door to William's office, taking the strength of both Kate and Sarah to pull it closed behind them. Kate heard the familiar voice of Olivia calling, "I will be with you in one moment. Please take a seat." She was coming from William's inner office with notepad in hand. "Kate, Sarah, it is so good to see the two of you."

Kate, removing her scarf with a short of breath, complimented, "You are looking well, Olivia."

"Thank you, Kate."

Olivia asked, "Have you been by the boarding house?"

"Yes, we have. That is how we knew you were here. It seems things are working out well for Violet, Adeline, and yourself. This is very good news."

With great appreciation in her voice, Olivia said, "We certainly have been blessed. I am sure William would like to see you, if you care to wait for a few minutes. He is in a conference at present." Olivia sat down at her desk.

"How are all the children and Jonathan?" asked Olivia.

"They are quite well, thank you. They are excited about Christmas this year," answered Sarah.

William excused himself for a moment and came from his office. "Kate, I am so glad to see you. I have something for you."

Stepping over to the files, he took out a sealed letter and handed it to Kate.

Kate looked at it, perplexed. She could not believe that she had a letter from Robert, for he had never before written her from the field.

William continued, "Washington sent me a number of documents by courier, and among them came this letter for you."

"Please excuse me. I cannot wait to read it." Kate stepped close to the window for better lighting. Her hands trembled as she broke the wax seal and opened the letter. "Oh, I can't believe it!" With excitement, she grabbed Sarah and began turning them both in a dancing circle. "Robert is coming home soon." Stopping, she clutched the letter to her chest. "He will be here for the holidays. This will be the best Christmas ever."

"We are so happy for you, Kate," exclaimed Sarah, with Olivia and William expressing their delight, as well.

On their ride home, Kate just could not get over the joy of her letter. "As far as I am concerned, my Christmas has just been delivered. I still can't believe it, a real Christmas."

"Kate seems unusually cheerful," noticed Jonathan. "What has brought about the change?"

"We stopped by William's after we left the boarding house. William received some documents from General Washington by courier, and among them was a letter for Kate. The letter was from Robert. Robert wrote that he will be home for the holidays."

After the children said their good nights and went to bed, Jonathan, Sarah, and Kate sat by the firelight, making various gifts for family and friends. Jonathan carved wooden toys and building blocks for the children. Sarah and Kate knit the warm winter clothing that was a necessity. The fire in the fireplace was beginning to burn low as the three finished up their handiwork. Kate, remembering once again how she and Robert's courtship had begun, had a piercing thought. "Jonathan, Sarah, how did the two of you meet?"

Jonathan and Sarah began to laugh.

"Well, Kate," replied Sarah. "It was so long ago. As you know, we came from a small town in Wales. Jonathan's father was the town blacksmith and owned the livery stable. My mother was a widow, a dressmaker. She also made ladies hats. We were small children and in town most every day, so we saw each other a lot."

Jonathan interrupted, "I saw this little girl in pigtails that was missing her two front teeth. I knew she was for me. I told my Pa, 'I am going to marry her when she grows her teeth back,' and I did."

Sarah hit at Jonathan in embarrassment.

"How did you come to America?" asked Kate.

"My father died, leaving his life savings to me. The taxes on the livery stable were so high that I sold it to pay the debt. With what was left, we bought passage to America. It was hard with a large family, but here we are and we are trying to make the best of it."

"That is a beautiful story. To think, you knew each other as children and that your love has prevailed all these many years. Thanks for sharing it with me." Kate folded her knitting to put it away.

Jonathan stoked up the fires for one last good burn before retiring.

It is the middle of December. Once again, the brutal winter weather returned. Robert, along with many of his troops, was preparing to take leave to visit with their families for Christmas and the New Year.

There was happiness in the house as Kate and Sarah cooked for the season.

"I can't believe I can cook as much as I can, thanks to you." Kate asked, "Remember the first meal you helped me cook? We went to the woods for greens and mushrooms. I have survived the hardships of this life only because of you and your friendship."

Sarah stopped stirring the cake and looked at Kate. "I can't believe you gave up your rich life in Ireland for this hardship. You think you are the only one that has had help these last two years. With a family as large as Jonathan's and mine, I don't know where we would be this Christmas without the help of you and Robert. I say we all have a lot to be grateful for."

The sun was setting. Kate stood looking out of the window through the uneven glass panes, dotted with tiny air bubbles and the condensation from festive cooking. She could hardly see as the first snow of winter began to cover the ground. Her excitement in Roberts's arrival was building, reminding her of the captivating courtship she and Robert had experienced. Kate's feeling of Christmas joy was invoked in the pure love of one human being for another. Walking away from the window and picking up Mary Margaret, she remarked to Sarah, "Robert didn't say what day he would be here. I just want him to come before a northeaster hits us."

I feel sure he will be here before that, Kate," encouraged Sarah, trying to ease her worry. Why don't you play for us? This house could use some holiday music."

"Perhaps I will play softly after the girls are down for the night," muttered Kate, taking the girls to their beds.

There was the stomping noise of boots being cleaned of snow and mud on the porch. The door opened, and Jug skirted by shaking the rain and snow from his coat, bringing in a wet dog smell. The two women assumed the commotion was Jonathan and Nathaniel coming from the barn after the evening chores. It was the men, but just behind them came Robert and behind him came another army officer.

Kate was saying good night to the girls for the evening when Sarah called, "Kate, look who is here!"

This time, Kate knew it was Robert. She quickly made her way to him. "Robert, you are home. I am so happy and relieved you made it before such bad weather hit us."

Robert picked Kate up, swung her around, and set her down gently, then gave her a long-awaited kiss.

"You look so good in your new uniform." Kate stepped back to admire him. "You look like a real soldier."

Short of breath, Robert answered, "Funding for the war helps." Still holding Kate's hand, Robert announced, "Kate, everyone, I want you to meet Major Michael Hayes. He is from Charleston, South Carolina. I have invited him to spend the holidays with us. Major, this is my wife, Kate."

"It is nice to make your acquaintance, Mrs. McCall. Please call me Michael."

Kate extended her hand. "We welcome you, Michael. It is good that a friend of Robert's can visit with us for the holiday season."

Robert continued, "This is Sarah and Jonathan Thatcher. They help Kate on the farm. The Thatchers have six children. Speaking of children, where are my girls?" asked Robert.

"They are in bed." Taking Robert by the hand, Kate led him to their room. "Be very quiet. Should we wake them, we will never get them to sleep again.

Once more, Robert looked down on his girls, just as in times past. "Kate, they are perfect and sleeping so peacefully. If there is anything that this war has taught me, it is the value of peace no matter where it might be found. Let them sleep."

Robert held Kate in his arms and tenderly whispered, "I have thought of this moment so many, many times. I missed you, Kate."

Kate shifted and snuggled into him. "I missed you as well, Robert. I lived each day in fear that you might be taken from me and that I would not be able to—"

Robert gently placed his fingers on her lips and told her, "Shhhh, I am here now. War is not easy for any nation. God has preserved me thus far, and I trust him. I know this. If we do not win sovereignty for this, our new country, there will be many more wars, as other empires try to take over this land. We left Ireland because we were subjected to the whims of one person."

"Of course, you are right, Robert. We must see this thing through, no matter the outcome. I realize and respect your deep commitment. This is one of the many reasons I love you so, Robert McCall," whispered Kate. "Now tell me more about Michael."

"Well, Michael is from a wealthy southern plantation family. He is very educated and a fast learner. General Morgan saw potential in him as an officer and advanced him to major. He is young, only twenty years old, but definitely mature for his age. We work very closely with the generals. I knew he was far from home and so young, so I invited him to spend the holiday season with us." Robert held Kate in the crook of his arm and gave her one last kiss for the evening.

"He certainly is a handsome young man and very polite. Does he come from a large family?"

"You know, Kate, I have never heard him mention his family. I only know what General Morgan has shared with me."

Kate and Sarah were up early as they cooked a hearty breakfast and then packed the foods that were to be taken to the boarding house for Christmas Eve dinner.

The men, along with Nathaniel, went in search of Christmas trees for both the house and the boarding house.

The children chose one of the two trees and carried it inside. Arianna and Nathaniel were in charge of the decorating while the rest of the family packed the food and loaded the wagon. The sun was shining, but a cold blowing wind made a very low chill factor. Everyone sat very close, wrapped in blankets, as the wind cut through them, burning their cheeks. The children crawled under their blankets to escape the blistering winds. The four miles into town could not end too soon.

Turning down Market Street on to Broad Street, one could sense the Christmas spirit in the air. The vendors were once again on the street corners, building their fires and waiting for the festivities. The aromas from roasting hot chestnuts, along with the cinnamon apple cider, filled the air. The lampposts were once again wrapped with cedar and red bows.

Approaching the boarding house, one could see the familiar candles were once again lighting the windows as they did before the British occupation. Cedar and red bows adorned the front porch banister and post. There was no longer a stained glass door reflecting its beauty, but love and warmth radiated from behind the door.

After unloading the wagon, the men unhitched the horses and sheltered them in the barn from the cold of the day.

Robert was reintroduced to Violet, Olivia, and Adeline, along with his new friend Michael.

The men and children took to the parlor, as all the women attended to setting the tables and preparing the food.

Sarah asked, "Adeline, what do you think of the nice officer Robert has brought to share the holidays with us?"

Adeline blushed and dropped her eyes in search of words for Sarah. "He seems very nice, Sarah."

"Kate and I think he is very handsome," grinned Sarah as she placed bread on the table.

Mrs. Fargo rang the dinner bell, calling everyone to the table. "Lilly and I wish to thank all our dear friends for coming to our home and sharing the bounties of the season."

Robert expressed gratitude by leading everyone in grace.

The dinner conversation did not involve talk of the war. Rather, everyone was grateful for a time to reflect on family, good friends, and a blessed bounty.

After dinner, Robert and Jonathan brought the tree from the front porch into the house for everyone to decorate.

William clinked his glass to make an eggnog toast, as everyone stood back admiring their handiwork and the perfectly decorated tree. "Everyone, I have an announcement to make." He shifted his feet, came to a very erect position, and cleared his throat. "I have asked Olivia to be my wife and she has accepted. You are all invited to a wedding on New Year's Day. We can't think of a better time to enter upon a new life for the both of us than the beginning of a new year."

No one was shocked by the good news. It was delightfully received.

Melancholy set in as Mrs. Fargo looked out the front window, remembering, "The street minstrels and carolers seem to be few in number this year. Many of Philadelphia's citizens fled with the invasion of the British. I suppose it will take some time for our city to return to its past glory."

Michael asked Adeline, "Would you care for an after dinner walk?"

"Yes, I would, that would be lovely to walk in the falling snow."

"So tell me, Ms. Kaiser, how long have you lived in Philadelphia?" asked Michael, as they walked the block.

"We have been in Philadelphia for only a few months. Prior to that we lived in Brandywine. My father and brother were killed in the battle of Brandywine. We came to the city to find work and stumbled upon the McCall farm. Our circumstances were very poor. The Thatchers and Mrs. McCall treated us very kindly and introduced us to Mrs. Fargo. Oh, I am talking way too much." She paused to catch her breath. Even though she seemed nervous, she realized that she was relaxed in his company. She thought, *He is so easy to talk to and so polite. I think I really like him.* Adeline continued, "Please, Michael, do tell me about yourself?"

"I would like to hear your story. By the way, you are not talking too much, please do continue," encouraged Michael.

"So far, I do like Philadelphia, the new friends, and the new life that we have made. Now, please, I am serious, do tell me of yourself."

"I come from Charleston, South Carolina. My family grows cotton for export. I am twenty years old. I am a major in Washington's army. Oh yes, one more thing, I have the pleasure of spending the evening with a very lovely young lady. The night is getting much colder. Perhaps we should start back," suggested Michael, surprising himself with his own flirtatious behavior as he wrapped Adeline's neck scarf a little tighter under her chin.

The evening at the boarding house ended with lots of love and well-wishing.

On the ride home, Kate told Robert, "The sky is so beautiful, and the stars are so many now that it has stopped snowing. See how the moonlight makes the snow look like crystal prisms. Last Christmas, we were all here at the farm along with Mrs. Fargo and Lilly. We dared not to go into town. Sadly, Christmas came and went without much fuss. The Christmas before last, in the northeaster, we took an entire day to travel four miles in the ice and snow. In the night, Ashley got so sick, it almost took me to my grave."

"I remember that Christmas very well. It was the night we crossed the Delaware River. The weather was treacherous, many of our troops froze to death," recalled Robert. "Lucky, Michael was not among us then."

Robert looked back at Michael. "Michael, you should have seen Washington that night as he led our troops, believing God to be on our side. God was on our side, for we did prevail."

The family returned to a warm farmhouse, for the fires had been well built before leaving. Jug anxiously hoped to be let outside since he had been left in the closed house all evening. The small children were carried to bed.

Michael helped Jonathan care for the horses, and Robert built the fires up for the night. Kate and Sarah put the leftover food away before all settled in for a good night's sleep.

Christmas morning came. The children were beside themselves; never before had they experienced a Christmas like this. The wooden toys, mittens, and scarves were happily received. Kate made the smaller children cloth balls filled tightly with soft chicken feathers. Each stocking held a stick of peppermint candy.

Robert and Jonathan were given warm mittens and a scarf. Kate had made an extra set, intending to give them to William. Instead, she gave them to Michael, for she could not allow a guest in her home to go without receiving a Christmas gift. Everyone but Kate and Sarah seemed to have a Christmas gift.

Jonathan took from under the tree a roughly wrapped package and handed it to Sarah. Opening it, she found a beautifully hand-carved set of extra-long-handled wooden spoons and a stirring paddle. The love spoons were of a young boy and girl kissing. Jonathan's family, being of Welsh descent, was famous for ornate spoon carving.

Robert put his arms around Kate and whispered in her ear, "Go look on the tree for a small blue bag and see what is inside."

Kate's eyes widened with excitement as she searched the tree high and low and found the small bag on an inside branch. Looking at Robert with a childish like grin on her face, she pulled the tiny silk string to open the small royal blue velvet bag. With a sigh, she said, "Robert, gold rings. How did you?"

Robert softly took her left hand and placed the ring on her finger. Then kissing the ring, he said, "Now the world will know you are taken, my sweet."

Kate placed the larger ring on Robert's left hand, expressing her love. "I am yours forever."

Then they embraced. It was as though they had recommitted themselves to a long life together.

It was midday, and everyone from the boarding house arrived at the farm. The farm had been decorated with green cedar and holly berries. A big red bow, tied around a spray of cedar, hung in the center of the roughly cut heavy door. The table was full of festive foods with elk roast, lots of carrots, potatoes, onions, and savory gravy, winter turnips, and greens. Kate had fried Robert's favorite chicken. The feast included pumpkin pie, egg custard pie, along with persimmon pudding and cooked cinnamon apples. Lots of fresh butter and honey in small bowls were placed alongside the breads on the table.

Everyone spent the day in laughter and Christmas caroling. Kate played the harpsichord while Jonathan fiddled. The other women bargained with Kate that if she would continue to play for them, they in return would attend to the cleanup.

No demands were placed on Adeline and Michael. The older folks could sense the spark beginning to burn between the two young people.

While the ladies cleaned, the men gathered in the corner by the fireplace, roasting chestnuts, cracking walnuts for the children, and discussing war strategies, as they tried to speculate Washington's next campaign.

Chapter 32

THE WEEK BETWEEN CHRISTMAS AND the New Year of 1779 flew by very quickly, with everyone preparing for the wedding. William and Olivia planned to marry at the boarding house, with only their very closest of friends. William asked Robert to be his best man. Olivia asked Kate to attend her. Violet would give the bride away.

The holiday decorations remained for the wedding. The staircase was dressed with an abundance of greenery with red holly berries. White bows added the finishing touches. Jonathan played angelic selections on his fiddle, making it sound as though it were a Stradivarius violin. Olivia descended the staircase, which led into the parlor. There, William stood waiting for her in front of the candlelit fireplace. The soft yellow glow of the warm fire and the many candles gave forth a romantic ambience of tender love.

Mrs. Fargo had given Olivia the wedding gown that she herself had worn thirty-five years earlier. She and Lilly had somehow hidden some of their cherished things from the British, and among them was the gown. The once snow-white French lace gown with scalloped edges had turned a beautiful ecru. In her auburn hair, Olivia wore a cluster of winter-white bayberry flowers. A single strand of white pearls graced her neck, accenting the white of the flowers. The pearls had once belonged to William's mother. The children had gathered fresh holly and bayberry, which had been tied with a white satin knotted streamer ribbon for a bouquet.

Sarah had baked an apple walnut wedding cake with heavy caramel frosting.

Afterward, while cleaning the kitchen, Sarah mentioned to Kate, "I think we have another romance in the making."

"I think you are right. Michael and Adeline seem to be spending a lot of time in proximity to each other. I think it could be a good match. He certainly seems to be of good character and highly educated. Robert told me that his family are very wealthy Charleston plantation owners."

"You don't say!" exclaimed Sarah, thinking of the possibilities of a new union.

The holidays fell behind them. Robert and Michael helped Jonathan replenish the porch with fresh cut wood. The three, along with Nathaniel, went hunting to extend the food supply for the remainder of the winter.

Robert felt strongly that before he left, he must tell Kate of the wedding rings and how he came by them. They were in their bedroom when he asked Kate to sit on the edge of the bed as he began the story.

"Kate, I did not buy the rings you and I are wearing, for I have no money. But there was a young corporal under my command, sort of like Michael. I saw that he was well-bred, and I was drawn to his solidarity, resolve, and especially to his patriotism. His name was Marvin Jones. His young wife had died shortly after they were married, and Marvin carried her ring close to his heart. Before his death, he asked me to take the rings for you and me and asked that we wear them in love."

"Oh, Robert," moaned Kate, "what a sad turn of events for such a young couple. I am pleased you shared it with me. We will wear their rings to carry on their love, as they remind us of our love."

It was time once again for Robert's early morning departure. The weather was fiercely cold. Kate, as in times past, had placed extra food along with clean clothes and bedrolls for Robert and Michael.

Kate stood with her wool shawl wrapped tightly around her. "I am not going to cry, Robert. The time we have had over this Christmas season will carry me forward. This time I have no doubt that you will come back to us."

Robert mounted his horse and pushed his saber out of the way as he bent low to give Kate one last kiss.

Michael also bid his good-byes, thanking Kate for a wonderful Christmas. Then turning his horse, he said, "Mrs. McCall, would you please tell Adeline that when the war is over, I will be back for her. I love her. I just could not tell her and then leave her."

Kate stood twisting her wedding band with tear-filled eyes, as Robert disappeared in the winter mist. With the tail of her apron, she wiped away the salty tears as they fell over her stinging cheeks. Turning, she faced the feeling of an empty dawn with the beginning of a new day.

Chapter 33

THE WINTER OF 1779 WAS as ruthless as that of 1777. Epidemics of dysentery and smallpox were brought into the city by the soldiers moving back and forth from New York City to Philadelphia. The family stayed close to home. Not many trips were made into town. Attention was given to indoor needs, such as spinning and ripping worn clothing apart to use the unworn portions to make warm quilts. Kate found time to make lace in the hope of selling it in town. Times were still very difficult for those living in the city, and few had little to eat, much less enough to barter for lace. Jonathan and Nathaniel spent time in the barn, making repairs on the wagons. They repaired and sharpened the plowing tools. Wooden sleds were used to move provisions from barn and cellar to the house. Waxing the runners made them glide much smoother. In the evening, by the firelight, they worked on horse bridles and harnesses along with resoling shoes. The leather came from the skins of wild deer and elk. Jonathan taught Nathaniel how to make brooms out of willow limbs.

One morning in March, as Sarah and Kate were scouring the front porch, cleaning off the mud and slush the winter had dealt them, Olivia and William came to visit.

"It is so good to see you. How are the newlyweds?" Kate asked as she propped her scouring broom alongside the porch wall.

"We are doing very well, thank you. It is Lilly. We have come for you, Kate, she is feeling very poorly and is asking for you. I fear there is not much time," expressed William, deeply concerned.

"If you can come, you are welcomed to ride back with us this morning," invited Olivia.

"Of course, let me freshen up a bit and gather a few things." Walking toward the kitchen, Kate untied her apron and hung it on the hook next to the stove. "I will be with you in just a few minutes."

Sarah saw the urgency in Kate and invited the McDonalds inside to wait. "Kate, do not worry about the children. We will care for them. Take as long as is needed. Give our love to Lilly."

Kate arrived at the boarding house and saw Dr. Franklin in the front parlor. "Dr. Franklin, it is so good to see you. It has been almost two years, and you are looking well."

"It is good to see you, Kate. How are the children?"

"The children are good. They are growing like garden weeds. Tell me about Lilly. How bad is she?" asked Kate. As she hung her coat across a chair, she realized Lilly was not there to take it as she so often did.

"It is her heart. I am certain that her time is short. It is very doubtful that she will last through the night," whispered the doctor.

Kate quietly went into Lilly's room. Mrs. Fargo had moved Lilly into the big house. Leaving Lilly's bedside, Mrs. Fargo came to Kate. "I am so glad you are here. She has been asking for you."

Kate sat by Lilly, taking her hand as she softly spoke to her. "Lilly, it is Kate. They tell me you are feeling poorly."

Lilly, in a much weakened voice, gasped, "Oh, Ms. Kate, youz come. Ize's so glad youz here. How is youz beautiful chillen? I did not want to meet my sweet Jesus without saying good-bye to you."

"Now, now, Lilly, you are not going to leave us. We don't want you to go." Kate rubbed her face ever so tenderly.

"Ms. Kate, youz is a very fine lady. Yes'em youz is. Youz has always treated me well with love and consideration." Lilly's voice weakened.

"Lilly, I do love you. You gave me strength to survive, you taught me to be a homemaker and mother to my children. These things will always remain in my heart."

Looking around the room and drawing in a very shallow breath, Lilly asked, "Wherz Isabelle?"

"I am here, Lilly, you can't leave me now." Mrs. Fargo, taking her hand, sniffled. "Why, you are my best friend. Whatever shall I do without you, Lilly?"

"Oh, Isabelle. It's time. My Jesus callez me home." Her hand dropped limply as she softly drew in her last breath and exhaled slowly. Gently, she left this life behind on her journey to meet her Sweet Jesus.

After Lilly's funeral, everyone met back at the boarding house. Mrs. Fargo languished with despair at Lilly's passing. Kate was grateful that she had been given a chance to say a final good-bye. Kate, very mindful of Mrs. Fargo's loss, took her thoughts back to Liz. She wished that she had a chance to say a final good-bye as Mrs. Fargo did. The four ladies had much in common, their devotion of serving and of being served.

Sitting in the parlor, Mrs. Fargo made an announcement. "I am now an old woman, and just like Lilly, my time will come. You are all my very best friends and have become my family. I have come to a decision. With William's help, I have made arrangements with Violet that she should remain with me and look after my needs. For this, she is to receive the boarding house, its contents, and the surrounding property."

Everyone agreed with the arrangement and let Mrs. Fargo know that they supported her decision.

Kate talked with Violet in the kitchen while making small sandwiches for the guests. "I have something to tell you. It concerns Adeline. The day Major Michael Hayes left with Robert, he told me that he loved Adeline and wanted to return for her. He did not tell her because he could not bring himself to tell her and then leave her behind."

Violet, stacking the sandwiches, concurred, "I, too, felt there was a spark between the two before Michael left. Have you told Adeline?"

Kate answered, "No, I have not. I wanted to know your feelings first."

"Adeline just turned seventeen in February. I see no harm in telling her. We are settled now," said Violet. "It is my personal opinion, Michael is a fine young gentleman."

Kate responded, "Robert told me that he has a fine education. He has impressed General Morgan and that is why his military rank was promoted to major. He is the son of a wealthy Charleston plantation owner. If they have a strong enough love, it would be a secure future for Adeline."

The two returned to the parlor with the fresh sandwiches.

Chapter 34

WILD DAFFODILS SPOTTED THE COUNTRYSIDE with the brightness of canary yellow, renewing the feeling that the world was still alive and had escaped the brutality of what seemed to be an endless war.

There was much outside work to be done. There was ground to plow, planting to do, and damaged roofs to shingle.

As Jonathan was replacing roof shingles, he could see a pair of horses and riders coming down the dirt road at a slow gallop. As the riders neared, he determined that it was Robert and Michael.

"Kate, Kate, someone here to see you!" hollered Jonathan.

Kate came from the back of the house where she had been planting in the summer garden. Rounding the corner of the house, she and Robert collided. Kate squealed, "I was so hoping it was you."

Robert was greeted with a surprise as well. Kate was in her fifth month of pregnancy, which was quite evident to Robert.

"Look at you. When are we due?" asked Robert.

"September this time, I hope it will be a son for you, Robert." Kate put his hand on her stomach. "John Robert, meet your father. I see Michael has come with you again."

"It is good once again to be home with you and the girls. I am sure Michael has come to see Adeline," muttered Robert as he and Kate walked around the house in search of the girls.

"How long is your stay this time?" asked Kate with her arms wrapped around Robert.

"We have a thirty-day pass. I am hoping with this much time, and with Michael's help, we can do some needed work here at the farm."

Robert reached for Ashley to give her a hug and kiss. Robert looked around among the children and asked, "Where is Mary Margaret?"

"She is down for a nap. I was working in the garden when you came," answered Kate.

At the supper table, Robert suggested, "It seems that more room is needed with another baby coming. What should we do? My thoughts are we can build another house for the Thatcher family or build a room and loft behind mine and Kate's room for our children."

Kate spoke up. "Well, Robert, not knowing how long you are going to be in Washington's army, I would much rather build just a room and loft for now. We are doing quite well with the arrangement as it is. It would be much easier on Jonathan as far as keeping up with our needs, such as winter wood for heat and cooking. The water issue is so easy for everyone in this house."

"I think Kate is right," agreed Sarah as she began cleaning up the dishes.

"The ladies have spoken." Jonathan nodded.

Robert drank the last of his milk and continued, "So be it. Sarah, Jonathan, when the war is over and I come home, we are going to build you your own home. I could not have left my family if it were not for you living here. We won't waste time tomorrow. I will go see if Charles, along with his team and wagon, will be available to work with us. With four good men, two teams of horses, and two wagons, we should finish by the time Michael and I report back. I am not so sure how much work we will get out of Michael, as he is here to court Adeline."

The table followed in laughter.

Michael blushed and realized that everyone seemed to recognize the true purpose of his visit.

Chapter 35

June ushered in another hot and humid summer. The farm had long ago lost its unlived-in, uncared-for look. Rocks lined a walkway that supported the border plants Kate and Lilly transplanted from the boarding house. The English ivy had now taken root and was maturing and covering the house foundation, giving the yard a well-cared-for appearance.

The new room addition was moving along very swiftly as the four men worked from sunup till sundown.

The women arose early to prepare a large breakfast and pack a substantial lunch. The men left for the north end of the farm just at sunrise.

"Ma, I am going to milk and feed!" shouted Nathaniel, reaching for his hat.

"Me too, Ma," chimed Arianna, who was willing to help her brother with outside chores. It gave her a much needed break from what seemed to be the never-ending babysitting, which always befell her.

"Come, Jug, you go too, boy," called Nathaniel as he always wanted the dog beside him.

Kate, Sarah, and the six small children were left in the house. Kate mentioned to Sarah. "Let's allow the children to sleep a bit later this morning while you and I catch up on a few long overdue chores."

"Jonathan told me that today should be the last day the men need to work away from the house. They should have enough timber cut with today's haul," continued Sarah as she strained the whey from the clabber cheese.

"I wonder what the guineas are in such a fuss over this morning." Kate was wiping her hands and looking out the opened window. "Sarah!" she yelled with much concern, turning around. "There are two strange men riding up into the yard. They are not businessmen, and they have a very unsavory look about them."

"We should be very cautious in dealing with them as they may be rogues. I am going to bolt the door." Sarah quickly dropped the wooden bar across the front door. She then rushed to the opened window, pulled the outside shutters closed, and latched them. At that moment, the men, being very loud and unpleasant, shouted, "Let us in, I say!" They pounded and kicked the door. Jug broke from the children and ran back to the porch. He grabbed the intruders by the pant legs as they dragged and kicked at him.

"What shall we do?" asked Kate.

"We can't let them in, Kate, you know they are up to no good."

Kate moved quickly to the stove where she had June crab apples boiling to make jam. Removing the boiling pot from the stove, she stood behind the door. "If they break through, I will douse them with this."

Arianna and Nathaniel heard the unusually loud commotion at the house and stopped what they were doing.

"We must go for Pa quickly!" Arianna yelled in a high-pitched voice. "Those strange men on the porch are scary. Why are they yelling so loud? It is best that we do not go back to the house."

Off they ran to the north field for their father.

With no hesitation or fear, the rogues broke through the door and landed hard. Kate, with all her might, threw the boiling apples over them. The scalding red apples and juice flew everywhere, with the steam rising from the floor. The strangers, in their astonishment and confusion, were trying to regain an upright position. All the while, they stumbled and slid in the hot syrupy liquid. The two intruders grabbed their faces, groaning in pain as they scrambled, crawling to the door.

"Joe, I can't see! Where are you?" cried one of the trespassers, stumbling in a cowering position. "Let's leave this place."

"Oh, I hurt. My face, it's on fire!" yelled Joe. "What in the blazes have you done to us?"

At the same time, Sarah had been beating them with the laundry stick. "Out of here, and don't you dare come back. Next time, we will tar and feather you."

All four men and the children came driving up to the porch in one of the wagons. Robert jumped from the wagon before Jonathan could bring the horses to a halt.

"What's going on here?" shouted Robert as Sarah continued beating the men off the porch with the stick.

Jug, doing his part, was still hanging on by the pant leg, as the men barreled out into the yard.

"We're going, we're going. Where's our horses, Billy? Find our horses," ordered the other man, rolling in the dirt.

Robert, brutally frank, pointed his gun at the men, giving orders, "It's best you take the advice of these women and leave quicker than you came. I had better never see you in these parts again."

Everyone gathered their composure and went inside. Kate recounted all that had taken place.

Sarah asked, "How did you know to come?"

"Arianna and Nathaniel came for us. They saw the strangers on the porch," answered Jonathan.

"They must have been a couple of deserters up to no good," interjected Robert. "That was very clever, fast thinking on your part, Kate. You could have hurt yourself in your delicate condition."

"They could have hurt us worse. Heaven only knows what they were up to," replied Sarah as she began to scrape and mop up the apples.

With a bit of pride in what his children had done, Jonathan complimented, "Arianna and Nathaniel, that was very wise of you to come for us."

Kate, being charitable, added, "If they would have come here like gentlemen should, we would have given them food if that was their purpose,"

"I don't think they will be back any time soon," added Michael. "Mrs. McCall, you may be small, but you are just like Robert says, a feisty little redhead." Looking surprised, he apologized to Kate. "I'm terribly sorry I said such a thing, please forgive me."

Everyone laughed.

"So that is what Robert thinks of me, a feisty little redhead?" chuckled Kate.

Robert stepped in to rescue Michael from his regretful slip of the tongue. "Her quick thinking has saved us from quite a few anxious moments. That's my Kate." He gave her an approving lighthearted kiss. With the expansion of the house finished, it was again close to the time for Robert and Michael to report back to their command post.

Michael talked with Kate and Robert about his feelings for Adeline and asked their advice about the wisdom of marrying so young.

Kate, being optimistic, shared, "Michael, a true and strong love can stand the winds of time."

Robert, being much of a patriarch, continued, "Michael, you have roots and a birthright here in America. You have a family who will support you and Adeline. Kate and I, we had to find our own way. With our love and much hard work, we have survived. I feel sure you and Adeline will do the same."

Michael asked to speak with Violet. Nervously, he asked for Adeline's hand in marriage. Violet gave her permission, knowing that Adeline would move to Charleston to a social lifestyle, far beyond her dreams. She would become the mistress of a Southern plantation. Violet gave tender loving advice to the couple. "Michael, you and Adeline have witnessed more in your young lives than anyone so young should have to endure. Be kind to one another. You both have paid a high price for the opportunity to begin a life together in a free democracy."

A perfect summer day was the setting for the marriage of Michael and Adeline at the little farm. Kate had a very compelling desire to make this day special for the two young lovers. Once again, her thoughts took her back in time to the night she and Robert had married, comparing the youthfulness of the two couples. She found herself with no special memories to cherish, except the genuine love they shared. For this reason, she wished to make this occasion unforgettable for the newlyweds.

Adeline asked Lisa-Jean, "Would you please be my flower girl?"

Lisa-Jean was ecstatic. "Oh, do you really mean it, Adeline, really, really? I can pick a nosegay of daffodils. It will be beautiful." Lisa-Jean went in search of her mother. "Mother, Adeline asked me to be her flower girl. May I please? Please say yes."

Sarah was happy for her daughter. Her heart sank a bit, realizing she was growing up so fast. "Yes, of course you can. I think that is a lovely idea. Did you thank Adeline?"

A little embarrassed, she said, "No, Mother, I didn't, but I will."

Lisa-Jean kissed Sarah and went in search of Adeline to tell her the good news.

Michael, with a chiseled look wearing his freshly pressed uniform, stood very erect and nervous under an outside willow arch covered in lilac vines. Adeline came to his side on the arm of William. She was attired in the same wedding gown worn by Olivia. Yellow roses, with white ribbon streamers, accented her chestnut brown hair. The afternoon festivities livened with the abundance of music and food. Michael and Adeline left on their way to Charleston where Michael was to await his next assignment. He would leave Adeline with his family. When Washington's army advanced southward, Michael would rejoin his regiment.

Kate counted another three months before the arrival of the new baby.

Robert, with orders from General Morgan, was on his way southward to the Carolinas. Knowing the time was close for Kate, he stopped by the farm as he passed through. It was a very wet and rainy September day. Everyone was forced to stay inside. Kate, now in her third pregnancy, easily recognized all the signs of child birthing and believed this was likely the day. This time, she did not have Lilly or Dr. Franklin to assist her, but Robert being with her made the pain tolerable.

Sarah cut the cord and turned to Robert. "Come see your son. Kate, it's a big baby boy, and he seems to be very healthy."

Kate, taking the baby in her arms, kissed him, and looking him over head to toe, whispered, "Welcome John Robert McCall the Second.

Robert, I am so glad you are here for the birth of our son. It is just as I wanted it to be."

Robert sat by the bed with Kate, taking her hand in his and feeling its roughness. He remembered once they had reminded him of smooth ivory as he told her, "Kate, thank you for this beautiful son and for our girls. Thank you for being the rod we cling to, for your strength that has built our family. Your work has been difficult as you have made a home for us without my help. I love you and our family. You know that is my reason for serving our new country."

The birth of his son was an endearing moment for Robert. His most inward and private thoughts were that through his new son, his name would be carried forth. He deeply desired that his son should not have to fight for a rightful place in history. Then Robert again left Kate with a new baby just days old, to join up with General Morgan in the south.

Chapter 36

WASHINGTON'S ARMY WAITED RESTLESSLY OUTSIDE New York City.

The British believed that the war could be won in the south backcountry. A new offensive prompted by the British general Clinton drove into the Carolinas and Virginia. The opinion of the British was that the plantation owners would not turn their guns away from their slave population. They believed the loyalists would prevail in the support of the king when the British forces arrived.

Washington and his worse-for-wear army continued to wait outside New York City.

Establishing a beachhead in the South, and together with the loyalists, the British drove north overland.

The year was 1780 when Charleston fell. Loyalists and backcountry rebels fought, pitting neighbor against neighbor and brother against brother, and then killing each other. Cornwallis did nothing to prevent his loyalist followers and his own troops from harshly mistreating Southern civilians.

On October 7, 1780, a victory was claimed at the Battle of King's Mountain by over-the-mountain men from North Carolina, Virginia, and Eastern Tennessee. These men used guerrilla tactics, carrying out hit-and-run fighting against British detachments.

The British had a major victory in Camden, South Carolina. Because of the American loss, Congress replaced Horatio Gates with Nathaniel Green. Green broke the conventional rule and divided his troops into two regiments. Gen. Daniel Morgan of Virginia was placed in command of a detachment of six hundred men. For two weeks in January of 1781, Morgan led Tarleton's troops on a cross country chase of the Carolina countryside, ending in an open meadow battle called Cowpens in Western South Carolina.

After his losses in the Carolinas, Cornwallis believed that he could still score a victory against the Continental Army. For his showdown, he chose the Chesapeake. For British pounds, Benedict Arnold had exchanged rebel secrets with Cornwallis. Arnold and Cornwallis fortified a site on the York and James rivers at a place called Yorktown.

At the end of September in 1781, 7,800 Frenchmen, 5,700 Continentals, and 3,200 militia sandwiched Yorktown. On October 9, 1781, Washington gave orders to fire the first cannon and began the ten-day encirclement of the small town. With each firing and pounding of heavy iron cannons, billowing gray smoke rose to the skies. Cornwallis surrendered to the rebels on October 19, 1781, in a very formal fashion as the two o'clock sun beamed down on silenced metal artillery. Drums sounded and battalions gathered as Reveille called troops to order.

Streets were lined as history was in the making. British battalions and bands marched to the British tune "The World Upside Down." Col. Robert McCall, along with Gen. Daniel Morgan, stood alongside Gen. George Washington. General Washington gave the order that his ragged American troops, along with the French in their gorgeous uniforms, were to stand in parallel lines in respectful silence as the British soldiers laid down their arms in surrender. General O'Hara, commanding British general of the conquered army, presented General Cornwallis's sword to General Washington.

There was a lingering quietness as everyone realized the deafness of the once resounding cannon fire had come to an end. The magnitude of what had just occurred stirred the souls of those gathered. Surviving and reflecting upon the brutality of this horrific war were those who fought on the battlefields and those who escaped its horrors. The British and French continued the war at sea.

The surrender at Yorktown ended the war for the United States of America. General Washington turned to Colonel McCall, saluting, then dropping his hand, he asked, "Well, Colonel McCall, now that we have defeated the British and will be able to more freely establish our own government, what will be in your future?"

Robert, being humbled and with a worn body but with a renewed faith in his country, was taken by surprise that after such a triumphant time in history that this great general would spend his first moments in conversation with him. With a grateful heart that he had been spared by the grace of God, he replied, "Sir, I will return to my loving wife and young children in Philadelphia to continue building my small farm and hopefully continue to weave the threads that will make the fabric of this land stronger and greater."

For this purpose, he was evermore committed to carry forth his posterity as he continued to help weave a new beginning in this newly founded republic in the United States of America, his new homeland. However, he thought, *I shall never forget the horrors of this war. They will forever play in the theater of my mind.*

Waiting for Robert's return with a renewing of hope in their future, Kate held in her work-worn hands the last remaining silver goblet. She traced with her fingertips the engraved king's crest. Slowly, she placed the goblet back in its proper place on the fire mantel. Her thoughts reflected back to her forever emerald-green Ireland, her childhood with her parents, and the affluence of her long-ago lifestyle. She thought, *Someday, I shall tell the children that they are noble and are of a royal birth.*

The End

Made in the USA
Middletown, DE
26 July 2017